Regards, Mia

BLUE RIDGE BOOK CLUB

JILL BRASHEAR

Cover Design by Sarah Kil Creative

Cover Photograph by Justin Zaffarese

Cover Model Jay Lam

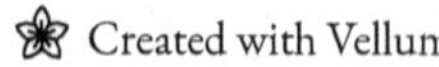 Created with Vellum

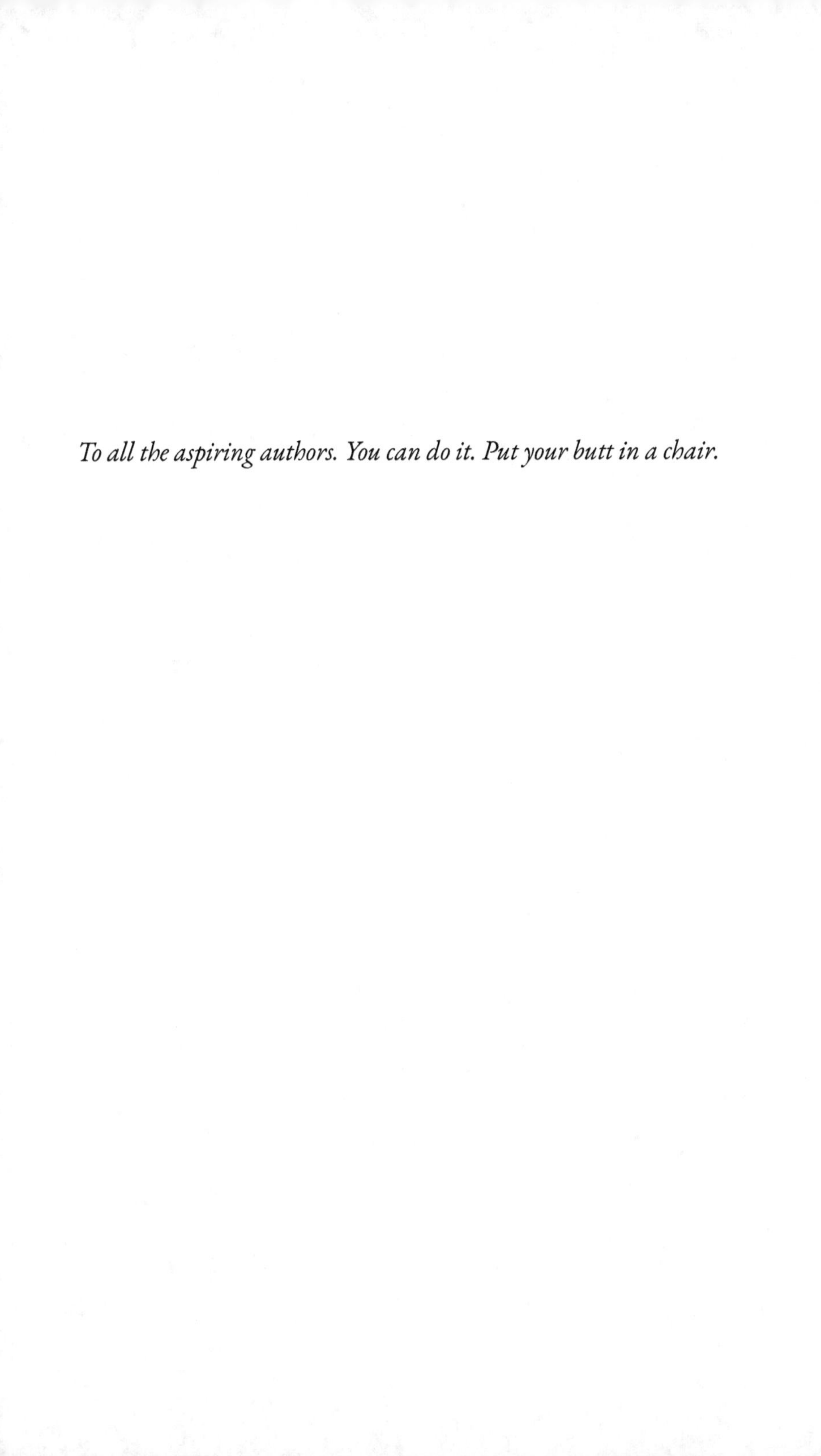

To all the aspiring authors. You can do it. Put your butt in a chair.

CHAPTER 1
Lucky Bastard

If I have to listen to one more description of a kitchen island, I'm out of here.

I started dating Harrison because he's boring, but he may be a little too boring. Even for me.

I've spent the last fifteen minutes pretending to listen to his ode to countertops while fantasizing about being at home in my warm bed reading my motorcycle club romance novel, *A Viper in the Flesh*. I daydream about Ryder Steelheart, the motorcycle club president with six-pack abs and a dark penetrating stare, sweeping me off my feet and carrying me away on his motorcycle.

At least the wine is good. It better be for two hundred dollars a bottle. When Harrison had ordered it, he'd assured me he could afford it thanks to a closing on a house in Dogwood Hills, the most exclusive neighborhood in Mossy Oak.

"To million dollar homes," he'd said, raising his glass before immediately launching into a detailed story about...countertops.

Spending time with Harrison is about as exciting as filling out paperwork at the dentist, but that's exactly what I need in my life. I get enough excitement at work. My dating life can't have drama. I need predictable and stable.

But Harrison is killing me.

I'd worn my sexy thong and push-up bra for no reason. I'm definitely not getting any action tonight. When I'd first met Harrison, I'd thought he had potential for a permanent-temporary relationship. Something casually long-term. Or at least thought he'd break my dry spell.

Harrison is perfect on paper. Charming, good-looking, if a bit on the short side, and disease-free! He checks the basic requirements to make it into my bedroom.

But our chemistry is sadly lacking. The first few times we'd kissed, I'd figured we'd warm up with practice. But, the ick has spread its icy fingers through my body, and everywhere that should be sizzling, is frozen.

Harrison takes a breath from his monologue and sips his wine. "This is excellent."

Stifling a yawn, I agree.

"A wine cellar would bring great value to any home," Harrison says, more to himself than me.

I take a bite of a breadstick, crunching loudly enough to drown out his voice.

"Oh, look!" He gestures across the room. "It's Emily from the office."

Harrison beams at Emily, and I see something in his expression that looks like relief. He's as glad for the interruption to our date as I am.

He's not having fun either. Time for me to make my excuses and leave.

"It's packed in here," Emily From The Office says. "The hostess said it's an hour's wait. My date will be here any minute, but we might have to go somewhere else."

"Why don't you join us?" Harrison points to the extra two seats at our table for four.

Emily blushes. "We couldn't possibly impose on you."

"It's fine," Harrison says, pulling out a chair for her. He suddenly remembers my existence, and a sheepish look crosses his handsome features. "You don't mind, do you Mia?"

"Of course not." I point with my breadstick. "Please, sit."

My phone buzzes with a text, and thank God, I see my boss's name on the screen. Here is the out I needed.

"Excuse me," I say, sliding my chair back from the table. "I need to make a quick call."

Harrison nods. "Work never ends. I had to leave a dinner party to show the Hampton residence." He picks up his glass of wine and toasts the air with a wink. "But it was worth it."

Emily leans forward, enthralled. "I heard they had the most fabulous kitchen island."

"You should see the tile work." Harrison pulls out his phone. "I've got pictures."

"I'll be back in a minute," I say.

Harrison glances up distractedly and nods.

Threading my way through the crowded tables, I make my way outside. The sidewalks are full of people celebrating First Friday, and it's hardly any quieter outside than it was inside the busy restaurant. At the end of the block, I duck into a side alley between the old brick buildings and dial my boss.

It doesn't matter that it's seven o'clock on a Friday Night, Jordan Adler is at work. As District Attorney for Azalea County, he keeps even less conventional hours than I do. Although it isn't unusual for him to call on a weekend, I feel a rush of worry before he picks up. Hopefully, he's just lost track of time and this isn't an emergency situation.

"Mia." Jordan says my name in two long syllables, dripping with honeyed charm. "Thanks for calling me back."

"No problem." A chilly blast of air sweeps in from the sidewalk, and I shiver. I'd been so eager to get away from the table, I'd left my jacket on the back of my chair. "What's up?"

"I'm afraid it's not good news."

Huddling against the side of the building for warmth, I run through all the cases I'm juggling, cataloguing every possible disaster. One case stands out in my mind. I can't afford bad news about Warner Mattson. The case is already hanging by a thread. I will Jordan to say any name but—

"It's Warner Mattson," Jordan says.

"Fucking hell. Mother fucker."

"Mia."

I wasn't done with my litany of fucks, but I bite my tongue. My skin crawls at the sound of that lowlife's name. A snake disguised as a southern gentleman, Warner Mattson is worse than despicable. He's one of the good old boys, whose family name means more than any pile of money ever could and he's been getting away with shit his entire life.

"What happened with Mattson?"

Jordan pauses for a long moment, then lets out a frustrated sigh. "We have to release him."

My fist clenches and unclenches, and my entire body tightens. The cold has nothing on the angry red heat sparking in my chest.

"Elena Rogers is an unreliable witness," Jordan says. "It's not a strong enough case."

A burning sensation radiates up my chest to my throat. "Elena is not unreliable." I bite out each word as if saying it slowly will make Jordan realize I'm right.

"She's got a record."

"So?"

"We'll lose," Jordan says.

"Without Elena, there is no case. Warner Mattson will get away with harassment and rape."

"We'll get him, Mia. A man like Mattson is bound to screw up again."

The thought doesn't comfort me. "You mean another victim."

Jordan doesn't say anything for a long moment. "My hands are tied," he says finally.

My throat feels thick with unsaid words. It doesn't take a genius to figure out why Jordan wants to cut Mattson loose. It's an election year.

"It's your call," I say, my mind already whirring with ways to get Mattson.

"I owed it to you to hear it from me directly," he says. "Sorry to ruin your night."

A dull ache pulses through my head. "It's fine."

Jordan laughs at the flat tone in my voice. "Date with the accountant not going well?"

I pinch the bridge of my nose. "He's not an accountant."

"Medical sales?"

"Real estate," I say. "I need to go."

There's no way I'm sharing details about my personal life with my boss. Jordan is the kind of man who uses every piece of information to his advantage. Who knows when the sorry state of my love life might come in handy to him?

"Enjoy the rest of your night," he says.

"Thanks."

I hang up and wrap my arms around myself. The crowds of people walking down the charming cobblestone sidewalks of Main Street have no idea a criminal is being set free to mingle among them.

God, I need a smoke.

Ducking further into the alley between the buildings, I reach into my purse for my emergency pack of cigarettes. I quit months ago, but it never sticks.

I step behind a dumpster and light a cigarette, feeling the immediate effects of the nicotine hit my system. I'm calmer, but the buzz of anger still vibrates through my body.

I'll never give up on Mattson.

Not until he's behind bars where he belongs.

Pulling out my phone, I tap out a text message to Elena, asking her to call me as soon as possible. Jordan gave me the heads up about Mattson, but I doubt he did the same for Elena. She needs to know what's going on, and she needs to hear it from me. We've been in this together for months.

The roar of an engine sounds, and I glance up from my phone

to see the headlamp of a motorcycle coming from the other end of the alley. I step back into the shadows of the dumpster and watch as a man stops the bike and cuts the engine a few feet away.

He's clad in all black, a combination of denim and leather, and he's a formidable presence on the bike. His shoulders are broad, his legs are long, and his overall size is larger than average. He dismounts with fluid grace, throwing his leg to the ground in a practiced move.

My heart thuds against the tight walls of my chest as he pulls off his helmet and shakes out a wavy mass of long, dark hair. A throb of desire races through me, because this guy looks like Ryder Steelheart, president of the Shadow Vipers Motorcycle Club, just pulled into Mossy Oak for the weekend.

Desire surges in my belly as the streetlight plays over his rugged features. He's dangerously handsome, with a close-cropped dark beard, and an intimidating presence. He's not my usual type—I prefer men with hair shorter than mine and safer modes of transportation—but there's no denying he's off the charts sexy.

"Is this the new smoking section?" he asks, pinning me with his dark gaze.

Oh, hell. I must not have been as much in the shadows as I'd thought. Now, I've not only been caught smoking, but also staring.

"Want one?" I ask, reaching for my purse. There are a few more in my emergency pack, and I'm feeling generous in my misery.

"I don't smoke," he says.

"Neither do I."

His dark brow lifts, and I try to explain. "This is an emergency."

He stiffens and glances around the alley. "What's going on?"

"I'm not in danger," I say. "I'm just fucking pissed."

His shoulders inch down, and his gaze zeroes in on me again. "You're gonna freeze your ass off dressed like that."

I'm not in the mood for a lecture about my smoking habits or my wardrobe choices, no matter how appealing the lecturer. "Gotta go somehow," I say on a long exhale of smoke.

In two long strides, he crosses the distance between us and peels off his jacket. "You want this?"

Without waiting for my answer, he drapes the jacket over my shoulders. It violates every instinct in my body not to shrug it off, but instead of tossing it off, I burrow deeper. The jacket is warm from his body and smells inticingly of leather and man.

"What's got you so pissed you're out here smoking an emergency cigarette without a coat?"

Light shines from the streetlamp directly on his face, illuminating the sharp planes and angles of his features.

"Bad news from work."

He crosses his arms over his chest, drawing my attention to the rounded biceps straining under his long-sleeved shirt. "What bad news?"

I feel the urge to confide in this handsome stranger, but there's nothing he can do to help me with my problem.

"Nevermind," I say. "It's nothing I can't handle."

He nods tersely. "I can believe that."

I crush my cigarette under the toe of my boot. "I should get back inside," I say, gesturing around the corner to the sidewalk. "I'm on a date at The Vine."

He cocks his head at me. "You must not be that into him."

My spine stiffens at the way he reads me so easily. I've been told I'm the Queen of Ice, my thoughts impossible to decipher, but this guy has sliced through all my walls in mere minutes. "Why do you say that?"

"Because you're out here with me, instead of inside with him."

A laugh escapes my mouth. "True." I take off his jacket and hand it to him. "I should go."

"I'll walk with you." He falls into step beside me. "I'm going the same way."

"Are you on a date with a woman you're not into?" I ask, feeling the blunt edge of jealousy stab my chest for absolutely no reason.

"I don't know yet," he says. "It's our first date." He checks his watch. "And I'm late."

"I guess that's my fault. You felt compelled to lend your jacket to a stranger."

His brow furrows. "I'm Jay," he says, offering his hand.

"Mia."

His strong, firm handshake sends a message to every cell in my body. *This man is good with his hands.*

"Now we aren't strangers." He opens the door to the restaurant for me. "Ladies first."

I step inside the warmth of the restaurant and turn to him with a reluctant smile. "Goodbye, Jay."

"I'll walk with you," he says, following closely behind.

"No need."

"There is for me. I want to see the lucky bastard who's having dinner with you."

My heart races, and a blush heats my cheeks. He's flirting with me, and God help me, I love it. I shouldn't. He's on a date with another woman, and I've kept Harrison waiting long enough.

With a guilty start, I see Harrison at our table, looking in our direction.

"Is that your date?" Jay asks.

I see Harrison through Jay's eyes. Fresh haircut, trendy suit, and perfect posture—he's the opposite of Jay.

"Yes. Why?"

Jay laughs softly. "Because that's *my* date sitting with him."

CHAPTER 2

No More Phones

My feet come to an abrupt halt. "Emily is your date?"

"It's a blind date. We've never actually met." He places a hand on the small of my back, urging me forward. "Funny thing, huh?"

I try to picture Emily and Jay together and fail. "She's a little young for you, isn't she?"

Jay winces. "Her sister said she was thirty, but she doesn't look it."

Jealousy rears its ugly head. Emily doesn't deal with criminals daily, which probably contributes to her fresh face.

"Maybe it's the ponytail," I say, watching her hair swing as she turns her head and sees Jay.

Then she *really* sees him.

Her eyes widen, her jaw drops, and two spots of color appear on her cheeks.

Oh yes, honey, I know how you feel. I felt the same way when I saw him for the first time.

Hot.

Bothered.

Tingly in all the right places.

Wait till she hears his voice. Deep and rumbly, Jay has one of those voices that stirs your soul.

We approach the table, and Emily shoots to her feet.

"You're taller in person." Her voice comes out in a squeak as her gaze drops over Jay from the tip of his motorcycle boots to the top of his head.

He's standing behind me, but I can visualize what she's seeing. Broad shoulders, impressive chest, long legs, then back up again to his sexy-as-sin face.

"I get that a lot," he says, sounding mildly annoyed.

I can sympathize. One of my biggest pet peeves is people commenting on my height. I know I'm short. I don't need anyone to remind me.

And of course Jay knows he's taller than average, an imperial mountain of a man.

"The wait for a table was over an hour," Emily says. "But my friends invited us to join them." She darts a glance between Harrison and Jay. "Is that okay?"

"It suits me." Jay raises an eyebrow at me, gesturing at Harrison. "Unless you two would rather be alone?"

I shake my head, taking the seat Harrison pulls out for me. "Please join us. No use waiting an hour for a table when we have plenty of room."

Jay helps Emily with her chair, then shakes Harrison's hand. This isn't selfish at all on my part. I'm only trying to be nice, not prolong my interaction with the sexy stranger who isn't a stranger anymore.

"Jay, this is Harrison and Mia," Emily says.

Jay takes the seat across from me. "I met Mia on the way in," he says.

Shivers tiptoe down my spine at the sound of my name on his lips. That deep rumble hits me in all the right spots.

"I know Harrison from work," she says to Jay.

He nods, his gaze flicking to Harrison. "Real estate?" he asks.

"That's right," Harrison answers, looking pleased. "Are you in the market for a house?"

Jay shakes his head. "I've got a place."

Emily laughs. "Harrison never stops working," she says. "That's why he won Mossy Oak's Best Realtor three months in a row."

Harrison waves his hand in the air, dismissing Emily's praise. "I'm just doing my job. Finding people their perfect homes is my passion."

I laugh, but the sound dies in my throat as three pairs of eyes turn to look at me. "Sorry," I say. "Thought you were joking."

Harrison shakes his head with disappointment. "My job may not be as glamorous as yours, but I'm just as dedicated as you are."

I force a smile. "I think you've been watching too much *Law and Order*. There's nothing glamorous about courtrooms and jailhouses in Azalea County."

"You work in the court system?" Jay asks.

I nod. "I'm an attorney."

There's another long pause in the conversation, then Emily says, "I love *Law and Order*."

"It's my guilty pleasure," Harrison says.

"What kind of work do you do?" I ask Jay. If I had to guess, I would say it was something labor intensive. Construction or landscaping would suit him. I can almost picture him swinging a hammer or hefting a small tree.

"I own a gym," he says.

"My sister is his manager," Emily says. "She set us up."

Harrison chuckles and pats his belly. "I should probably get a membership," he says. "I've been working so much, I don't have time for exercise."

My phone buzzes. I glance down at where it's lying face up on the table and see it's Elena. My heart jumps into my throat, and I grab my phone as if it's a lifeline. "I need to take this."

"Again?" Harrison asks.

I nod, scooting my chair back from the table.

"Mia James." Harrison shakes his head. "She never stops working."

His tone makes it clear it's not a compliment, but I don't have the time or inclination to apologize. I have to answer before Elena hangs up. Hurrying away from the table, I hold the phone to my ear before I'm even a few feet away.

"Hello?"

"Ms. James?"

"Yes."

"Is this a good time to talk?"

"Of course." I rush into the restroom and lock the door behind me.

"It sounds like you're out somewhere," she says.

"I am, but it's important we talk." I take a deep breath. "It's about Mattson. You should know they are releasing him."

She laughs shortly. "I knew it."

"We can still get him," I say. "I just need your help."

"What can I do?" Her exhausted voice sounds over the mewling cries of a baby in the background. "No one believes me."

I grit my teeth. "*I* believe you."

Elena hushes the child. "I have to go," she says.

"Wait. Let's meet up and talk."

"Why bother?"

I run a hand through my hair, facing my reflection in the mirror. The determined glint in my eyes is a little scary, even to me. "We can't let him get away with this," I say.

Elena sighs heavily. "I'll think about it."

"Text me when and where," I say. "I'll be there."

Elena agrees to let me know, and we hang up. Feeling more confident about nailing Mattson, I drop my phone into my purse and apply another coat of my signature red lipstick. With Elena's cooperation, I'm sure I can get enough evidence for Jordan to change his mind. Maybe I can get her to meet with him and wear a wire. There's got to be a way to convict him.

I'm contemplating my strategy as I weave through the restaurant toward our table, only to stop short when I see Jay is sitting by himself. Harrison and Emily are gone.

"Where did they go?"

"They had a real estate emergency," Jay says.

My brows lift. "Both of them?"

He shrugs. "I think we just got ditched."

"What?"

"Our dates would rather be with each other than us," he says in a dry voice.

"You're saying Harrison and Emily went home together?"

"Definitely."

A surprised laugh escapes my mouth. For the life of me, I can't figure out why Emily would choose Harrison over Jay. Maybe she hit her head on one of those lovely tile countertops.

I glare at the bottle of wine on the table. "He better have paid for that."

Jay picks up the bottle and squints at the label. "Never tried it."

"It's one of the most expensive bottles on the menu," I say, seething with frustration. "He said he was celebrating."

"Don't worry about it." Jay waves it off. "I got it."

"No. That's not fair."

I'm all about justice. And not too happy about being dumped and stiffed with the bill.

Jay stands and pulls out the chair Emily vacated. "Mia, have dinner with me."

My body instantly reacts to his command. I'm tingly all over, a pile of mush where I'd been so hard with annoyance only moments before. That voice will do it. All he has to say is my name.

"Harrison is paying for that wine," I say, swiping my phone to life with renewed determination.

Jay reaches over, plucks my phone from my hand and drops it into my purse. "No more phones."

My shoulders stiffen at the absurdity of his suggestion. "What if there's an emergency?"

He takes the chair next to me, scooting in so our legs brush. "Let someone else handle it."

"But..."

He runs his finger down the menu. "Have you eaten?"

I watch the slow glide of his finger down the menu selections, imagining how it might feel against my skin. "Not yet."

He catches our server and orders a few appetizers and another bottle of wine. "Anything else look good to you?"

Besides him? "No, that's fine."

The server disappears, and it's just me and Jay, sitting close together as if we are intentionally on a date. "I can't believe I just got ditched. Without even a text."

Jay shrugs. "It's actually not the first time it's happened to me."

I turn my head to look at him, my eyes widening with disbelief. It's hard to believe any woman in her right mind would turn him down. "Guess you and Emily aren't going on a second date."

He shakes his head. "Her sister is probably going to give me hell for it."

"But it's not your fault."

He lifts a brow, but doesn't add to the conversation as the server comes back with the wine and pours a sample. She hands it to Jay, but he gives it to me.

"Taste it," he says.

A bolt of desire shoots down my spine. Usually I'm not the type to take orders, but I'm all too eager to do anything this man says. The quiet confidence in his voice, combined with the sexy package of it's owner, makes me jump to do as he commands.

I lift the glass to my lips and take a sip. One taste of the rich, spicy wine, and I'm sent straight back to my summer studying abroad in Italy.

"Where's this from?" I ask.

"Sky Valley Vineyards," the server says with more than a hint of local pride. "Do you like it?"

I nod, my gaze colliding once again with Jay's. "It's surprisingly good."

When she's gone, silence stretches between us, but it's not unpleasant.

"Are you sure you're okay with this?" He lifts the wine bottle, pausing to meet my gaze before he fills my glass.

He's giving me an out, letting me go if that's what I want. What do I want? To be home, tucked under my covers, reading about motorcycle mafias? Or sitting here with what is quite possibly the real thing?

I tilt my glass toward Jay and wonder what I'm about to get myself into. "Pour."

CHAPTER 3

Just My Type

Mia forks the last bite of tiramisu and holds it up to my mouth. "Eat this before I do."

I usually skip dessert, but I open my mouth obediently. I've known Mia all of two hours, and she's already got me wrapped around her little finger. She could ask anything of me in that low, silky voice and I'd do it.

I'll go back to chicken and vegetables tomorrow. Tonight it's tiramisu, and if I'm lucky, Mia.

From the moment I saw her, I wanted her. After sharing a meal and conversation with her, I don't just want her. I need her. I'm a sucker for a strong, confident, shit-talking woman. Some might call them bitches or Ice Queens, but I call them Just My Type.

Mia leans forward and points to the corner of my mouth. "You've got chocolate sauce."

I lick my lip, and her eyes track the slow sweep of my tongue. Anticipation vibrates between us, thickening the air with a sense of urgency. I need to kiss her, but I hold off, teasing out the tension between us like foreplay.

When we kiss, it's gonna be combustible, inevitably leading to one place. Someone's bedroom.

Mine. Hers. Doesn't matter. We're going there, and we're going to stay all night.

Her pale blue gaze is sucker punch that steals my breath. My face gives away my thoughts, and Mia reads me easily, a slow smile curving her mouth.

"Excuse me." A voice sounds from above. "Sorry to interrupt, but can I get you guys anything else?"

I reach for my wallet. Mia starts to protest, but I wave her off. "I've got this."

A determined look I'm starting to love crosses her face as the server leaves the table. "I'll split it with you," she says. "The wine—"

I cut her off. "Come back to my place."

She tilts her head at me. "You're a cocky bastard."

"It's part of my charm."

She shakes her head, staring at the tablecloth. "You ride a motorcycle," she says, more to herself than to me.

I bump her shoulder gently with mine. "Want to take a ride on it?"

"Ha!" Her gaze leaps to mine. "Never!"

The horror on her face makes me smile. "Want to take a ride on something else?"

Laughter spills from her lips. "You're fucking kidding me. You did *not* just say that."

I shrug. "I did."

Her head cocks to the side, and her hot gaze scorches over my face. I can almost hear her inner thoughts whirring.

I'm not her typical guy.

We don't know each other.

I could be dangerous.

Seconds tick by, and neither of us says a word. The server drops off the check and I sign it, then tuck my card back into my wallet.

Mia finally breaks the silence. "I'm not getting on that motorcycle."

Is that all that's stopping her? Easy fix. "My place is a short walk."

She eyes me for another beat, then nods and pushes back from the table. A thrill runs down my spine, and I scrape my chair away from the table, shooting to my feet to help Mia with her jacket. She's tiny, barely up to my shoulder despite her high heels. Her diminutive size brings out the caveman in me. I fight the urge to haul her up and carry her out of here.

"Let's go."

She laughs at the rough edge of need in my voice. "I don't take orders," she says.

My arm slides around her waist, locking her against my chest. Desire surges through me as her curves flatten against my body. "I'll let you call all the shots. But we need to get out of here."

Her face lifts to mine, and our lips collide. I steel myself as pleasure scorches my veins. Every muscle in my body tenses as I fight the urge to claim her mouth. I hold back, making sure Mia knows the next move is all hers.

She could push me away.

Maybe she should.

But she doesn't.

Her mouth parts under mine, and her tongue sweeps past my lips. My nerves sizzle in response to the slow, tantalizing caress of her tongue. She tastes of chocolate and wine, filling me with the need for more.

Her palm flattens on my chest, fingers sliding under the open collar of my shirt to steal a fleeting touch. My heart slams, crashing hard against her palm. She's all fire, wrapped up in a petite package I'm dying to open.

She drops her hand, easing back to end the kiss. "I don't usually go home with men I don't know."

I pull in a breath, willing my senses to stop sparking. Hopefully there's a word she left off. I supply it for her. "But?"

She blinks up at me, clearing the haze from her eyes.

"Tonight, I want to stop thinking about something. I think you could help with that."

Frustration stabs my chest. "You want to use me?"

She nods. "Maybe."

After a moment, the frustration ebbs, and I'm surprisingly okay with being used. "Okay."

She rewards me with a grin. "How far to your place?" she asks. "I'm wearing heels."

Anticipation ripples through me, replacing any lingering doubts. "We can walk slowly," I say.

Mia's eyes sparkle like ice on a clear mountain lake. "Not too slowly."

Jesus. This woman is going to kill me.

CHAPTER 4

Spider's Web

I lift my chin to take in the brick building. "This is a gym."

Jay's shoulders stiffen. "*My* gym."

I squint up at the repurposed warehouse. Thanks to a revitalization movement a few years ago, a lot of spaces downtown had a new lease on life. Jay's gym had probably been a factory or mill, but now it boasts a boxing logo over the entrance.

"I think my friend Thatcher trains here," I say. "Do you know him?"

"I know Thatcher," he says, a muscle in his jaw ticking. "He has a lot of women friends."

"We're in a book club together," I say. "We're just friends?"

"Just friends?" He lifts a brow at me, his gaze raking over me in the dim light of the moon. "Are you sure?"

I step closer, wrapping my arms around his neck. "Positive."

He lowers his mouth to mine, kissing me hungrily. Now that we are alone, his kiss is less tame than it had been in the restaurant. I feel it down to my bones. His mouth covers mine, taking with fierce possession.

"Want to come inside?" he asks between heated kisses.

"Yes." My voice is breathless.

He takes my hand and leads me around the back of the

building to a private entrance. Unlocking the door, he tugs me inside and climbs the stairs. I follow at a slower pace, enjoying the view of his tight ass in dark denim.

He pauses to unlock another door and tugs me inside. I get a glimpse of shiny wood floors, brick walls, and large, masculine furniture before his mouth is on mine again, dragging me under his spell.

His lips are hard and soft at the same time, and the tickle of his beard is much more erotic than I would have thought.

I've never kissed a bearded man before. I've never tasted a tattoo.

But that's what I want now, more than anything. I want to see what's under his clothes, get more than a peek of what's beneath the denim and leather.

My fingers slide to his shirt, fumbling to undo the buttons as his mouth continues to scramble my brain.

Thank fuck, I get the first button open. I skim my fingers over his skin, feeling the soft, curling hairs on his upper chest before diving back in for the next button.

Jay's hands are just as eager as mine. He slides them into my hair, tugging gently and then with more force. My head falls back, and his lips trail from my mouth, along my jaw, to the exposed column of my neck. He bites softly, licking a path to my collarbone as one hand fists in my hair and the other wraps around my waist, bending me backward.

His hot mouth and firm grip almost make me forget my goal to lick his tattoos. But my desire to taste him can't be forgotten so easily. I tear at the next button, feeling it give with a snap.

"Shit." Never have I ever torn a man's clothes off before. "Sorry."

Jay's chuckle vibrates against my neck. "Doesn't matter." He shrugs his jacket off his shoulders, then reaches for the remaining buttons on his shirt. His long, nimble fingers make quick work of them, and he spreads it open, allowing me my first glimpse of his chiseled torso.

My jaw drops as he spreads open the fabric of his shirt, revealing muscles, tanned skin, and ink.

So much ink. So much for me to taste.

RESPECT is inked in traditional script across his upper chest.

A hum of appreciation runs through me. This word means more to me than he could ever know. If there is one thing I've always craved, it's respect. I trace my fingers over the capital letters, imagining the pain that went with every prick of the needle.

Lower down, the feathered wings of a proud eagle spread over his pecs and a black-and-red dragon with two heads coils across his abdomen.

His tattoos are beautiful, intricately drawn by an artist's hand.

I lick my lips, but before I can bend to my delectable task, he grabs my face and kisses me.

His tongue streaks possessively into my mouth, then slides across my lower lip. He takes, then teases, takes again. The glide of his tongue seduces me, makes me come undone.

I wonder how it would feel on the rest of my body.

As if I've said the desire out loud, Jay trails a path of kisses down my neck. His hands glide up my ribcage and skim lightly over my breasts.

My nipples peak under his brief touch. Shameless nipples, standing at attention, begging for more.

He flicks his tongue in the hollow of my throat, then bends down to brush his lips over my nipple through my blouse. I gasp at the sensation of lace and silk rubbing against my sensitive skin.

A satisfied smile curves his lips as his gaze roams over my chest. "You're so fucking hot, Mia."

I feel the same about him. He's dangerously hot. I'm going to get burned and enjoy every fucking moment in the fire.

I'm really doing this.

My dry spell is about to end, and I don't even know the man I'm going to bed with.

I don't know his sexual history.

I don't care.

He backs me up, guiding me across the large expanse of open living space until I'm pressed up against the back of a sofa.

"That's why I gave you my jacket," he says, pressing his knee between my legs to part them. "You were only wearing this top." He plucks at the tiny buttons on my blouse, his fingers big, confident and extremely knowledgeable of women's garments. "You were cold, and I could see the outline of your nipples."

His fingers slide down the center of my chest, between my breasts, down to my navel, then slowly back up. I gasp as he rubs his thumb over my aching nipple.

He kisses my neck, his mouth caressing my skin, his breath warm and inviting.

"I got instantly hard." He pinches my nipple through the lace of my bra, and goosebumps ripple across my skin. "And possessive."

His fingers continue playing with my nipple as his other hand gathers my skirt, pushing it up my hips. I ache to get closer, and part my legs for him, scooting back so I'm perching on the back of his plush leather sofa, giving him all the access he wants.

All he has to do is take it.

I've never wanted to be taken so badly in my life.

His deft fingers push down the lace of my bra over the top of my breast, exposing my nipple. Bending his head, he swirls his tongue around the hardened flesh and sucks deeply.

A moan escapes my mouth, and my hands go to his hair, holding him close as he draws my nipple between his lips, sucking and licking until my pulse hammers in my ears.

So good. His mouth is so good.

His hands are even better.

He's somehow managed to get my panties off and is gliding his long, agile fingers along my throbbing flesh. One finger pushes between my wet folds, and drags up to my clit, working me with teasing strokes.

"I couldn't stand the thought of anyone else seeing these hard nipples." He pushes down the other side of my bra and takes his time admiring me before tonguing a hot path across my chest, all the while stroking me with his expert fingers.

I whimper as he sucks and kisses my chest, fucking me with his hands and his mouth until I can't control the words coming out of my mouth. I have no idea what I'm mumbling, but whatever it is makes Jay chuckle softly against my aching flesh and increase the pressure between my legs.

Pleasure ripples across my skin wherever he touches.

My fingers tangle in his hair, and I cinch my leg around his hips, arching to get closer, to grind against his hand. He obliges my demands with an increase of pressure. Another finger plunges into me and his thumb flutters over my clit in a merciless rhythm.

Without warning, the orgasm crashes over me, drawing a sharp cry from my mouth that Jay smothers with his kiss. His tongue plunges into my mouth, devouring my pleasure as his fingers work slowly and deeply inside me, sliding through my arousal.

My heart pounds, my chest heaves, and my pussy aches for more of Jay than just his skilled fingers.

All my adult life, I've avoided men like Jay. Men who looked and acted tough. Men who wore something other than a suit and tie to work.

This is what I've been missing out on?

Fuck that.

I didn't realize I'd said the words aloud until he pulls back and gazes down at me through heavy-lidded eyes. "Don't worry," he says wrapping his arm around my waist and setting both my feet on the ground. "I plan on fucking you. After I make you come a few more times."

He takes me by the hand, turns and walks me toward the archway separating his king-sized bed from the rest of the large, open loft apartment. My gaze roams over his shoulders, along the mountains of muscle, and then I see it.

The tattoo spreads out over the back of his arm, up his tricep in intricate detail. A spider's web radiates from the central point of his elbow halfway up and down his entire arm.

I freeze. My feet refuse to budge another inch. My mind reels.

"Is that...?" I swallow hard and force myself to finish, even though I already know the answer. "Is that a *prison tattoo*?"

Jay stops in his tracks, his muscles bunching across the tops of his shoulders. He glances back in my direction, his gaze meeting mine before dropping to the back of his own arm. Looking at the tattoo as if he forgot it was there, he pauses, drawing out the moment when he has to answer. Finally, he nods, affirming my worst fear.

"You've been to prison."

He nods again, turning slowly to face me. The absolute beauty of his body stuns me for a moment. Undoubtably the most gorgeous man I've ever laid eyes on, his body is a work of art. His tattoos are more decoration on top of taut muscle and smooth, tawny skin, and his face is that of a dark angel, gracing Earth.

His body is rigid, as if he's holding himself back from touching me until I manage to find my tongue and speak first.

"I want to leave," I say, hastily pulling my blouse closed.

His eyes widen. "Now?"

I shove down my skirt and glance around for my panties. Where the hell did they go? My blouse gapes open, and I grip it tightly as I bend down and search for my missing undies. "Yes, now."

Jay laughs, a hollow bark of a sound. "Because I did time you don't want me to fuck you anymore?"

A hot throb of desire quakes through my entire body at the sound of the growl in his voice when he says the word *fuck*. My body wants what it wants, but my mind is strong.

It knows best. And my gut is rarely wrong either. Both are telling me to get the hell out of Jay's apartment before I do something I will deeply regret.

Forgetting about my panties, I stumble toward the door grabbing my jacket and my purse from the floor.

"I'll take you," Jay says, his voice all business from a few feet away.

Disappointment breaks through the cracks in my judgement. I hadn't expected him to give in so easily. He's not even going to argue. "Your bike is at the restaurant," I say.

"I have a truck," he pulls on his shirt with fluid movements, unbothered by the turn in events. "I'll drive you."

I turn away from the sight of him buttoning his shirt. "I'll walk."

"Mia."

My head jerks up at the sound of my name on his lips. I'm still helpless to obey him. If he tells me to stay, I know I will. I can't say no to him, not when I've experienced the exquisite pleasure he's capable of giving me.

Damn my body. I should have procured a fuck buddy just to prevent situations like these. I'd been too long on my dry spell, that must explain why I'm even entertaining the thought of fucking a man who is entirely wrong for me in every possible way.

But all he has to do is say one word. One syllable. And I'm willing to ignore all the red flags waving in my peripheral vision.

Stay.

But he doesn't.

"You're not walking alone at this hour," he says. "I'll walk with you."

A burning feeling spreads through my lungs, and I taste something bitter. "This is Mossy Oak. Not New York City."

His voice snaps like a whip, leaving no room for argument. "I'll walk with you."

There is no use arguing. I stride out the door he holds open, leaving my favorite panties, and any fantasies of fucking a bad boy behind.

CHAPTER 5

Little Hustler

Nothing works. I can't get Mia off my mind.

After walking her to her car and saying goodbye, I spent a sleepless night drinking expensive scotch, feeling sorry for myself, and playing the piano badly.

I finally passed out and woke before dawn with a terrible hangover. Instead of trying to go back to sleep, I decided to punish myself further with a brutal circuit workout.

Anything to forget the woman whose scent still lingered in my apartment.

Ninety minutes into a circuit of pull ups, jumping rope, and punching the heavy bag, my front desk manager unlocks the door and turns on the bright overhead lights. She nearly loses her shit when she sees me jumping rope in the back corner.

"What are you doing here?" she shrieks.

I drop the jump rope and shoot her the evil eye. "Last time I checked, this was my gym."

"Yeah, but..." She pulls out her phone, her eyebrows knitting together as she swipes the screen. "Emily just sent me a picture. I thought you were still there."

Holding up her phone, she shows me a picture of Emily reclining against a headboard, a satisfied grin on her face.

"That smile is no thanks to me," I say, scowling as I pick up my gloves.

"What do you mean?" Laura steps in between me and the bag. "Did you or did you not take my sister on a date last night?"

"Well…" I'm not sure how to have this conversation. "She left with another man."

Laura's mouth opens but no words come out.

I drop my gloves and grab a towel. "Next time you want to set me up with someone," I say, wiping sweat from my face. "Do us both a favor and don't."

"Jay!" Laura follows as I head toward the front door. "What the hell?"

"Ask your sister," I say. "I'm going for a run. I'll be back in a few hours."

"Jay!"

Laura's shrill voice stops me in my tracks. My chest aches with longing for a woman who doesn't want anything to do with me, and all I want is to get her out of my system the only way I know how—to sweat her out. The last thing I feel like doing is answering questions about Emily, who obviously had a much better night than I did. "What?"

Laura frowns up at me. "Are you okay?"

Her question draws a frustrated sigh from the depths of my chest. "I will be."

The front door opens, and Out of the Box's first client of the day steps into the gym. Laura greets him, and I take the opportunity to slip out the door.

My feet know the way. I don't even have to think about which way I'm running to do my usual six mile loop to Gingercake Acres Park and back.

It's still early enough for a chill in the air, but I'm working up too much of a sweat to be cold. I jog along the cobblestone sidewalks lining Main Street, my mind circling back to Mia on an endless loop.

She's hot as fuck, but so are plenty of other women. I've never had one stick in my mind like Mia.

Even after her blunt rejection, I still want her.

They say you always want what you can't have. And I can't have Mia James.

* * *

An afternoon break from the gym at the indoor shooting range seems like the perfect way to blow off steam. Target practice always clears my mind.

Just me and my Smith and Wesson thirty-eight special. No small talk. No questions. No need to be polite to strangers.

The noise-canceling ear protection and whir of the ventilation system make conversation difficult, and most people aren't at the range to socialize.

I must be giving off the don't-fuck-with-me vibe I've honed so well over the years, because no one attempts more than a greeting. It's been months since I've been to the indoor range, but I feel right at home as I stride past the other shooters honing their skills to the empty lane near the end of the row.

Then I see someone familiar.

Fuck me.

I blink slowly, thinking I might have conjured her up with my obsessive thoughts. Because unless there's another five-foot-two blonde bombshell in Mossy Oak, it's Mia James in all her glory.

She's stuns me in a pair of painted on jeans, high heels and a V-neck T-shirt that skims her chest in a way that leaves nothing to the imagination.

She tosses her head in my direction, and our gazes clash. Her eyes widen, and a brief look of longing flashes in her eyes before it is quickly replaced with irritation.

What did I do to annoy her? Besides make her come?

You're welcome, babe.

She dismisses me with a greeting and turns her attention to the target. Aiming down the lane, she fires off six shots in rapid succession.

My dick responds as if she stuck her hand down my jeans and

stroked it.

Fuck me twice.

I'm instantly rock hard. I've never seen anything sexier than Mia with a gun.

I don't need to look at the paper target to guess her accuracy. The confident flash of her smile tells me everything I need to know.

She straightens and pushes her safety glasses up on her head; her pale blonde hair falling in a straight, silky curtain around the ugly plastic. Her blue eyes assess me with cool detachment. A smirk lifts one corner of her lips. "They let you have a gun?"

Ouch. There goes an enormous chunk of my pride, crashing to the rubber-tiled floor.

Mia doesn't know my history. What I've done or what I've been forgiven for. I remind myself I've paid my dues, done my time.

And I would do it all over again in exactly the same way. I have no regrets about my jail time. I'm the man I am today because of my sentence.

My only regret is the one right in front of me. A pint-sized moral crusader with a body built for sin.

"They let you in here wearing that?" I ask, letting my eyes linger on her chest. "That T-shirt is quite the distraction."

Her blue eyes fire beams of ice at me. "That's your problem. Not mine."

I take my position in the cubicle next to her, vowing not to look at her.

"Care to make a little wager?" she asks.

I make sure my gun is pointed at the targets and unzip my bag. "What did you have in mind?"

She replaces her target and presses the button to send it down the lane. "Best of three rounds?"

My inner competitor can't resist a challenge. "What's the prize?"

"Winner's choice," she says.

I pin a target, thinking of the prize I'd like most: her. My mouth waters at the thought of her submitting to me. "You've never seen me shoot," I say, thinking she has no idea what she's gotten herself into.

"You've never seen me shoot." She levels me with a confident stare.

My competitive spirit overrules my practical side. "I'll take that bet."

"Want to go first?"

"Sure." I load my gun and take my stance. Mia makes a little noise that sounds like a laugh and a moan rolled into one. It sets my blood on fire.

"You look seriously hot with a gun," she says in a low smoky voice.

I glance over and see her running her finger over the v of her neckline. Jesus. She's trying to kill me with those curves. I focus on the target, take aim, and only miss one shot.

"Not bad," Mia says.

She spreads her feet and brings her arms up, holding the gun with a two-handed grip that makes my dick strain against my jeans. She fires off her shots, smiling as she pushes the button to bring back the paper target. "Looks like that one goes to me," she says.

"Not so fast." I fire off a perfect round, debating on whether I will ask for a blow job or an apology. Maybe both. I like the thought of her on her knees begging me for forgiveness. "You're up."

Mia shoots perfectly, then tosses me an unapologetic smile.

She's playing me.

Two can play games, though. I focus all my thoughts on the target and fire my gun. I don't miss.

Take that, little hustler.

"You're not bad," she says. "But I'm better."

I place my unloaded gun on the bench and step into her cubicle.

Her chin jerks up, making her blonde hair swing against her shoulders. "You can't be in here."

"You distracted me on my first round." I step close enough to catch the subtle scent of her shampoo. "It's only fair I do the same to you."

"You..." She pushes against my chest, her eyes going wide when I don't budge an inch.

"Just keeping things even," I say. "If you can shoot perfectly during a distraction, I'll give you..." I drop my eyes to her mouth, then further down her body. Her nipples stand out against the cotton of her tight-fitting T-shirt, telling me everything I need to know. "Whatever you want."

She turns around and takes her stance. "You're not going to beat me."

I slide in behind and put my hand on her hip. One tug and she's flush against the hard ridge of my aroused cock. "See what you do to me?"

Her gasp of pleasure sends my blood straight to my crotch. She leans into me, pressing her ass against my hard flesh. I let my hand glide across her hips and over her thigh and lower my mouth to her ear.

"What do I do to you?" I whisper. "Are you wet for me?"

She shifts slightly, rubbing against me like a cat. "Wouldn't you like to know?" Raising her arms, she fires off a perfect round, tossing a grin over her shoulder at me as she stows her gun. "Looks like I won."

"Fuck."

She laughs, zipping up her case. "Don't be a sore loser."

When she tries to move past me, I block her exit. "Not so fast. What about your prize?"

My hands burn with the need to touch her, but I need to let her make the first move. Damn if I can't wait to taste her, kissing that cherry red lipstick right off her mouth.

She looks up at me, her big blue eyes wide with innocence. "I want you to forget about me," she says.

CHAPTER 6
Emails to Book Club

Email message from James.mia@azaleacounty.gov
To: Blue Ridge Book Club Members

Hello friends,

I'm excited to be hosting book club for the first time! I will provide adult beverages. Thatcher will be provide snacks.

Thatcher—please refrain from bringing pizza. You have plenty of notice to bring a decent snack.

If you are unable to join, please let me know by Thursday, 3 pm at the latest.

I've attached a list of the books we will be discussing and a sign up for next month when we will be choosing books for the entire year.

I finished my book last night and will have my review in by end of day. I'm looking forward to reading everyone's reviews!

If you are struggling with uploading to the site, feel free to reach out.

. . .

Regards, Mia

Email message from Lacey_donovan@hyperbolesbookshop.com
    To: James.mia@azaleacounty.gov

Help! I can't get my review to upload no matter what I do!!!

Love, Lacey

P.S. Sorry for all the exclamation points

Email message from yogagirl@gmail.com
    To: Blue Ridge Book Club Members

Guyzzzz!!

I'm sorry to miss book club, but I have decided to stay in Puerto Rico for another week. The yoga instructor scheduled for next week cancelled, so they asked me to stay and teach.

I must admit, they are paying what I make in a whole quarter for one week. I can't say no to that!

Don't have too much fun without me.

Namaste, Kennedy

Email message from xoxovalentina@gmail.com
    To: Blue Ridge Book Club Members

. . .

Hi everyone,

Can't wait to see you! My latest book inspired me to take up surfing! Too bad there is nowhere around here to practice.

XOXO,
Gabi

Email message from Sloane@skyvalleyvineyards.com
To: Blue Ridge Book Club Members

I might be a little late because we have a new chef and he wants us to do a tasting menu. I'll be there as soon as I can.
Mia—I can't wait to see your new place!

Cheers, Sloane

Email message from James.mia@azaleacounty.gov
To: Sloane@skyvalleyvineyards.com

Sloane,

Can you get your hands on a bottle of Sangiovese? I can't find it anywhere.

Regards, Mia

. . .

Email message from Thatcher@Hyperbolesbookshop.com
     To: Blue Ridge Book Club Members

Is everyone okay with pepperoni?

CHAPTER 7

I Understood the Assignment

Lacey takes a long look around my apartment, smiling as she tries to find something nice to say. "It's very clean," she says, finally.

Gabi swoops in to the rescue. "Mia hasn't had time to decorate yet," she says. "She just moved in."

I glance around my apartment, appreciating the calming effect of the monochromatic color scheme. After a stressful day at work, all I want is soothing colors and soft lighting. It might look undecorated to them, but it's perfect to me.

My furniture is the height of modern function. The clean lines and absence of clutter are more than enough to satisfy me.

"Wait until you see the view from my bedroom balcony," I say. "It more than makes up for my lack of interior design talent."

I lead the way up the stairs to my beloved outdoor space. The balcony with the views of the Blue Ridge Mountains is the reason I bought the condo.

Lacey and Gabi follow me to my bedroom and onto the balcony. I have a coveted end unit. No one to my right, and to the left, I'm screened from my neighbor's identical balcony by a row of tall potted plants.

"This is serenity," Lacey says, looking out over the swelling mountain peaks under the hazy blue sky.

Gabi points to an ashtray filled with lipstick-stained butts. "This is a death sentence."

"That's old," I say, dismissing it with a wave. "I quit, remember?"

Gabi gives me the mom glare she's perfected from raising a teenager. "See that *you* remember."

The doorbell rings, and I hurry downstairs to open the door to Thatcher. He's grinning and holding a pizza box in his hand.

I prop my hand on my hip. "No, you didn't."

He strides inside. "Of course I did."

"Asshole."

"Very nice," he says, sweeping a critical gaze around the first floor of my condo. "Very organized."

"And clean," Lacey says from the stairs.

"Mia said no pizza," Gabi says, pointing at the box in Thatcher's hands.

"I love pizza," says Lacey.

"I don't," I say. "I have a bridesmaid's dress to fit into in less than a month. And Chelsea purposefully ordered a size too small."

"That woman is so annoying," Gabi says. "Whatever size you are is already perfect."

"Try living down the street from her," Thatcher says. "She knows everything about everyone."

"Don't even start." I roll my eyes. "She's about to be my sister-in-law."

"This will make you feel better." Thatcher opens the pizza box with a flourish.

Under the lid is an array of girls' night out finger food. Tiny sandwiches, cut vegetables, olives, dip, crackers, and cheese line the pizza box in a rainbow of colors.

Gabi claps with appreciation. "A pizza box grazing board. How original."

Thatcher's grin widens. "I understood the assignment."

Lacey nudges him with her elbow. "You're such a show off."

I take drink orders for wine and beer and head into my kitchen to fill the requests.

The six of us bonded over our love of books, and have been meeting every month for the last year. We each review our own genres of books and pick one to discuss as a group. I'm so obsessed with my job that I don't make time for friends, but these guys are like family.

When we settle down to discuss our chosen books, Thatcher lets us in on the local gossip. "I have a new neighbor," he says. "Pressly Vinroot."

"Beckett's sister," Lacey says, taking a cracker and loading it with cheese. "Sloane's boss," she continues. "Thatcher's first love."

Thatcher looks away with a long sigh. "I might have blown it with her already. And she's not my first love."

Gabi puts her arm around his shoulders. "You still have a chance with her. Just be patient."

"Out of all the places in the entire town, why did she have to buy the house next to mine?"

"Reality is a bitch," Lacey says. "That's why I read."

We all tap our glasses to that and sip thoughtfully. My mind wanders to Jay, where it's been traveling ever since I met him. "Are you still training at that boxing gym?" I ask Thatcher.

"Yeah. Why? You gonna come take one of my self-defense classes?"

"I should be the teacher of that class," I say, taking a sip of wine. "You know I have a black belt in Brazilian Jui Jitsu."

"Yes, we know, Mia." Gabi tosses an almond into her mouth. "And you were first in your class in college. Captain of the archery team."

"Not everyone has an archery team," Lacey points out.

"I'm just saying, I don't need to take self defense."

"Maybe you should come show the other students a thing or two?" Thatcher suggests. "You can be my assistant."

I rise from the sofa, suddenly restless. "How well do you

know the owner?" I ask, an image of Jay shirtless flashes in my mind, and I'm instantly hot.

"Jay?" Thatcher strokes his stubbled chin. "He's a good guy. A little stand-offish, but what do you expect from a champion?"

"He's a champion?" I rest my hip on the back of the sofa, leaning in.

"Heavy weight and Cruiser weight. He held both titles in his mid-twenties."

He's a champion. No wonder he radiates raw power and grace.

"He has a record?" I ask, bracing myself for the details.

Thatcher nods. "He did time."

I lean closer, starved for the details I didn't dare ask. "For what?"

Thatcher raises a brow. "Why all of the sudden interest in Jay? How do you even know him? Can't imagine you two running in the same circles."

"We don't."

Gabi gives me a look only a mom could pull off. "Spill," she says.

I shove a carrot stick into my mouth, pretending to focus on chewing.

"If she doesn't want to tell us she had sex with a guy called *The Savage,* she doesn't have to." Lacey pats my back in sympathy, but the gleam in her tells a different, more curious story.

The doorbell rings, and I hurry to answer it, glad to have some distance between me and the conversation. Sloane has arrived, bearing the wine I asked for, which makes me think of Jay and our evening together. When we kissed, I tasted the sweetness of black cherries and pomegranate on his lips, felt the scrape of his soft beard, and hungered for more.

But as Sloane barrels in with her abundance of peppy energy, the conversation takes a turn toward books. Any chance I have of pumping Thatcher for information about Jay is lost. And it's a good thing, since I'm supposed to be forgetting all about him.

I shouldn't be wondering about what he's doing tonight. If he's thinking of me, even better, touching himself in my honor.

I'm guilty of letting him occupy more space in my thoughts than he should. I've never even considered dating a man who has been to jail, but Jay is... He's so tempting. And I still want to lick those tattoos.

CHAPTER 8

Consider an Upgrade

I'm a fighter, not an accountant. I close the spreadsheet and rub my eyes. None of this makes sense to me, but it's unavoidable. I have to order towels, pay my employees, and make sure everyone is getting their dues in on time.

I'm pulled in a dozen different directions on a daily basis, and managing everything sometimes feels like I might rip apart.

The kids' team, Champion's Corner, is losing money hand over fist. The fees are on a sliding scale, and right now there are more scholarship kids than paying kids. If I don't attract some kids who can afford to pay the full tuition, the program will go under.

I've taken donations from sponsors and done fundraisers with car washes and lotteries, but if I don't figure something out to make some money for the program, all my dreams will be flushed down the toilet.

I lean my elbows on the desk and rest my head in my hands. I've got to think of something big, something to keep the sinking ship afloat.

My mind works better when I move, so I push back from my desk and head down to the gym. Even though it's past ten o'clock, it's never too late for a workout. And I like the gym at night. It's quiet and peaceful.

I flip on the overhead lights and survey the space with a satisfied sweep of my gaze.

Out of the Box is my place.

Plenty of blood, sweat, and tears have gone into making this place what it is. But there's no denying it's all mine.

As I walk the floor, an idea forms in my head.

The gym where I first started training to fight used to hold fight nights featuring amateur and professional boxers.

Every first Friday of the month, the gym had been crowded with spectators and fighters. There had been music and food and so many people, some had to be turned away.

If I could find a fighter worthy of a main event, I could plan the entire event around him—or her. A few promising candidates pop into my mind immediately, and I know I'm onto a good idea.

In North Carolina it doesn't take a lot to go pro. Pass a health screening, be under a certain age, pay the fee, and welcome to professional boxing.

If I can get a few athletes on board, and a few of the older teens from Champion's Corner, I'll have myself an event. I even know the perfect public relations person to promote for me.

Cassandra Darling is not only fabulous at her job, she's also gorgeous with a banging body. I've done some private security jobs for her clients in the past, and we've hooked up a few times. Just casual. Friends with benefits. Cassandra is the perfect remedy for my little Mia James obsession.

The best thing about my idea is it can happen quickly. If we move fast, we can have something set up for the first weekend of the month.

My footsteps echo in the gym's silence, and then I hear another noise. Something that doesn't belong. I'm used to the faint groan of the HVAC system and the rumble of the ice machine.

This is different.

My ears perk up as I stealth-walk toward the locker rooms. I hear hushed voices, then a thump. A chill runs down my spine as I creep closer.

If someone is breaking in, they aren't very good at it. Besides a few jump ropes or some hand weights, there isn't much a thief can walk off with in my gym. I don't keep cash around, and it's not like they are walking off with a punching bag or a treadmill.

I hear more hushed conversation, the click of a door, and then the unmistakable sound of female laughter. A muffled crash comes from the sauna.

I approach the door and listen. Moans and muffled grunts come from the other side of the door.

Sex noises.

Someone snuck into my gym to have sex in the sauna. Anger flares in my chest as I grab the door and yank it open.

On the wooden floor are two teenagers locked in an embrace. Their clothes are half off, and their hands are full of each other. They are so busy making out; they don't even notice me.

I clear my throat loudly, and finally they look up. The girl I've never seen before, but the boy is a regular at Champion's Corner. George, called Turbo in the ring because of his lightning speed, is one of the scholarship kids. He can't afford to pay the fees, but thanks to our sliding scale tuition, he has a spot.

George is a good kid. He gets along well with others, trains with focus, and never bitches about doing chores. I've never met his parents, but I get the feeling they aren't super involved in his life.

"Shit," says George, struggling to wrangle his jeans into place.

Since the underage girl's chest is on full display, I turn around. "My office, George. Now."

I don't wait for him to argue as I turn and march straight to my office. My temper flares as I wait by the door. Every second that ticks by fuels my anger. When George finally slinks down the hall toward me, avoiding eye contact, I'm simmering and ready to boil over.

He doesn't say a word as he brushes by me and enters my small office.

"Where's the girl?" I glance toward the locker rooms.

"She left."

"She has a ride?"

"She has a car."

I point to the sofa pushed against the wall. "Take a seat."

He sits and hangs his head, worrying his hands in his lap. When I slam the office door, he jumps. "Jesus."

"Mind your fucking mouth."

His head jerks up, brows raised, but he quickly swallows his protest and nods respectfully. "Yes, sir."

I push aside some papers and lean my hip on the desk. "How the hell did you get in here?"

George lifts his gaze halfway up to my face, but can't quite meet my eyes. "I broke in. I didn't think you were here."

I'd been at my desk most of the night. Besides a quick dinner break, I hadn't moved. Sneaky bastard. How the hell did he get past me? "What about the alarm?"

He finally looks up at me. "It's an outdated system. You might want to consider an upgrade."

Anger mounts in my chest. Something tells me this isn't the first time he's snuck in here. "Have you done this before?"

His mouth clamps shut, but I wait him out. After a long silence, he finally cracks. "I sleep here sometimes when my dad puts me out."

My jaw flexes. I've never actually met George's dad. Unlike the other parents, he doesn't come to competitions. And George has never mentioned his mom.

Call me a sucker, but my heart goes out to the kid. I may not have had a lot growing up, but I did have a mom who loved me. It made up for a lot of the other shit going on in my life.

"You're this close to getting kicked out of Champion's Corner," I say.

The color drains from George's face. "I'm sorry, I won't do it again. I'll do anything to stay. I need to stay."

I hold up a hand to stop Georges groveling. I know what Champion's corner means to these kids. For some of them, it's the only stability they have in their lives. If they don't do well in school, or have a good home to go to, they can come here.

I move around to my desk and sit down in the chair, leveling him with a stern gaze. "You can't break in here anymore," I say. "You want to go to jail? I can tell you, it's not a fun place to be."

"I won't get caught."

I stare him down. "Seems to me you just did."

"I wasn't stealing anything."

"Shut up, George." My voice is quiet, but deadly.

His gaze skitters away from mine, all pretense at bravery vanished. "Sorry, sir."

"You and this girl are having sex?"

His face goes up in flames, and he looks like he wants to crawl under the desk. "Yeah."

I hold back the urge to swear. "You're sixteen years old."

"So? I'm sure you were bonin' some chick when you were sixteen."

I stand up, looming over him. "Are you staying safe?"

"I know about all that. You don't have to lecture me."

"Don't be an asshole!" I nearly bite his head off. "You want a kid at your age?"

"No." A sullen look crosses his face. "But I can't buy rubbers at the Blanchard's. Miss Bella would rat me out." He cocks his head. "Guess I could lift them."

I glower at him. "No stealing."

He sighs, looking miserable.

"If you're gonna have sex, use protection. Not just the pill," I say. "There are other..." I hesitate, trying to figure out exactly how I got myself into this conversation.

"You don't have to give me the talk. I'm not a baby."

I grab a notepad, write down my cell, and rip out the page. "Call me if you need a place to stay. You can crash here."

The color fades from his cheeks and his eyes widen. "You mean it?"

I nod and force the paper on him. "I mean it. But no girls. This isn't your bachelor pad."

"Alright."

His hopeful face embarrasses me. "If I catch you breaking in here again, I won't call the cops. But I will make sure you learn your lesson. You hear me?"

He nods, pocketing the paper. "I got it."

"And first thing tomorrow, I need you back here at the gym. You're gonna scrub down the sauna before I open in the morning."

He pulls a face. "But I've got school."

"Then I'll see you before. Bright and early." A thought comes to mind, and it makes me cringe. Where else has George been bringing girls? "All week you're gonna stay after and help me with chores."

George doesn't even attempt to protest. He knows he's getting off easy.

"You got a place to stay tonight?"

When he nods, I point to the door. "Get lost."

He scrambles to the door. On his way out, he turns to look at me, and I swear I see tears shining in his eyes. "Thanks."

I stack a folder on my desk, pretending to be busy, and nod. "Bright and early tomorrow," I remind him.

He leaves, and I wait until I hear the door close before following him out. If a sixteen-year-old can break in, my security system needs revamping.

At least it will give me something to occupy my mind other than my problems.

CHAPTER 9
Knight on a Shining Harley

I've been at my desk all day, and every muscle in my body is cramped. The text messages come at the perfect time, reminding me I need to leave. Thatcher is renovating the house his uncle left him, and we've all been roped in to helping him pack up his uncle's library.

Almost everyone is gone for the day. Everyone except me and Jordan, which is like every other night. Both of us are workaholics who often stay late, ordering takeout for dinner.

Not tonight.

I have plans. I have a life. I'm not chained to my desk. Nope. Not me.

My bones creak as I stand from my chair and stretch.

A knock on my door sounds a moment before Jordan steps in. "You want Chinese or Mexican?"

"Neither." I roll my shoulders, which ache just like the rest of me. I feel one hundred years old after sitting in the same position for hours.

"Thai?" Jordan looks up from his phone.

"I'm leaving," I say. And I don't feel bad about it. I've been working like a dog for months.

"Hot date?"

I grab my purse from the bottom drawer and catch a glimpse of the invitation to my brother's wedding, which reminds me exactly how pathetic my dating life is. I'd planned on asking Harrison to be my date at Max's destination wedding, but those plans are forgotten now. "Not a date," I say. "Book club."

"You and your book club," he says, tapping on his phone. "You guys are tight."

I shove the invitation to the back of the drawer. Maybe I could ask Thatcher to be my date. Thatcher is handsome and charming, and we are close enough that he could fake being my boyfriend to impress my family. If they knew I was single, I'd never hear the end of it. My baby brother is already getting married before me, which my mom never tires of reminding me.

Grabbing my jacket off the back of my chair, I tuck my purse under my arm. "See you tomorrow."

Jordan looks up from his phone, his brow creased. "Wait. There's something I need to talk to you about."

My heart jumps to my throat. Not more bad news. "What?"

Jordan pinches the bridge of his nose. "I received a threat."

"Someone is threatening you?"

He shakes his head. "Not me. You."

"Oh." My shoulders relax. "I get threats sometimes. Don't we all?"

Jordan winces. "Not like this. I'm concerned for you."

I pull on my jacket. "What kind of threats?"

"It's better if you don't know the specifics, but trust me, they are worth taking seriously."

"I take threats seriously," I say. "I just don't let them intimidate me." I've put a lot of people in jail over the last few years. Threats are part of the package. It's one of the reasons I have a concealed carry license.

"How is your home security?" Jordan asks.

My alarm system came with the condo. I haven't given it much thought. "It's fine."

Jordan reaches out and takes my shoulders, looking deeply into my eyes. I don't think we've ever been this close before, and the intense way he's looking at me is unnerving.

"Fine isn't good enough." His jaw flexes, a muscle ticking under his five o'clock shadow. "I want you safe."

"Don't worry about me."

His hands grip my shoulders tighter. "This is serious."

His touch makes me feel trapped, and I take a step back. "I can handle it."

Jordan shakes his head. "I know a guy who does private security. A professional bodyguard who knows his shit. He'll check out your security and watch your back."

A muscle twitches in my neck. I don't need anyone watching my back. The last thing I want is someone trailing behind me, getting in my business, telling me what to do. And how would it look to everyone? Like I'm weak. Like I can't take care of myself. *No way.*

I force a laugh, dismissing his concern. "I don't need a bodyguard."

Jordan blocks my exit. "You're important around here. The state will pay to make sure you're protected."

Frustration builds in my chest, but I press it down. "Jordan, this is ridiculous. The budget doesn't cover security."

"It does if I say so. I want you safe, Mia." He pins me with a sharp stare. "You're vital to this office."

My heart softens, and some of my frustration fades. It's good to be appreciated. It almost makes up for Jordan underestimating me.

Still...

"Thank you. But I don't want personal security." I stand to my full height, wishing it was more for the millionth time in my life. If I was taller, people would have to take me more seriously.

"We'll discuss it later." Jordan opens the door, allowing me to exit. "I'll walk you to your car."

I don't attempt to argue. These threats must be bad if Jordan is so riled up. He insists on waiting until I've started my car before leaving the parking lot.

Jordan's worry has me paranoid. I feel like someone is watching me, and I imagine a car following me as I pull onto Main Street.

I need a cigarette.

My emergency pack is empty, so I make a quick detour out of town. I don't buy cigarettes at Blanchard's because Miss Bella is nosy as hell and the worst gossip in town.

I'm relieved that the headlights are no longer behind me as I leave Mossy Oak and drive one town over, to a convenience store.

They have a decent selection of wine, and I grab a bottle to share with the book club.

"Anything else?" the clerk asks.

I point to my brand of choice. "I'll take a pack of those, please."

"I thought you didn't smoke."

My head whips around at the familiar voice, and I see the sexiest guy in town standing right behind me. Jay lowers his chin, pinning me with those gold-flecked brown eyes.

My heart crashes against my ribs at the sight of him. I don't think I will ever get used to the sheer magnitude of his masculine presence. He's wearing his usual black, and he's carrying a box of condoms.

I stare at the box in his hand. It burns me up that he's buying condoms. It shouldn't. I'm the one who rejected him. But still...

"Planning on getting lucky tonight?" I ask.

His eyes widen, and he glances down at the box of condoms in his hands. "It's not what you think."

I swipe my card through the reader and grab my wine and cigarettes. "Safety first," I say, pushing past him.

My blood heats as I stride through the door. *What a player.* He probably has dozens of women lined up. I was nothing to him.

Feeling justified in my decision to reject him, I turn the corner of the building only to run into a man.

"Sorry." I suck in a surprised breath. "I didn't see you."

Rough hands clamp on my arms, pinning them to my sides. "You should be sorry, Ms. James," he says with a low chuckle. "You tried to ruin my life."

My eyes adjust to the darkness, and I see it's Warner Mattson looming over me. He's taller than he seemed across the courtroom, and broader. He's wearing the clothes of a businessman—a pristine suit, a crisp white shirt, and an understated tie—but his eyes are wild.

His grip on my upper arms tightens, and he pushes me back into the shadows against the rough brick of the building.

I know I should move. I should scream. I should taser him in the nuts.

But I can't do anything. I'm frozen to the spot, my body locked in the stranglehold of terror. Nausea twists my belly, and my vision clouds. A taunting voice echoes in my head.

I'm gonna give you what you want.

You're gonna love this.

It hadn't been what I wanted. And I hadn't loved it.

"Not so high and mighty now, are you?" Warner's hot, sour breath brings me back to the moment.

I scream, but the sound ricochets in my head, never making it to my mouth. My heart races, and a shiver runs through me. I can't breathe as Warner closes the space between us, sucking up all the air.

"Take your fucking hands off the lady right now," a deep growl sounds from a few feet away.

It takes me a moment to recognize Jay's voice. I've never heard it so low before.

Warner loosens his grip and takes a step back, but doesn't let me go. "Relax, man. We're just having a little chat."

"Chat's over." Jay takes two long strides, and there is suddenly a human wall between Warner and me. His arm pushes me slightly behind him, and his broad back blocks my view.

Warner's casual laugh sounds. "Sure, man. No hard feelings. We were just catching up, right Mia?"

"Get lost," Jay says, widening his stance. Tension radiates off his body, sending a message even clearer than the deep growl in his voice.

Warner would have to be an idiot to challenge Jay. And even though he is a dirty criminal, he's not stupid. "Good catching up with you," Warner says in a casual tone. "I'll see you soon."

His footsteps fade away, and Jay turns to face me. "You okay, Mia?" His voice is softer now, gentle.

A shiver runs through me, and I drag in a breath. I smell the familiar scent of Jay. Leather and pine, he smells like the fresh outdoors. His eyes spark with anger and frustration, and he's vibrating with the effort to suppress it.

But he's restrained with me, patient, and kind. He doesn't touch me, or get too close, but he watches with a protective gleam, his body coiled and ready to pounce on anyone who gets too close.

Shame surges through me. I've acted like a coward, showing vulnerability when I should have been tough. It's fucking embarrassing.

"I'm okay." My voice is a thread pulled too tightly, ready to snap. "I don't need your help."

A storm clouds Jay's dark eyes. He reaches out, but lets his hand drop before touching me. "What was that about?"

I grimace, remembering how I'd frozen like a scared rabbit when I should have kicked Warner Mattson in the balls, rendering him incapable of reproduction. "Nothing."

Jay's eyes narrow. "Old boyfriend?"

I cringe at the thought, my skin crawling at the memory of Mattson's touch. "No."

"You're shaking." His brows pull together, eyes tight in the corners. "Let me walk you to your car."

"I don't..."

He cocks his head at me. "Just let me, okay?"

I sigh and stalk to my car, not looking over my shoulder as he follows and waits for me to get inside.

Resting his hand on the roof of the car, he leans down. "You okay to drive?"

I nod and look pointedly at the plastic bag in his hand. "I'm sure you have somewhere to be."

He tucks the bag behind him. "Thatcher asked me to come over and help pack up his uncle's office."

An ache builds behind my eyes. "Really?" *I'm going to kill Thatcher.* "It was supposed to be just our book club."

Jay shrugs. "He needed some muscle."

I can't help but stare at Jay's biceps, bulging beneath his jacket. "We could have managed without you."

"I'll follow you," he says.

"You don't have to." Sweat trickles down my back, and a chill spreads through me.

"We're going the same way," he says. "It's no trouble."

He strides off toward his bike. I watch him climb on with effortless grace, irritation bubbling in my chest.

Breaking my rule never to smoke in my car, I light a cigarette and take a deep drag. I don't know who I'm more angry with— Mattson for trying to intimidate me, myself for freezing up, or Jay for coming to my rescue.

Myself. Definitely myself.

And now, unless I want to bail on one of my best friends, I have to spend the entire evening with my knight on a shining Harley Davidson.

CHAPTER 10

Love Always Wins

Thatcher lives in the fancy part of town. The wide streets lined with ancient trees, manicured lots, and stately homes couldn't be more opposite to the trailer park where I grew up.

He inherited both the house and his bookstore from his uncle. He's a hardworking guy, with a backstory only a few people know about. I'm one of them because I tried to get him to renew his license as a professional boxer. I thought he had the size, strength, and talent to be a champion, but he assured me his days in the ring were over. His reasons why were enough to make me back off. Him trusting me with his story is the reason we are more than just a gym owner and member. We're friends.

It's not the first time I've helped Thatcher at the dilapidated house he inherited. I was there when he ripped out the cabinets in the kitchen, and I helped him cart off the disgusting carpet from the upstairs bedroom.

Thatcher is a good guy, but all his friends are women. None of them are strong enough to help knock down walls or carry heavy equipment. Thatcher had said he was inviting his book club friends to help box up the library, and I'd volunteered for one reason—Mia.

I'd known I'd see her tonight. I'd even stopped by the wine

store and found a bottle of Chianti similar to the Sangiovese we'd had at the wine bar. I hadn't expected to run into her while buying condoms for George at the convenience store. And I definitely hadn't expected to chase off some asshole who'd been groping her in the parking lot.

I haven't lost my temper in years, but I was close when I saw the slime ball's hands on Mia. My first instinct was to knock him out, then ask questions later.

She'd looked so lost and afraid, like a little girl facing a nightmare in the dark. And even though she'd insisted she was fine, I'd seen the terror in her eyes.

My teeth grind in frustration as I pull to a stop behind Mia's silver Lexus and climb off my bike. I never want to see that look on her face again.

She gets out of her car and marches toward Thatcher's house without a glance in my direction.

I grab the bottle of wine from my bag and follow her up the sidewalk, catching up with her easily.

"You can stop following me now," she says, tossing a glare at me over her shoulder.

"Kinda hard when we're going to the same place." I gesture to the traditional brick home with four columns and a wide front porch.

She stops abruptly, a challenge in her pale blue eyes. "What are you doing here, anyway? There are no men allowed in our book club."

I hold back a smile. "What about Thatcher?"

"He doesn't count." She balls a fist and plants it on her hip. "He's harmless."

I shift closer, invading her space. "And I'm not?"

Her gaze drops to my mouth, and she pulls in a sharp breath.

She feels the tug of energy between us just like I do. Whenever we are close, there is the need to get closer. We are definitely a dangerous combination, a bomb ready to detonate.

"You're annoying," she says.

"And *you* are the epitome of charm."

"Big word." She tilts her chin to glare at me. "Do you even know what it means?"

I reach up and cup her cheek, my thumb tracing the tight muscle in her jaw. "It means you have me enchanted, and I have no idea why."

Her eyes soften, going from Ice Queen to cool inviting waters. She touches my chest, her hand flattening over my racing heart. Every muscle in my body goes taut when she looks at me like that. I dip my head, and she rises up on the balls of her feet.

"Hey ya'll!"

Mia startles and jumps away from me, putting at least a foot between us. Her cheeks bloom with color as she looks toward the sidewalk. "Hi Chelsea."

"Having a little party?" Chelsea walks up the sidewalk with her dog, staring at me with open curiosity. "Jay Sanchez, right?"

"That's right. Chelsea Taylor. Kickboxing."

Her face brightens. "You remember me?"

I nod. I remember everyone who comes into my gym. "Thanks for being a member."

"It's the best workout in town," she says. Transferring her gaze to Mia, she frowns. "You haven't sent in your RSVP yet."

Mia's entire body tenses. Frustration rolls off her in waves. "You know I'm coming," she says, smiling falsely. "I'm in the wedding."

"Of course." Chelsea's gaze darts to me, then back to Mia. "Do you have a plus one? You're not dating anyone, are you?"

Mia's lips pinch together. "I'll let you know," she says in a tight voice.

"No worries," Chelsea says in a tone that sounds exactly the opposite. "I just want to make sure everything is perfect for Samantha. She's got so much on her plate."

Mia clenches her jaw. "We all do."

Chelsea scoffs. "But she's the bride."

"Everything will be perfect," Mia says with a long-suffering sigh. "Max adores her. That's all that matters."

Chelsea's dog pulls on his leash, and she turns to go. "Love always wins," she says in a sing-song.

Mia glares at her as she walks away. "God, she's insufferable."

"What was that about?"

"My brother is marrying her sister." Mia grimaces. "I can't believe I'm going to be related to her."

"When's the wedding?" I ask.

"Six weeks," she says. "It's a destination wedding on this little island off the coast of Florida." She rolls her eyes. "It's their family tradition to get married there."

"And you don't have a date."

Her head snaps in my direction, and she glares at me. "I'll have one by then."

I bite back a smile. "Harrison?"

Her gorgeous eyes glitter with annoyance. "It's none of your business."

"You could ask me. I could use a vacation."

She takes a step back and starts up the stairs to the front porch. All the warmth between us a few moments ago evaporates with the icy glare she gives me.

"I won the bet," she says. "Forget about me. It's for the best."

"I tried," I say. "I can't."

"Try harder."

"Maybe we need a new bet. I think you cheated. Plus, I saved you from that asshole, so you owe me one."

Her entire body stiffens. "I didn't ask you to save me." She strides up the steps and looks down at me. "And I didn't cheat," she says. "I'm just better than you."

Flames of heat sizzle up the back of my neck, and I drop my gaze before she can see all my secrets. Maybe she didn't mean for it to come out like that, but it's too late, the words are between us. I know without a doubt; she believes she's better than me. And not just at shooting targets.

A dozen years stand between me and my jail time, and hundreds of miles separate me from the desolate trailer park where I grew up, but I feel like I am right back there again. I'll never be good enough for a woman like Mia.

The thought burns in my chest, making me struggle to catch my breath.

Mia stops at Thatcher's door and turns around to look at me. "You coming?"

I nod tersely. "Just a minute."

It's best I put some distance between us and remind myself of the bet Mia had won. She's right. Forgetting her is best for both of us.

CHAPTER 11

Rethinking My Goals

I stow my jacket and purse in my office and take a cautionary sip of my overly caffeinated coffee. I hardly slept at all last night, thinking about how I'd done everything wrong with Mattson. Then I'd treated Jay like shit, alternately ignoring him, insulting him, and scowling at him all night. My friends had called me out for acting like a bitch, and I had no excuse for my behavior. It's not like I could tell them what happened with Mattson. They would freak out, insist I spend the night with one of them. Or worse.

I throw myself into my job, spending hours catching up on emails and making calls. The day flies by, and just as I'm getting ready to take a late lunch break, I get a message from Elena. She can meet me tomorrow at Ginger Cake Acres, near the kid's park.

Adrenaline buzzes through my system at the thought of getting closer to nailing Mattson. After yesterday's stunt, I'm more determined than ever to make him pay. I forget lunch and keep working. I don't realize how late it's gotten until my phone dings with an appointment reminder.

I have a fitting for my bridesmaid's dress. Oh, joy! Not only will I get a warning from the dress shop about how they can't let my dress out if I gain weight, I'll also get to see Chelsea.

On my way out, I stop in to tell Jordan I'm leaving.

I used to dream of having his office one day. It's the nicest one in the building, with a closet and a window. Lately, I've been rethinking my goals. District Attorney James was a title I once craved, but everything changed when Jordan declined to prosecute Warner Mattson.

I'm not sure where I'll end up in a few years, but I can guarantee it won't be Jordan's office—even if it does have a window.

I knock lightly on his door before entering.

Jordan doesn't look up from behind his mountain of paperwork. His hair is disheveled, his tie is loosened, and there are half a dozen empty coffee cups on his desk. The unmistakable scent of cigarette smoke stings my nose, stirring a craving I fight with every bone in my body.

"Mia," Jordan says, looking up from his desk. "Come in." He flicks his wrist for me to enter.

"I'm late for something," I say, stepping all the way into the office.

Jordan leans back in his chair and loosens his tie. "Another hot date with the CPA?" he asks, raising one brow.

"Real estate agent," I say.

"Right. That's what I meant." He stacks folders on his desk and pushes them aside. "You only date one type of guy."

It's true, I tend to stick with safe, predictable men with white-collar professions. Except for Jay...

"I've got about five minutes," I say, shutting off the part of my brain that called up a picture of Jay's shirtless torso, sculpted to perfection. "If you want to waste it talking about my dating life, that's your call, Boss."

Jordan sips from one of the coffee cups, grimacing as he swallows. "Close the door."

I shut the door behind me and walk over to the window, which is slightly cracked, allowing a chilly mountain breeze to drift inside. There are telltale ashes in the window sash, giving away Jordan's secret. He *has* been smoking in here.

"Care to tell me what you're up to?" Jordan asks.

I spin to face him, my hands raised in an innocent gesture. "I have no idea what you're talking about."

He cocks his head at me, giving me the look he's perfected with hostile witnesses. "You can't hide things from me in my own office."

I shake my head, wondering how he found out about my meeting with Elena. I didn't say anything to anyone or write it down in my calendar. And then I realize that Jordan is bluffing. He doesn't have anything on me, he's just trying to get me to spill.

"I'm not hiding anything." I force a smile, checking the time again. Chelsea is going to flip if I'm late.

Jordan gives me one long look before nodding tersely. "Good. That's good, Mia. We need to trust each other, right?"

I nod in agreement. Jordan has definitely been at his desk too long. "Right."

Jordan rises from behind his desk and crosses to the window to stand next to me. "I have to come clean with you."

My lips twitch as I suppress a smile. He's going to admit he's smoking in his office. But why call me in here for that? Jordan has been working too hard. He's losing it. "What?"

"There have been more threats," he says.

I cock my head at him, noticing the new gray hair at his temples. Jordan isn't a day over forty, but the job has aged him. "What kind of threats?"

He shoves his hands in his pockets and rocks back on his heels. "Some pretty nasty stuff online. Pretty specific." He winces. "All directed at you."

A shiver runs down my spine. *Fucking Mattson.* I know it's him. Dirty bastard is trying to get under my skin. "Thanks for the heads up."

"It's time to bring in outside help," Jordan says.

"What?" My thoughts scramble as I try to catch up. "I told you I don't want that." I force a laugh. "Internet threats don't scare me." And if Mattson bothers me again, I'll be ready for him. I won't react like a scared puppy, cowering in the shadows.

Jordan touches my shoulder, and I jump at the contact.

He squeezes gently, his expression softer than usual and filled with concern. "You're shaking."

I shrug his hand off my shoulder and blink back a sudden torrent of tears. "I'm fine. It's just cold in here." I gesture at the window. "You left the window open."

"I can't have you in danger. You're too important to..." He pauses and swallows hard before continuing. "To this office."

A flush of genuine pride fills my body. Jordan has never given me more than the cursory compliment. He's always been a good boss, but he's never been kind.

Jordan holds my gaze for a long moment before striding back to his desk. He opens a folder and takes out a business card, handing it to me with a concerned expression. "This guy is good. He's local and discreet."

I glance at the black business card with gold embossed lettering. "I don't need someone following me around." The humiliation is almost too much to bear. "I can take care of myself."

Jordan clamps his mouth shut and rubs the back of his neck. I feel almost sorry for him, but I still don't want a bodyguard getting into my business.

"Just promise me you will think about it," Jordan says.

I nod briskly, eager to be finished with this conversation. "Will do, Boss. Anything else?"

He holds up his coffee mug. "Can you start a new pot on your way out?"

"Sure." I escape before he can add anything else, and pour a hefty helping of decaffeinated beans into the brew I fix for him. He's had enough caffeine for one day if he thinks there's any way I'm getting a bodyguard.

CHAPTER 12

Worth Your While

I circle the boxing ring, watching Manny and Thatcher exchange punches. It's just a sparring match, but with Fight Night coming up in a few weeks, every second of training counts. Manny looks distracted, and I try to bring his focus back to the training with direct instructions.

"Keep your hands up. Move your feet. Jesus Christ, look alive, will you?"

Even though we've planned for several amateur fights, including a debut from a Champion's Corner fighter, the entire event rides on the main card, which is Manny "The Killer Bee" Perez verses "The Hitman" Logan Malone.

Cassandra and her firm have done a great job stirring up interest on social media, and the event is nearly sold out. The ticket sales, plus concessions and sponsorships will be enough to fund another season of Champion's Corner.

"You need a break?" I ask Manny.

He shakes his head, throwing another punch that Thatcher easily dodges.

I shift my focus from Manny to Thatcher, noticing his agility, his strength, and the look in his eye that says he's determined to crush anything in his way.

"Move your feet, Manny."

Thatcher throws a punch Manny can't duck, and he takes the hit with a muffled oaf. I transfer my attention to Thatcher, watching him instead of Manny. Thatcher has the whole package, and he's the most dedicated guy I know. He never misses a day of training, and his involvement at the gym goes beyond his personal goals. Thatcher volunteers with the self-defense classes and the youth group. He's an army veteran and business owner, a perfect role model for the kids. And his recent photograph in the Men of Mossy Oak Calendar clad in his boxer briefs will bring an audience of women to the fight.

Maybe I should add him to the card. A celebrity match. An idea forms in my mind, fleshing out by the minute as I watch Thatcher hold his own against the best fighter in the gym.

Cassandra would have a field day with Thatcher Hayes. He's got a great personality, and he'd look great on a social media post.

"Take five," I tell Manny. "Hey, Thatcher? Come here a minute. I want to run something by you."

"Sure. What's up?"

"You ever thought about getting in the ring for real?"

Thatcher nods. "Pretty much all the time."

Perfect. "If you ever want to step back in, let me know."

His eyes spark with interest. "I'll think about it."

"Hey, Coach?" George comes up next to the ring, interrupting us.

"Just a minute, kid." I don't take my eyes off Thatcher. "What aren't you saying?"

Thatcher shakes his head. "I'll tell you later."

I glance over at Manny, who is watching us curiously. "You ready to look alive?" I ask.

"Ready."

"Get back to it. Keep those hands up." I take my eyes off them and look at George, who has been waiting patiently. "What do you want?"

"Can I go? The bathrooms are clean."

The kid looks exhausted. He's been coming in early every day for weeks. "Check with Laura and see if she has anything for you, then you can go."

"Thanks, Coach."

"Get home safe, George," I call after him.

I'm looking at George when the worst thing that could happen happens. Manny throws a punch, Thatcher doesn't dodge, and the howl of pain from Manny's mouth can only mean one thing.

He's hurt.

* * *

Two hours later, I'm sitting in the emergency room waiting to hear the results. But I already know. Manny's hand is broken.

Fight Night is in jeopardy.

My first call is to Cassandra.

"We've got a problem," I say as soon as she picks up her phone.

"Hello Jay, always good to hear from you."

"I'm at the hospital."

"Shit." The teasing tone in her voice vanishes. "Are you okay?"

"It's not me."

"You almost gave me a heart attack. Don't scare me like that."

I pace back and forth in the waiting room, wearing a path out on the linoleum tile. "It's Manny. His hand is broken."

She releases a long sigh. "That's not the end of the world. Is it?"

I shove a hand through my hair. "It could be the end of the event. That fight is the main draw."

"Do me a favor, will you?"

I pace to the end of the room and peer into the hallway, hoping to catch a glimpse of a nurse who can keep me informed. "What?"

"Take a breath and chill out. Everything is gonna be just fine."

Her smooth voice has no effect on me. Not when the kid's

program I've fought for can't make it without a serious influx of cash. I was counting on Fight Night to save the program. Now everything is unraveling. Guilt and regret are like a double-edged sword in my gut.

"Breathe, Jay."

"I'm breathing." I suck in a breath so she can hear it.

"I wish I was there to make you feel better." Cassandra's voice is soothing in my ear, but there's only one woman I want to make me feel better. And she made me promise to forget about her.

"What should we do?"

"Don't worry. I can spin this. You just need to find another fighter and convince Malone to accept the change."

"I don't have another fighter." *Except maybe Thatcher.*

"You have an entire gym full of fighters. You can find someone."

"None of them are ready, and the fight is in two weeks."

"What about you?"

My stomach clenches. I haven't fought in years. "I'm retired."

"You can come out of retirement. You're in shape, aren't you?"

"That's not the point. I don't fight anymore."

"Why not?"

A rumble of anger and frustration threatens to break free from my chest, but I choke it down. The waiting room is filled with people. I can't lose it in front of an audience.

"I don't fight anymore."

"Okay, okay," Cassandra says, letting it drop. "You can find someone else."

"I might have someone in mind."

"See? Don't panic," Cassandra says. "It's going to be an amazing event."

"Thanks, Cassandra."

"No problem. Don't forget to breathe. And if you need me to come to Mossy Oak, I'll be there."

"No. I've got this." I don't have a choice. The nurse who took

Manny back comes down the hall, looking for me. "I've got to go."

"I'm only a phone call away," Cassandra says before hanging up.

I walk over to the nurse only to find out that Many has a broken hand just as I suspected. They are treating him and it will be another hour before he's released.

"You can see him if you want," she says.

I shake my head. He's got his wife with him; he doesn't need me.

As I'm leaving the hospital, my phone rings with a number I don't recognize.

"Hello?"

"Is this Savage Security?" A man's voice asks.

"Yes." I haven't had time for a job in months, and I don't have time now. Luckily, I'm freelance and can pick and choose my clients. "What can I do for you?"

"This is Jordan Adler from the district attorney's office. I'm reaching out to see if you have availability in your schedule to do a private security job for us."

I push through the exit doors and walk through the parking lot to my truck. The fresh mountain breeze is a welcome change from the stale air in the hospital room.

"My schedule is pretty full."

"The pay will be worth your while," he says.

"How worth my while?"

He throws out a number that gets my attention. "What's the timeline?"

"You'd have to start tonight," he says.

My night is already over thanks to Manny and his broken hand. "I can arrange that. What's the location?"

"I'll text the address."

My phone dings with the address, which is only a few blocks away in a part of town popular with young professionals. I can drive by and check it out on my way home to grab some gear.

I get a notepad and pen from my glove box. "Who's the client?"

"She's very important," he says. "I need you to make sure she's well taken care of. And you need to be discreet."

"No problem." Keeping my mouth shut is part of the job.

"Is it a witness?" I ask.

"No," he says. "It's a fellow prosecutor."

An alarm goes off in my head. Mia is an attorney with the county. "Which prosecutor?"

"The best one we have," he says. "Mia James."

No way. I can't take this job. Protecting Mia means spending time with her. A lot of time. I'm not signing up for that torture.

"I may have a conflict in my schedule," I say.

"Okay," he says after a brief pause. "But I've heard you're the best. I want the best for her."

"Yeah?" When he puts it like that, it's impossible for me to say no. There's no one else I would trust Mia's safety with, especially after seeing that prick put his hands on her outside the convenience store. "Send the email," I say, throwing my truck into gear. "I'll take the job."

CHAPTER 13

Let Me Take Care of You

After a long day at work, followed by a dress fitting where I'd been warned not to gain a single ounce before the wedding, the only thing I want is a glass of wine and a romance novel.

I pull into my condominium complex and wind along the meandering streets to my section, trying to put Chelsea and her annoying comments about my figure out of my mind. She's ordered matching swimsuits for us to wear and let me know I still had time to get my bikini body.

When I pull into my parking area, I immediately notice the familiar motorcycle parked in the lot. The man sitting on the bike has his back to me, but there's no mistaking Jay.

Black denim, black leather, with a side of sexy. He's perfectly wrong for me, but oh so delicious.

Don't trip.

Don't drool.

He climbs off the bike and shakes out his hair.

Fucking hell.

He is the hottest man of the year. Who am I kidding? I can't deny how much I want him. He's seduction on legs. When he strides toward me, shifting his helmet from hand to hand in a fidgety gesture, I see the longing in his gaze and liquid pools between my thighs.

He must be here to beg me for another chance. Has he been thinking about me non-stop? Thank God he didn't listen when I told him to forget me. He stops a foot in front of me, his body radiating tension and barely concealed restraint.

"Jay. What are you doing here?"

His eyes soften, dropping down my face and lingering on my lips. "Waiting for you."

And just like that, I'm slick with desire. "Why?"

He steps closer, lowering his face to whisper in my ear. "I'm your bodyguard."

The hair on the back of my neck stands up. "What?"

He places his hand on my shoulder and gently turns me toward my unit. "Let's talk inside."

His hand is firm, guiding me toward my unit. "Wait. You're what?" I sputter, trying to fit the pieces together. Jay isn't here to win me over, he's here on a job. A job I didn't approve of. I'm going to kill Jordan. I whip out my phone. "No way."

"Yes," he says, stopping in front of my door and scanning the parking lot behind us. "Let's talk inside. I don't know how safe it is out here."

He's right. It's better to take this discussion indoors away from any nosy neighbors who might want to get an eyeful of Jay. Who could blame them?

I open the door to my condo, and Jay goes in first. He strides through my living room into my kitchen and peers out the blinds to the tiny patio.

"This is ridiculous." I follow him, clamping my hand on his arm as he reaches for the back door. "You can't be my bodyguard."

His arm stiffens under my hand. "Why not?"

"I don't need a bodyguard."

Jay brushes past me, walking back through the living room toward the stairs. "Wait here while I check upstairs."

"Wait." I hurry after him. The rest of my house is pretty clean, but my bedroom is a disaster. "I wasn't expecting company."

He turns on the stairs and places his hands on my shoulders. "Stay."

My blood simmers. "I'm not your dog. And I don't need a bodyguard. I have a taser, a gun, and I know self defense." I raise my arms in a fighting stance. "Want to see?"

Jay's lip curls. "You don't want me to answer that."

Desire crashes through me at the low growl of his voice, followed quickly by annoyance. "Don't underestimate me."

"I wouldn't dare." His expression hardens. "Can I check the rest of the place now?"

"I don't need..."

He sighs heavily. "Don't argue, Mia. Just let me do my job. If you want to take it up with Mr. Adler, that's fine, but let me make sure your place is safe."

I narrow my eyes at him. "What did Jordan say?"

"Only that you are in possible danger." He leans on the bannister. "Can you let me take care you?"

For fuck's sake, I've been doing nothing but fantasizing about how this tall, sexy man can take care of me. I straighten and school my expression into neutrality and nod. "Go ahead. Check under my bed for monsters."

He strides up the stairs and opens my bedroom door. I cringe at what he must be seeing. The unused treadmill, stacks of romance novels next to my unmade bed, and piles of laundry yet to be put away. I must look like a pathetic loser. It's so embarrassing I want to hide. Instead, I wait patiently at the top of the stairs.

"Nice view from the balcony," Jay says, coming out of my room. "Who lives next door?"

"No one," I say, pushing past him into my bedroom. I grab the stacks of clothes and hurry into my walk-in closet to put them away. "It's for sale, and guess who's the agent?"

"That oily prick from the restaurant?"

I laugh at his description of Harrison and take off my jacket, hanging it next to the others. "Chelsea Taylor. My future sister-in-law." Who is currently number one on my hate list.

"Let's talk about your security system," he says.

I reach into my jacket pocket and pull out the card Jordan gave me. *Savage Security.* "This is you?" I ask, showing Jay the card.

He nods. "That's me."

"I thought you owned a gym."

"Ten years of private security paid for that gym," he says. "I still do the odd job when I feel motivated."

"What motivated you to take this job?"

"You."

A thrill races through my body. "Me?"

"I don't like the idea of someone out to get you. Especially after what happened…"

"When I acted like a rabbit caught in a trap. That won't happen again." I move past him to sit on my bed and unzip my boots. "I'm prepared now."

"You don't have to be prepared. That's what I'm for."

I swallow thickly, unable to meet his gaze. "I can't have a bodyguard."

"Why not?"

"It's fucking embarrassing. I'm a grown woman."

"No one has to know."

I laugh, looking up at him looming over me. "Look at you. You ride a motorcycle and are covered with ink."

"I have a truck just like every outdoor lover in this town. And you'd be surprised how much I can blend in when I need to."

I doubt that. "What am I supposed to say if people see you hanging around?"

"Tell them we are work associates."

I can only imagine how well that will be received, but it's a problem I don't have the bandwidth to think about at the moment. I'm still trying to process the fact that Jay is going to be the one watching over me.

"Can you give me a minute to change?" I ask.

He nods, reaching for the door. "I'll be downstairs. I'm gonna call a guy about your security."

When he's gone, I throw on a pair of leggings and a sweater, run a brush through my hair, and touch up my makeup. It looks like I'm stuck with Jay unless I call Jordan and try to talk him out of it. But that will just land me with another bodyguard, a stranger who won't be Jay.

When I walk downstairs and see him examining the lock on my front door, I feel more confused than ever. God, I want him so badly, even though he is the last man I should want.

I need wine.

"This might take a while," he says. "Your security system sucks."

I feel his eyes on me as I walk into the kitchen and grab a bottle of wine from the pantry. "What's wrong with it?"

"You need exterior cameras, new deadbolts, and window locks. My consultant is meeting me here tomorrow to update everything, but until then you shouldn't be alone. I'll stay the night."

I nearly drop the bottle of wine on the counter. "All night?"

Jay comes into the kitchen and takes the wine bottle from my hands, expertly opening it with a few twists of his wrist. "I'll sleep on the couch."

"No." My chest squeezes at the thought of him on my couch, feet hanging over the side. "You're too big."

"I'll be fine," he says, setting the wine on the counter.

I pull two wine glasses out of the cabinet and begin to pour, but Jay stops me, covering my hand with his. "None for me. But I'll have some water."

I grab Jay a glass of water and pour wine for myself.

"Have you eaten?" he asks, eyeing my full glass of wine.

I take a step toward the fridge, but my kitchen is so tiny, it's hard to move without bumping into him

"I don't have much in here," I say, swinging open the fridge door.

Jay reaches past me to snap the blinds over the sink to the closed position. "We can order in. I'll charge it to your bill." Pulling out his phone, he scrolls through the delivery options. "What do you like?"

I reach for my wine and take another long sip, trying to put up my mental barriers again.

Do not think about how good he smells.

Do not picture him shirtless.

Fucking hell, this is going to be a long night.

CHAPTER 14

The Black Sheep of the Family

A scream from upstairs chills my blood. I drop my toothbrush in the sink and race upstairs to Mia's bedroom. Storming into her bedroom, I don't bother to knock. My heart stammers when I don't see her anywhere.

Silence echoes through the room.

I check her bathroom, her closet, then bellow out her name.

"Mia!"

"Out here!"

My gut twists at the sound of her voice. It's coming from the balcony, the one place of entry I couldn't protect from my position downstairs. Gaining entry could be as easy as a rope or a ladder.

I push aside the floor-length curtains with more force than necessary and rush onto the balcony, expecting the worst.

Mia held at knifepoint.

Mia bleeding.

Mia almost dead.

My pulse slows a fraction at the sight of her standing in a bathrobe with a towel wrapped around her head. Seemingly unharmed, she's standing with her back to the priceless view, holding a cigarette between her first two fingers. A quick scan of the balcony assures me she's safe and alone.

Her gaze drops over me from head to toe, and color flashes on her cheeks. She seems transfixed, frozen in time, with her mouth gaping open. "Oh, my God."

I look down and see I've lost the towel that had been wrapped around my waist.

I'm naked. And it's fucking freezing outside.

Ignoring my state of undress, I stride forward and grip her shoulders. "Are you okay?"

"I'm fine, Jay." Her voice is so low I can hardly hear. "But you're naked, and Chelsea is staring." She unwinds the towel from her hair and wraps it around my hips.

"Chelsea?"

Mia tilts her head to the side, indicating the neighbor's porch where a female figure is wedged between the tall potted plants. Chelsea Taylor leans on the railing, staring openly at us. At me.

"Good morning," she says cheerfully.

I drag my gaze back to Mia. "What happened?" I ask, shivering as a blast of wind whips through the trees and threatens to snatch the towel from around my hips.

"I came out here to watch the sunrise," she says. "Chelsea scared the shit out of me, and I screamed."

I glance at the stubbed-out cigarette, then back at Mia. "The sun rose fifteen minutes ago."

Her bright blue gaze is colder than the winter wind. "What do we do about Chelsea?" she asks under her breath. "She's still staring."

I'm staring too. At Mia. I have never seen her like this. She's always perfect in her makeup, silky hair, and sophisticated outfits. But she's even more perfect now with none of her armor.

Underneath it all, she's a natural beauty with flawless skin, sparkling blue eyes and the most kissable mouth. Her hair falls in damp waves to her shoulders, fragrant with the sweet scent of her shampoo.

I clasp her shoulders, pulling her close so that the only thing between us is the frosty cloud of our breath. "I thought something happened to you."

She shakes her head. "I'm fine."

She's small, but capable, and I'm reassured by the feel of her coiled strength. "Don't scream like that unless you mean it."

"Sorry."

"It's okay." I stare down at her for a long moment, resisting the urge to stroke her cheek.

"Chelsea," Mia mutters under her breath.

"Still staring?" I ask quietly.

"Ogling," she says. "Maybe you should put some clothes on."

I lift my head and look at Chelsea. Curiosity is written all over her face.

"I didn't realize you two were together," she says.

I stay silent, waiting for Mia to take the lead, but she says nothing. We hadn't planned on this other than claiming we were working together. But me naked at seven in the morning at her place makes that a tough fact to swallow.

Chelsea, bless her, has given us the perfect out. Shifting, I place my arm around Mia's shoulders and pull her close to my chest. "I'm her boyfriend."

Chelsea's face lights up. "Really?"

"It's new," I say.

"Very new," Mia says, digging her elbow into my side.

Chelsea's eyes nearly pop out of her head. "This is so exciting."

Mia stares at me, her lips pinched tightly.

"So exciting," I say, smiling down at her.

"That means you will be coming to the wedding?" Chelsea asks.

Color blazes in Mia's cheeks. "You probably can't make it, right?" she asks, trying to communicate with her eyes.

"I really could use a vacation."

Mia stomps on my foot.

"But I'm not sure, yet," I say.

"Oh, that's too bad," says Chelsea. "I hope it won't be too uncomfortable for you being the only one without a date for the wedding."

Mia stiffens. "I'll be okay."

"Everyone will be coupled up," Chelsea says. "It must be so hard for you to see your younger brother get married when you don't even have a date for the wedding."

My blood simmers, and I pull Mia closer, securing her to my side. "I can take some time off from the gym," I say. "After Fight Night, I should be free."

"How wonderful! Everyone will be thrilled to meet you, Jay. We've been so worried about Mia. We felt so sorry for her."

Frustration bubbles up inside me, and I place a possessive kiss on top of Mia's head. "No need to worry about Mia," I say. "I've got her."

Mia grabs my hand and tugs me toward the door. "I need to get ready for work," she says. "Come on, Jay."

I secure the towel with my free hand, making sure Chelsea doesn't get another glimpse of my assets, and follow Mia inside.

"See you later," Chelsea says in a cheerful tone.

Mia waves and shoves me into her room, glaring at me. "Boyfriend?"

"Sorry," I say. "I couldn't think of anything else."

"I would never date a man like you."

I pace across the room, my fists balling in frustration. "I think you've made that perfectly clear."

"There's no way you can come to the wedding with me. My family would never believe I was dating you."

A headache forms behind my temples, and I rub at my forehead, trying to ward off the pain. "Chelsea bought it, didn't she?"

Mia scoffs. "Chelsea saw you naked."

"What does that mean?"

"It means..." She pauses and looks me over with an appreciative glance before tearing her gaze away. "You know what it means."

I stalk closer, erasing the distance between us. Tension pulses between us as our eyes clash and hold. "Why don't you spell it out for me, counselor?"

Mia tosses her head, making her hair kiss the tops of her shoulders. "You're fucking hot as hell, and you know it."

My heart rate kicks up a notch, and my breath becomes shallow. Every muscle in my body tenses. "Thank you."

She waves a hand in the air, dismissing me. "My entire family is going to know about you within the hour."

I grimace. "Would that be so bad?"

"I haven't introduced them to a boyfriend in a decade." She laughs without humor. "Maybe more. I'm the black sheep of the family. Never getting relationships or anything else right."

Interesting. Mia a black sheep? I just can't see it. "Seems to me you're doing okay. You have a great career, your own place, plenty of friends." I rest my hands on the towel at my waist. "Your taste in men sucks, but other than that, you're pretty amazing."

Mia laughs, her blue eyes turning up in the corners, her shoulders shaking under the terry-cloth robe. She's so sexy when she laughs, I feel a tent forming under the flimsy towel I'm wearing. I imagine her soft skin under the robe, and the tent becomes more pronounced.

It's the first time I've ever gotten a hard-on at work, and I immediately feel like the scum of the earth. Mia's safety is my first priority, and now that the threat has been proven false, it's time to remember what I'm getting paid for.

"My security system guy is going to swing by this morning," I say, hitching my towel tighter on my hips and crossing the room to shut the balcony door. "Can you spare a few minutes to talk to him?"

Her eyes track my movements. "Yes. I'm not going straight to the office this morning. I'm meeting someone at the park."

I make my way to the door. "What time?"

"Ten-thirty."

"I need to rearrange my morning, but it's doable."

She raises a brow. "I wasn't asking your permission."

"Well, you should be. Unless you're at the office or at home, I'll be with you until this is resolved."

Mia's jaw flexes, and she tightens her robe around her. "This is bullshit, Jay."

I open the door to her bedroom. "Take it up with your boss. And until the cameras are installed, *do not* go back on that balcony."

Mia follows me to the door. Placing her hand on it, she cocks her head and smiles up at me. "Anything else, sir?"

"No, that's it." I glance around her room, noting the windows as a possible entry point. "For now."

"Okay then." She jerks her chin up at me and slams the door in my face. "Fuck off."

I step back and make my way down the stairs to the bathroom where I left my clothes. Despite getting cussed out, I feel lighter than I have in weeks.

CHAPTER 15

That One Looks Like Trouble

Jay's security expert looks like he's barely old enough to drive. I watch him with fascination as he clicks away on his laptop at warp speed.

"This is the most basic system I've seen in a while." He glances up at me, eyes dancing with humor. "Circa two thousand and eight," he says with a shake of his head.

I squint down at him, noticing the peach fuzz on his upper lip. "Were you even born then?"

Jay interrupts before the kid can answer. "George knows his stuff. He's brilliant."

George looks up at Jay like he worships the ground he walks on. "Thanks, Coach."

Jay nods once, then moves through the small kitchen to the back door. He gestures at the patio. "You got motion detector lights out here?"

"I'm not sure," I say, enjoying this different side of Jay more than I thought possible. He's a natural leader, easily assuming charge.

"Add that to the list," he tells George.

"Already on it." George finishes up on his laptop and shoves it

83

into his backpack. "Everything should arrive by tomorrow afternoon. I can stop by after school and help you install it."

Jay agrees and walks George to the door, discussing something I can't quite hear before the kid leaves.

"After school?" I ask as Jay comes back into the living room.

He shrugs. "He's the best. He redid my whole system. After he broke in a few times." Jay grabs his jacket and throws it over his shoulder. "Now no one has a prayer of getting in my gym. You're lucky to have George."

I pull on my jacket and grab my laptop bag. "He broke into your gym, but now you're friends?"

"Pretty much." Jay opens my door and steps outside in front of me, scanning the parking lot before allowing me to exit my own condo. "He's a good kid."

"He's a criminal."

He walks me to my car and waits until I'm seated inside. "I believe in rehabilitation."

"I never said I didn't."

Jay raises a brow and leans on my roof looking down at me. "I'll see you there. Drive safely."

He shuts the door, and I watch him walk away and climb on his motorcycle. I don't think I can ever get enough of watching him walk away, or watching him climb on his bike. He is too sexy for ten in the morning. I can't handle it.

On the short drive to the park, I clear my thoughts of Jay Sanchez and focus on Warner Mattson and Elena. I've got to come up with a compelling enough reason to convince Elena to meet with her former boss. Last night I found a few very interesting leads on scumbag Mattson. I just need Elena's help in nailing him. This meeting is crucial.

When I get to the park, Jay is already waiting for me in the parking lot. He opens my door and walks with me to the play area where Elena and I plan to meet. Even though the weather is still chilly, young children are playing on the swings while their mothers keep a close watch on them. I spot Elena over by a toy train setup and carefully plan my approach.

"You have to wait here," I tell Jay.

He stops short and crosses his arms in front of him, surveying the play yard with an eagle eye. "How long will you be?"

"I'm not sure, but don't blow this for me. Okay?" I glance up at him, noticing how he does not blend in like he promised he would. At the park mostly populated by young mothers or nannies, Jay sticks out like a sore thumb.

"Don't worry." He reaches down and kisses my cheek, giving me a pat on the ass. "I'm just your boyfriend waiting for you."

I glare at him over my shoulder. "Don't get any closer."

He nods and takes a seat on a bench, somehow looking relaxed yet ready to pounce at the same time. This giant of a man, who should look extremely out of place at a playground, somehow looks perfectly at ease.

Elena takes her eyes off her two children for a moment to greet me, then goes back to facing the playground, watching them intently. "Who's that with you?" she asks.

"My boyfriend," I say. The lie rolls off my tongue more easily than I would have thought, and I can imagine myself saying it to my close friends, my family. Would they fall for it?

Elena spares Jay a glance. "He's cute."

I laugh under my breath. Calling Jay cute is like calling a grizzly a pet. "Thanks for meeting me."

Her small shoulders lift in a shrug. Elena is young, only twenty-five. A single mom with a criminal record for petty theft and a GED, she has had a tough road in life. "I don't see what good it will do. *Jeremy!*" She yells at a kid on the playground. "Don't push your brother!"

"I found something I need you to verify."

Elena shakes her head. "Whatever it is, just forget it. That man will never go to prison. His type doesn't have to pay."

My mouth turns down in a grimace as I picture Mattson's

superior smile and arrogant gaze. "He isn't any better than the rest of us. He did the crime, he should pay for it."

Elena laughs. "You're naïve as they come, Ms. James."

I don't agree with her assessment. "I'm determined to put him away."

"Some people don't have to pay." Her voice is flat, more resigned than outraged. "Some people do. I'm one of those who pays more than her share."

Anger simmers in my blood. "Not on my watch. I'm going to put him behind bars. All I need for you to do is verify that these were customers at Mattson Payroll Services while you were there."

"What does that have to do with sexual harassment and rape?" she asks.

"Nothing," I admit.

Elena shakes her head at me. "This is total bullshit."

She starts off in the direction of the playground, but I catch her arm, stopping her. "Please. Let me explain."

Elena gives me a stern look that probably works wonders on her children. "Go ahead, but it better be something better than tax fraud. That's never gonna work."

My chest pinches as she easily guesses my intentions. Tax fraud had been my brilliant plan. It doesn't seem so genius anymore.

"What if you confronted him?" I ask, getting a wild, desperate idea. "What if you met him, somewhere safe, a public place, and got him to admit what he did?"

She looks skeptical. "I don't know. Would I have to wear a wire?"

I shake my head. "You can use your phone. It only takes consent from one party to record a conversation."

She bites her lip, deep in thought. "I'll let you know."

"So, you'll think about it?" I sense victory on the horizon.

"We'll see." Elena hurries off to the playground, gathering up her children and herding them off toward the swings.

It's not a promise, but it's better than what I could have hoped for. I watch Elena wrangle her children, emotions churning in my gut. Envy rears its ugly head before I remind myself how rough she has it and how much better off I am being single, childless, and alone.

"Everything okay?" Jay asks, coming up beside me.

His gaze scans the playground as if looking for a sign of danger.

"That one looks like trouble." I nod at a boy hanging upside down on the monkey bars.

Jay's lips twitch in what appears to be a tiny smile. "Not as much as her," he says, pointing out a little girl with bright red hair poised to push a little boy off the slide.

"Shouldn't we stop her?"

"She won't really do it," he says.

The little girl looks like the devil himself, her pigtails jostling like red horns. "How the hell do you know?"

"Watch."

I watch as the little boy steps out of the way, letting the little devil girl go ahead of him. She flashes a tiny-toothed smile at him and scoots to the top of the slide.

"See? I told you." His eyes are softer than I've ever seen them, filled with amused affection.

"You like kids?" I ask, feeling the familiar pinch of regret in my chest.

"Sure. Who doesn't?"

A cold fist closes around my heart. "Me."

His gaze shifts to me, assessing my expression with a sweep of his dark chocolate eyes before turning back to the playground. "Want to swing?"

"What?" I laugh.

He puts his hand on the small of my back, easing the tension I hadn't realized was there. "I think you forgot how to play, Counselor James."

His teasing tone makes my belly flutter. "I certainly did not."

"Prove it."

I can't resist a challenge, and before Jay can react, I take off toward the swings as fast as my high-heeled boots will allow. "Last one there is a rotten egg!"

CHAPTER 16

Work Emails

Email message from Adler.Jordan@azaleacounty.gov to James.mia@azaleacounty.gov

Mia,

It has come to my attention that you were late this morning without clearing paid time off with administration. I know you are working hard and need a break, but cavorting at the park on the state's dime is unacceptable.

Please refrain from such behavior in the future.

If you have any questions or concerns, don't hesitate to make an appointment with me to discuss. Remember, I'm on your side and here to support you in any way possible.

Respectfully,
Jordan Adler

· · ·

Email message from James.mia@azaleacounty.gov
    To Adler.Jordan@azaleacounty.gov

Dear Jordan,

I was unaware that I had to schedule every minute of my day with you. In the future I will be sure to involve you more in my schedule.

Just as a reminder, in two weeks, I will be gone Thursday-Sunday for my brother's wedding. Since I haven't taken any vacation days in three years, I plan to also take Wednesday off in order to prepare. I must look my best, and I have booked a hair appointment, a mani/pedi, and a Brazilian bikini wax. I will keep you informed with any additions to my schedule.

It is currently my time of the month, so I might need an emergency run to Blanchard's for tampons, but other than that I will be sitting tight at my desk.

Regards,
    Mia

P.S. Let me know if you need anything from Blanchard's

CHAPTER 17

How Was Your Day, Dear?

Jay quickly becomes a fixture in my life. Since George installed the high-tech security system in my condo, he no longer spends the night, but he is the first person I see in the morning and the last person I see before I go to bed.

He waits for me after work, escorts me home, does a sweep of my condo and locks me in for the night. The next morning he's back. He sees me off to work and is waiting for me when I leave the building.

He's a quiet shadow, keeping me safe but never intruding on my boundaries.

Although I've seen him every single day, we've barely spoken more than a few words. I know little more about Jay than I did that first night we met. Except now I've seen him naked, and I know he was blessed by superior genetics in the manhood department and he isn't tattooed *everywhere.*

He's physically the most perfect man in every imaginable way. His body looks like he's been honing it for years. Not an ounce of fat dares to cling to his muscular frame, and his proportions are more than adequate. *Quite a bit more.*

After checking in with Jordan to let him know I'm running off to Blanchard's and won't be back until the following day, I step outside for the first time in ten hours and scan the parking lot for the familiar Harley Davidson.

Despite the chill in the air, warmth fills my body as I see Jay, leaning against his motorcycle. He's wearing all black as usual, and his hair is pulled back from his face in a ponytail at the nape of his neck. Dark sunglasses cover his eyes, but I can feel the intensity of his gaze sweeping over me.

He pushes to his feet and walks toward me with a purposeful stride that eats up the distance between us before I can blink. The man moves like a predator, and I am ready to be devoured.

Ugh. These thoughts come out of nowhere when Jay is around. I'm normal one minute, and then I'm so hot and bothered I can barely breathe the next.

Must be the pheromones. His scent is undeniably sexy.

"Hey—"

He takes my arm and pushes me slightly behind him. "Stay behind me."

My heart lurches into my throat. "What's wrong?"

"I don't like the look of that Lexus," he says.

"Which one?" The parking lot is full of Lexuses, including my small SUV.

"Just stay behind me," he says, leading the way to my car. "Got your key out?"

I grab my key from my purse and press the unlock button as we approach my car. Jay hands me inside and stands between me and the open door.

"Go straight home," he says.

I plant my hand on the door as he tries to close it. "I need to go to Blanchard's," I say. "I've got nothing to eat."

He scans the parking lot, then backs up a few feet. "I'll meet you there."

"You don't need to come with me to the grocery store. How am I going to explain you following me around the aisles?"

"I'm your boyfriend. We can shop together."

He closes the door, giving me no chance to protest.

By the time I park in the lot at the grocery store, Jay is already there, waiting for me. He escorts me to the store, then stands aside as I pull out a shopping cart. It's funny to see a man like Jay at the market. His bad boy image doesn't add up to buying toilet paper and bananas.

Inside the store he hooks his sunglasses in the pocket of his black leather jacket and strolls slightly in front of me, his watchful gaze scanning everything in sight.

"Don't be so obvious," I say. "I doubt anyone is going to kill me at Blanchard's."

He slows down and walks beside me, but his serious expression doesn't change.

"How was your day, dear?" I ask, heavy on the sarcasm.

To my surprise, he doesn't ignore me. A rare smile lights his face. "It was a good day."

I'm temporarily stunned by his gorgeous smile and nearly trip over my own feet. If Jay notices, he doesn't comment.

"What made it a good day?" I ask, regaining my composure.

"Thatcher is going to step in for my fighter who broke his hand."

"Thatcher?" I can't keep the skepticism from my voice.

"You don't approve."

It's not that I don't approve, I'm just surprised. "I thought he quit fighting."

"It's only one fight," Jay says. "And it's for a good cause."

Thatcher is a grown man. If he wants to get in a ring and pummel somebody and be pummeled in return, who am I to stop him? "As long as it's for a good cause."

Jay nods. "It's for Champion's Corner. The youth program at the gym."

"The program is important to you?"

A muscle in his jaw flexes. "It's everything."

Jay is a man of few words, and I know I'm not likely to get more out of him.

We continue down the aisles; me checking the list on my

phone for the items I need and Jay scrutinizing anyone who gets within twenty-five yards of us.

I'm terrible in the kitchen, so each week I challenge myself with a new recipe in hopes of improving.

"You like to cook?" Jay watches me select ingredients for an early spring dish that is easy and delightful according to the online recipe.

"Not really."

He winces as I add a sad-looking bunch of asparagus to the cart. "What are you gonna do with that?"

"I'm going to bake it with a creamy mushroom sauce."

Jay wrinkles his nose, letting me know exactly how he feels about the dish.

"Care to join me?"

His gaze transfers from the cart to me, and a hum of excitement plays on every nerve in my body as I wait for his answer.

"Only if you let me cook."

"That's the best offer I've had all day."

"If we are gonna pretend to be a couple at your brother's wedding, we should practice sharing a meal together."

I grab a bottle of wine and add it to the cart. "You don't have to come to the wedding."

Jay grabs another bottle of wine and inspects the label. "Do you have someone else?"

His voice sounds strange, like he swallowed too much air.

"No." I take the bottle from his hands. "Have you tried this one?" I ask. "It's more than decent."

"You're really selling me." He selects another bottle and shows it to me. "How about this one? Is it more than decent, too?"

"Yum. This is one of my favorites."

Jay puts it in the cart.

"It's pricey," I say, choosing another bottle. "This one is a better deal."

Jay's dark eyes narrow on me. "You have this preconceived notion of me that I can't afford wine." He takes the bottle from my hands and puts it in the cart. "But the truth is, I can afford more than one bottle."

"I didn't say you couldn't afford wine. It's just a better deal for the money."

Jay walks ahead of me a few steps. "I don't always care about the better deal," he says, turning around to let his gaze drop over me. "Sometimes I just want what tastes good."

A shiver runs through me from head to toe. I know exactly what he means.

CHAPTER 18
Hard To Believe

At Mia's condo parking lot, there is no sign of the suspicious black Lexus, but I get the feeling that danger is lurking around the corner.

There have been no further threats since I came on board to watch over Mia, which raises a red flag for me. I don't trust the quiet.

If I'm right, the man hasn't given up; he's planning.

When Mia pulls into her spot and cuts the engine, I'm there to open her door. "Let's get inside."

"Can I at least grab the groceries?"

I shake my head and haul her out of the car. "I'll come back for the groceries."

She begins to protest, but smothers the urge and allows me to escort her to the door. I know she thinks everything I do is overkill, but that doesn't stop me from ordering her to wait inside her locked front door while I do a full sweep of the entire condo, including the balcony.

When I'm sure everything is secure, I go back outside to get the groceries. The parking lot is quiet, but I can't shake the feeling that something is wrong.

"Everything okay?" Mia asks, reading my expression.

We've spent enough time together over the past few weeks that we are beginning to communicate without saying a word. I know when Mia's had a bad day or slept poorly. Or when she's had a satisfying day at work.

"Stay inside," I tell her, slipping out the back door to the small patio to give it a quick inspection.

When I come back, Mia is opening a bottle of wine. She has kicked off her high heels and shed her blazer, looking more relaxed than I've seen her since our first night together.

"You'll join me for a glass," she says, popping the cork.

"Is that an order?"

She quirks a brow at me, pouring two glasses of wine. "I am technically your boss, right?"

"No. You're my client."

She raises her glass to mine. "Drink, Jay."

I raise my glass to hers then to my mouth. She's right, it's delicious. I shouldn't have gotten so uptight at the store about affording the wine. But after the way she judged me for my tattoo, I couldn't help jumping to conclusions.

Maybe I judged Mia a little bit too. Her condo isn't anything like the lavish home I pictured her living in. It's a small place, practical and neat. There is a tiny living room, a galley kitchen, and an office. Her furniture is high quality, but completely devoid of personality. The walls are painted builder's beige, and the hardwood floors are bare.

"Did you just move in?"

"I've been here almost two years. Why?"

"This place reminds me of a hotel suite."

She laughs. "Coming from a man whose apartment smells like sweaty gym socks, I'll take that as a compliment."

I step around her to unpack the ingredients for our chicken marsala dinner. "Can you chop this?" I ask, handing her the onion.

It's a small kitchen, but we manage to work together to

prepare dinner. Mia chops while I sauté, and in no time dinner is ready.

I'm no master chef, but Mia praises my humble chicken dinner as if she's never tasted anything so good in her life. "This is amazing."

I take another bite. She's right, it's pretty damn good. "It's one of the few things I can make," I admit. "I don't have a lot of time to cook."

"Me neither." She sips her wine. "Most nights I end up getting take-out at the office with Jordan."

I can't help the wave of jealousy that ripples through me. "You two are pretty close?"

"Not really. Jordan isn't a friend. He's my boss."

"He's obviously worried about you."

"Jordan doesn't really care about anyone but himself."

Mia doesn't know it, but Jordan is the one paying my bills. I consider telling her, but it isn't my place to interfere.

She finishes off her meal and lays down her fork. "I shouldn't have eaten all that. I have a dress to fit into. Fucking Chelsea ordered me the wrong size, and I've been dieting for a month trying to fit into it."

Whatever size she is, she's perfect. "Couldn't they get you another dress?"

Mia puts her chin in her hand. "You'd think so, right? But it won't get here in time, so I had to lose seven pounds."

"I know how you feel. I had to lose thirty pounds for a fight once."

"Thirty pounds?" Mia's eyes widen. "How did you do it?"

"Protein and veggies. No alcohol. Miles of running."

"Sounds horrible."

I laugh and finish my wine. "It wasn't that bad."

Mia leans forward on her elbows, looking at me intently. "Tell me about Champion's Corner."

"What do you want to know?"

"What made you start it?"

I plan on giving her the usual story about how I saw a need in the community and blah, blah, blah, but something makes me change my mind.

"I grew up pretty rough," I say.

Mia tilts her head at me, listening intently.

"I used to get beat up a lot when I was a kid." They made fun of my clothes, my accent, and most of all my address.

"Hard to believe."

We are sitting close together at the dining room table, our plates empty and forgotten, our fingers brushing occasionally. It's almost like we are on a real date.

I pick up my story where I left off. "I was pretty skinny. Then, I had a growth spurt, and I started fighting back."

Just remembering my childhood is painful. There had never been enough to eat. But then my mom got a job as a night shift waitress, and she started coming home with food every morning. I got bigger and stronger, and pretty soon no one messed with me.

"I was fourteen the first time I had a street fight. Bare knuckles and no ref. We fought until one of us couldn't get up. I made sure I was the one getting up."

"Fourteen? You were just a baby."

My throat tightens as memories fill my mind. I shove them away. "I was already six-foot two."

"So? You were still a kid."

I shake my head. "I stopped being a kid a long time before that. I was only five years old the first time I saw a man hit a woman."

Her eyes narrow shrewdly. "Your mom and your dad?"

Emotion swells in my chest as I remember the shouts, the silence, the bruises. "Yeah."

"Okay, so you weren't a baby," she concedes. "But you were still a kid."

"Kids fight," I say. "That's what Champion's Corner is all about. Giving them a safe space to do it."

"I doubt you were fighting kids your age. It was grown men, wasn't it?"

I shrug. "I was big. Then I got this tattoo." I lift my shirt and show the LOYALTY tattoo that stretches across my stomach. "I looked older." I drag my gaze away from hers. I can't stand the way she's looking at me with pity. "Boxing saved me. It gave me an opportunity to be somebody. It gave me…"

"A way out," Mia says, finishing my sentence for me.

"Exactly."

Back then I'd fought more for money than pride. If I won, I made more money. So I won. I'd fought and won until I'd made enough to move out of the trailer park. We could afford gymnastics lessons for my sister, and my mom quit working the graveyard shift.

"I want to give kids a chance to experience the good side of boxing. The structure, the sense of accomplishment, the family."

"You're a good man." Her hand covers mine. "Really decent."

A smile tugs at my mouth. "You seem surprised."

"Maybe." She trails her hand up my forearm, her eyes following the path.

I shift closer to her, breaking every rule I've ever made regarding clients as I lower my mouth to hers.

Just before our lips touch, the doorbell rings. We jerk apart as if we've been shocked, and I jump up from the table.

"Stay there," I say, moving quickly to the door. I look through the peephole, and wrench open the door.

No one is there, but a manilla envelope rests just outside the door frame. I snatch it off the doormat and step outside, telling Mia to lock the door behind me.

"What is it?" She's on the other side of the door, trying desperately to see over my shoulder into the parking lot.

"Stay inside." I slam the door shut between us. "Lock the deadbolt, Mia."

When I hear the bolt click into place, I tuck the envelope into the waistband at the back of my pants and duck into the shadows.

I track the perimeter of the building, but there is no one around. Nothing unusual catches my eye, and the only people are a young couple walking their dog.

"Excuse me, did you notice anyone over there?" I point to Mia's unit.

"Just a delivery guy," the man says.

"Did he get the right unit?" the woman asks. "People are always mixing the addresses up."

"Thanks," I say, backing away.

"Sure. No problem."

I hurry back to Mia's house and knock on the door. "It's me. Open up."

Mia pulls the door open, stepping back a few inches to let me in. She slams the door behind me and locks it.

"No need for that." I nod at the gun in her right hand.

She relaxes her grip on the gun and points the barrel at the ground. "Who was it?"

I pull the envelope from the waistband of my pants and examine it. Mia's name is printed on the front in large block letters. "A delivery."

Mia places her gun on the coffee table and reaches for the envelope.

"Wait." I pull the envelope out of her reach. "This is evidence. Do you have any gloves?"

Mia goes into the kitchen and comes back with a pair of yellow gloves covering her hands. "This is the best I can do."

I hand her the package, my heart in my throat as she lifts the flap. She spills the contents onto the coffee table, and relief spreads through me when I see it's only newspaper clippings.

Mia makes a choked noise. I get a glimpse of the headline—*Sex, Lies, and LAX*—before she shoves everything back inside and clutches it with a death grip.

"What is it?" I ask.

She doesn't answer. Her face is deathly pale, and I know her well enough to see she's on the brink of tears.

Without wasting any more time, I pull her into my arms. At first she's limp, but after a moment, she wraps her arms around me and holds on.

"It's okay." I smooth my hands up and down her back. "It's just an old newspaper article. It can't hurt you."

She trembles. "I know I need to quit smoking," she says. "But I could really use a smoke."

I'm not about to tell Mia what she can or can't do. Although I'm not a fan of cigarettes, now isn't the time to take a stand. It's clear whatever was in the article broke through the walls she'd erected to protect herself.

"You'll quit tomorrow." I take her gloved hand and lead the way upstairs to her balcony.

CHAPTER 19

Your Turn

Jay waits patiently while I pull off my gloves and shake a cigarette from the pack. I hold it to my lips, but I'm trembling so badly, I can't light it.

He grabs the lighter from my fingers and flicks the button, holding it up to the tip of my cigarette. I inhale deeply, then blow out a stream of smoke. It doesn't make me feel any better.

I know I need to quit, but it never seems like a good time. There's always a crisis that makes me crave the brief calm provided by the nicotine.

Memories of that horrible night crash over me. I know I'm safe, but I feel helpless just like I did that night nearly fifteen years ago.

Tears prick my eyes, but I blink them back. I can't cry in front of Jay. It was humiliating enough to break down in his arms and let him witness my weaknesses.

"I was assaulted in college," I say, keeping my explanation simple. Jay doesn't need to know the details about how I was nearly raped at a frat party by my own boyfriend.

He grits his teeth. "I'm sorry."

I'd been sorry for a long time, too. Then I'd snapped out of it and used my anger to direct my future. "Don't be," I say. "It made me who I am today."

I take a long drag off my cigarette and pace to the railing. Blowing a stream of smoke into the air, I close my eyes and block out the image from the newspaper article. But it does no good. I can still see those boys with their neat haircuts and smirking faces. My boyfriend with his guy-next-door good looks and the cocky angle of his chin.

A shiver runs through me as the cold night finally breaks through the heat of my adrenaline.

Jay drapes a jacket over my shoulders. I hadn't realized he left the balcony because he moves like a jungle cat, hardly making any noise at all.

"Do you want to talk about it?" he asks.

To my surprise, I do. "The boys all had rich parents, scholarships, and legacies."

"Boys?" Jay's skin pales under the moonlight. "There was more than one involved?"

"You might have seen it in the news. It was everywhere. The boys' lacrosse team was accused by multiple women."

"The team?" He grits out the word.

I nod. "They manipulated women into thinking they wanted to have sex with them because they were the most popular boys on campus."

"Assholes." His eyes turn dangerous.

"I testified at the trial. My boyfriend was one of the guys, so I didn't make a great witness." I cringe at how much Elena and I have in common.

A storm crosses his features. "Whoever sent this knew you were a witness."

"It was a public trial."

"Bastard. He's been planning this." Jay's posture changes. He's suddenly on full alert, scanning the woods beyond my yard as if he senses danger. "How close are you to getting this guy?" he asks.

Not *if* I will get him, but *when.* Jay has more faith in me than I do in myself. A strange, prickly sensation buzzes through my body. Maybe it's the nicotine, maybe it's Jay, but I feel my heart stutter and race.

"I won't stop until I get him."

Jay covers my hand with his and squeezes. His big hand is warm and comforting, and it sends a jolt of awareness through me. "Good girl."

Hearing his praise sends a shiver of longing down my spine. That deep voice makes me ache.

"Can I ask you something?"

A shell hardens around me as I brace myself for his question. "Go ahead."

"Did the assault make you want to be a prosecutor?"

It's an easy question. "Yes." I take a drag and blow smoke into the air. "I switched to pre-law after the trial and never looked back."

We are quiet for a moment, then Jay breaks the silence. "Your turn," he says.

"What?"

"Ask me something."

I play stubborn. "There's nothing I want to know."

"You sure?" He's perfectly relaxed, his face an unreadable mask.

I know he'll be open with me. Jay would never lie, but I'm not sure I want to know the answers.

He pushes up his sleeve and shows me his right elbow. "You want to ask about this?"

Curiosity burns inside me. "Yes." I brace for the answer, knowing nothing he can say will justify his crime.

"What do you want to know?"

Even if it will change everything between us, I have to ask. "What happened?"

He focuses on the sloping line of the dark mountains in the

distance. "Assault with a deadly weapon." His voice is cold and emotionless, as if he's talking about someone else.

I should be afraid of this man. He's been convicted of a violent crime and I'm alone with him in my house. But I'm not scared. This is Jay. He's sworn to protect me. He wouldn't hurt me.

"Knife?" I ask.

He shakes his head. "No."

"Gun? Bat?"

Again, he shakes his head, then holds up his hands. He has big, powerful hands with broad palms and long fingers. I know from experience his touch is rough but gentle.

He curls his fingers toward his palms, making two fists. "Just these," he says.

A ghostly finger brushes down my spine, causing a chill to break out on my skin.

"Your fists?"

His head bobs once in confirmation.

"But how?"

"I'm a trained fighter. They argued my hands were weapons."

My brows raise. I'm impressed. "That's brilliant."

Jay laughs tightly. "Not so much for me. But yeah, the opposing attorney was smart as hell." One dark brow wings upward, and his gaze slides over my face. "Kind of reminds me of someone else I know."

The compliment swells in my chest. I can't help leaning a little closer. Electricity crackles between us. Just before the doorbell rang with the unwelcome delivery, I could have sworn he was about to kiss me.

"Any more questions?" he asks.

"Not at the moment."

I need to come to terms with the fact that Jay nearly killed someone with his bare hands. Those same hands that I've been fantasizing about touching me everywhere.

"I'll sleep on the sofa tonight," he says.

"You don't have to do that."

He steps away, toward the door. "No arguments."

I pull his jacket tighter around me. Without Jay's warmth, I feel the chill in the early spring air. "What if I have plans?"

His brow creases. "Do you have a date?"

"Maybe."

He narrows his eyes. "Get rid of him."

"I don't have a date." I hadn't had a date in weeks. Not since my date with Harrison which had ended at Jay's apartment. "All I want is a hot bath and my bed."

"I'll leave you to it," he says, exiting the balcony. A smile lifts one corner of his mouth as he turns around to look at me. "If you need me, just scream."

CHAPTER 20

Is That All She Handles

Leading up to Fight Night, I split my hours between guarding Mia and training Thatcher.

Our relationship moved solidly into the professional category. No more dinners or sleepovers, and our time together was often spent driving across town to work or the gym. Mia attended some self-defense classes, which she was obviously not in need of, and I balanced my books from her kitchen table using my laptop.

We are surprisingly alike, in that we are devoted to our jobs, and neither one of us has much in the way of a social life. Also, neither one of us owns a television.

There have been no more threats on Mia's life through email, the website, or in letter form, but that doesn't mean I feel comfortable leaving her alone.

The day of the fight, Cassandra is in town to help on the media end, and I am so busy, I've had to call in reinforcements. Since George owes me big time, I've subcontracted him to keep an eye on Mia while I focus on getting Out of the Box ready for its premier Fight Night.

George might only be sixteen, but he is smart and strong. He hooked up her security without a glitch. I trust him to keep her safe.

As the first fight of the evening begins, I spot Mia at a VIP table with her book club friends. George hovers nearby, ready to take action if anyone gets too close to her.

She looks so gorgeous; I have to drag my gaze away from her. Taking a page out of my book, Mia is wearing all black. Her platinum blonde hair is scraped back from her face in a tight ponytail, and her eyes are made up with dark eyeliner. She looks badass. Like she belongs in a rock video.

Cassandra approaches me, taking my arm to steer me out of the shadows. "You should say hello to the guests," she says.

I roll my eyes, and she stabs me in the ribs with a sharp elbow.

"I'm no good at public relations," I say. "That's your job."

She tugs me onto the main floor. "It won't kill you to say thank you for coming. Try it out," she urges.

"Thank you for coming," I tell a table of guests who have purchased an eight-person VIP table. The cost of the table will fund an entire month of Champion's Corner, so my appreciation sounds sincere.

Cassandra smiles encouragingly at me. "Very nice," she says in her silky voice. "Next time, try smiling."

We make our way to several more tables before the announcer gets on the stage to introduce the next amateur fighters—two women who have only fought a few times.

As they face each other for the first round, I duck into the men's locker room to check on Thatcher. He dutifully pedals a stationary bike, looking unnaturally calm.

"Are you ready?" I ask, handing him a water bottle.

He pushes it away. "Doesn't matter."

His gaze is trained on the far wall of the locker room where a poster of him and "The Hitman" is tacked to the wall, and he pedals rhythmically as if in a trance.

In the image, Thatcher looks like his nickname, "Pretty Boy." He is classically handsome, with golden brown hair, and a lean physique. Jake "The Hitman" Malone, on the other hand, looks like a beast.

His bare chest is thick with muscles, and his face is set in a permanent grimace. A nose that has been broken too many times dominates his face, and the ferocious gleam in his eye leaps off the poster.

"You're the underdog," I say. "Use that to your advantage."

He gives me the side-eye. "Are you trying to motivate me?"

"Yeah."

"It's not working."

"Don't worry about winning," I say. "Just do your best."

Thatcher stops pedaling for a second and stares at me. "You're the worst at pep talks," he says.

I huff out a breath of frustration. "Maybe I'm no good at this," I say. "But you are. You've put in the training, made weight, stepped up when we needed you. Go out there and do your thing. You might not be favored to win, but we both know you're fully capable of beating him."

Thatcher starts pedaling again. "Is she here?"

"Who?"

"Don't fuck with me. You know who?"

Thatcher had a lady neighbor who had been occupying his mind. She would have been sitting at the table with Mia and her book club friends.

"I don't know." The President of the United States could have been sitting at the table with Mia and I wouldn't have noticed him.

"Can you go check?"

I leave the locker room, promising to return with news. Cassandra is waiting outside the locker room for me, insisting I make more rounds. We stop by a few more tables, getting closer to the table Mia occupies with her friends. I make an effort to look for Thatcher's woman, but she isn't here yet.

Mia meets my gaze, and I feel like I've been clapped with a bolt of thunder. I haven't seen her all day, and it feels like it's been years.

"I want to introduce you to a potential sponsor," Cassandra says, steering me away from Mia's table.

"No." I say it with more force than necessary.

"Jay." Cassandra touches my shoulder. "You're paying me to help you."

I nod stiffly. "I know."

She flashes her perfect smile. "So let me help you."

I can't help but remember the brief period we'd given dating a shot. We had fizzled out, not because of the distance between our homes, but because the chemistry was severely lacking. Although Cassandra was one of the most beautiful women I'd ever seen, there was no spark between us.

"Give me a minute," I say, glancing in Mia's direction.

"It's your dime," she says, backing off.

I make my way over to Mia's table and give George a squeeze on the shoulder. "Everything look okay?"

He nods, taking his eyes off Mia for a moment to watch the fight. "Gemma is kicking ass," he says.

"Watch your mouth."

George smirks. "Sorry, Coach, but she is. Look at her go!"

I watch Gemma kick some serious ass before sitting astride the chair next to Mia. "Thanks for coming," I say. The phrase sounds more sincere than it has all night.

Mia's brows pull together in a frown. "How's Thatcher?"

I cover her hand with mine. "Don't worry. He's ready."

A tight smile stretches her mouth. "Who's that?"

I follow her gaze to Cassandra and see her through Mia's eyes. Cassandra is gorgeous. Her dark brown skin shines under the bright lights of the gym, and her killer body, poured into a neon pink dress that fits her like a glove, turns every head as she walks by.

"That's Cassandra Darling, my publicist. She handles all the media."

Mia pins me with a curious gaze. "Is that all she handles?"

I hear the jealousy in her voice, and it tugs at my heartstrings.

A grin lifts my lips, but I force a neutral expression before Mia can spot it.

"These days? Yeah," I say, enjoying the fire dancing in her eyes. I link our fingers for a brief moment and squeeze.

"She's gorgeous." Mia's gaze is trained on our joined hands.

"It's not like that between us. Not anymore."

Mia turns her attention back to the fight. "You don't have to babysit me in public," she says, dismissing me.

I release her hand. "I'll see you after."

"If you insist."

Frustration makes my vision cloud as I get to my feet. "I do."

I lock eyes with George, and he steps closer to Mia's table, guarding her while I fulfill my duties as gym owner and trainer.

My nerves are on edge until Thatcher and Malone enter the ring, and then I forget everything else as I watch my fighter do everything right and take his first win with a knockout.

CHAPTER 21
Emails from Mia to Jay

Email message
　　From: James.mia@azaleacounty.gov
　　To: Jay_Sanchez@OOTB.com

Dear Jay,

Good morning. I hope this email finds you happy and well after an incredibly successful night. Congrats to you and everyone else who won!

As you know, my brother's wedding is quickly approaching. I wanted to make sure you were updated on the specifics. The wedding will take place on Serenade Island, a small island off the coast of Florida.

Due to the fact that one of the guests is a celebrity, extreme security measures are in place. No one without an invitation will be allowed entry, which means there is no safer place for me to be.

It also means you are off the hook for accompanying me.

I appreciate your willingness to go above and beyond your duty as my body guard, but it is not necessary for you to be my date to keep me safe.

. . .

Regards, Mia

Email message
    From: Jay_Sanchez@OOTB.com
    To: James.mia@azaleacounty.gov

Mia,

Thank you for the congratulations and for being there last night. It means a lot to me that you came.

I'm glad you will be safe during your brother's wedding weekend, but that doesn't mean I want to back out of the trip.

What kind of boyfriend would I be if I didn't show up to your brother's wedding?

Jay

P.S. Who is the celebrity?

Email message
    From: James.mia@azaleacounty.gov
    To: Jay_Sanchez@OOTB.com

Dear Jay,

Since you aren't really my boyfriend, it isn't necessary for you to come to the wedding. And I am not at liberty to discuss the identity of the celebrity.

.   .   .

Regards, Mia

Email message
   From: Jay_Sanchez@OOTB.com
   To: James.mia@azaleacounty.gov

Mia,

Will you please allow me to be your date to your brother's wedding?

Jay

Email message
   From: James.mia@azaleacounty.gov
   To: Jay_Sanchez@OOTB.com

Dear Jay,

I hope you are not volunteering to be my date because you feel sorry for me. I don't need your pity.

But if you are serious about accompanying me to Serenade Island for Max and Samantha's wedding, please have a look at the website www.serenadeislandresort and choose your top three activities for the weekend.

. . .

Regards,
    Mia

Email message
    From: Jay_Sanchez@OOTB.com
    To: James.mia@azaleacounty.gov

I don't feel sorry for you. It's you who should feel sorry for me. I haven't had a vacation in years.

Email message
    From: James.mia@azaleacounty.gov
    To: Jay_Sanchez@OOTB.com

Dear Jay,

When you put it that way, how can I deny your need for a much deserved vacation. Since you didn't select any of the activities from the website, I took the liberty of signing you up. I will be busy with wedding luncheons, spa visits, and photo sessions, so you will be left to your own devices.

Attached please find the weekend itinerary and suggested packing list.

I think it's best if you keep your shirt on at the beach. I don't want to answer questions about your tattoos.

If you have a problem with that, please let me know.

If you want to make a change to your activities, you can email the manager of the resort at Linda@Seranadeislandresort.

. . .

Regards, Mia

P.S. I have attached a full panel STD test and would appreciate if you send yours as well.

Packing list:
Swim shorts
Suit jacket (not black)
Teal blue tie (please see attached photo of my dress for matching purposes)
(2) Casual long sleeve shirt
Flip flops
Hat
Golf shirt
Dress slacks
Dress shoes
Sunscreen
Underwear
Toiletries

Itinerary:
Day One:
1pm Arrive on the island
2pm Golf (Jay)
2pm Bridal Luncheon (Mia)
7pm Rehearsal
8pm Dinner and Karaoke

Day Two:
11am Ziplining tour (Jay)

12pm makeup and photo shoot (Mia)
6pm Wedding

Day Three:
11am Goodbye Brunch
2pm Flight home

Email message
From: Jay_Sanchez@OOTB.com
To: James.mia@azaleacounty.gov

Golf and zip lining? WTF?
And why do you need STD test results?

Email message
From: James.mia@azaleacounty.gov
To: Jay_Sanchez@OOTB.com

Jay,

Please email Linda if you'd like to change your activities.
As for the test results, it's just in case.

Regards,
Mia

.   .   .

Email message
    From: Jay_Sanchez@OOTB.com
    To: James.mia@azaleacounty.gov

Just in case of what?

CHAPTER 22

Smoldering Embrace

"No. No. No."

I pull all the clothes out of Jay's suitcase and toss them onto his bed.

"What's wrong with these?" He rescues a pair of athletic shorts and holds them up. "These are my favorite running shorts."

"When do you plan on wearing them?"

"When I go for a run."

I grab them and toss them into the suitcase. "Fine. You can bring them. But you're only allowed to wear them for running."

He quirks a dark brow. "Why else would I wear them?"

"I have no idea." I shake my head, grimacing at the pile of discarded clothes. They are wrong. All wrong. They are never going to fool my family.

Jay rescues a black T-shirt from the heap. It's a luxury brand with the tags still on. "What about this? It's new."

I cross my arms over my chest. "Did you even read the packing list? It said long-sleeved shirts." I glance at the tattoos peeking out of the shirt he has rolled to his forearms. "It's best to keep as much of Jay covered as possible."

"I read it and everything else you attached." The golden

streaks in his eyes sparkle. "Congratulations on not having chlamydia."

My cheeks heat, and I turn toward the door. "The mall closes in two hours. If we leave now, we can make it in time."

Jay's hand closes around my wrist, and he spins me around—right into the hard wall of his chest. My heart lodges in my throat, pounding so hard and fast I can't breathe. We haven't been this close in weeks. And although he's always there, he's usually just out of reach, fully in protector mode.

His touch makes me remember that night we first met. The strength and gentleness in his calloused fingers sends my mind reeling, and my body into an uncomfortable state of awareness.

Time slows down as his hand trails up my arm from my wrist to my elbow, heating my skin despite the layer of clothing between us. I want to feel his touch against my bare skin, and taste every dip and curve of his mouth.

He smells so fucking good. I want to lean in and inhale deeply, filling my nose with his scent. If Jay was a cologne, he'd be called something like, Smoldering Embrace. Bottles of him would fly off the shelves no matter what the asking price. Every man would want to smell like Jay.

Spicy.

Sexy.

Undeniably masculine.

My gaze locks on his full mouth. His soft, firm lips are so close, almost within reach. My mind floods with memories of us locked together, his tongue gliding against mine, his taste filling my mouth.

He tightens his grip on my elbow, tugging me even closer. My head tilts back, and our gazes collide. Heat blazes in his dark eyes, sparking a fire deep inside me.

"I got my results back," he says. "Want to see them?"

I blink up at him, my brain scrambling to catch up with his words. "What?"

His lips curve upward for a brief second, and the gleam in his eyes says he knows exactly where my mind had been. "The test results you asked for," he says with the patience of a saint. "Do you want to see them?"

"Oh." I ease back, a blast of heat scorching from my chest to my cheeks. "Sure."

He tugs my hand, keeping me close while we walk through his living room to the kitchen. His long stride forces me to lengthen mine in order to keep up.

Jay's apartment is one long, open room with a wall of windows overlooking the Blue Ridge Mountains, highly polished wooden floors peeking out under antique rugs, and rustic wood-beamed ceilings.

The first time I'd been in Jay's apartment, I'd been too busy getting my world rocked to observe anything, but now I notice the book shelf overflowing with books, the contemporary art on the walls, and a shiny black piano tucked in the corner near the kitchen island.

"Do you play?" I ask, adding another potential detail to the list of *all things Jay.*

"A little." He grabs an envelope from a drawer in the kitchen and hands it to me.

It looks official, alright. The clinic's name is at the top, and it's addressed to Jay. It's still sealed. "You want me to open it?"

He crosses his arms over his chest and nods. "Go ahead."

I finger the edge of the flap. "But you haven't looked at it yet."

"Don't need to," he says, frowning down at me. "Why do you need my test results, Mia?"

A shiver of anticipation ripples over my skin. I might be imagining us in bed together, his body pinning mine to the mattress as he thrusts deep inside me. "It's just a precaution."

He cocks his head at me, dark eyes crinkling at the corners as he studies my expression. "Are you thinking about having sex with me?"

My heart speeds up, beating so fast it feels like it's going to explode. Busted.

"I..." The words get caught in my throat as his gaze slides over my body. "I, I... just want to be safe."

He stalks closer, his dark eyes hot and hungry on mine. "I don't remember you asking for my test results the last time you were here." His gaze shifts to the oversized leather sofa he'd pinned me against as his talented fingers brought me to ecstasy.

Desire streaks through my body. My breasts ache, nipples tightening at the thought of his sensual mouth and teasing tongue. "I don't know what I was thinking."

He makes a noise low in his throat that is part laugh, part growl. "Hmm." His hand skates up my arm, closing around the nape of my neck. He pulls me closer, bending his head to mine. "You told me to forget about you."

My eyelids flutter shut, and I tilt my head back, inhaling his delicious scent. The last thing I want is for Jay to forget about me. "I changed my mind."

He steps back, releasing me so fast it makes my head spin. "That's too bad," he says. "I don't have sex with clients."

Jay is halfway across the room, grabbing his leather jacket and shrugging it on. "Where are you going?"

"The mall," he says, pulling open the door. "I'll let you pick out some clothes for me on one condition."

My blood hums, and I hope his one condition is something that will ease the throbbing ache inside me. "What's that?"

"I get to pick out an outfit for you, too."

In the men's department, a sales person greets us with a warning. "We close in thirty minutes."

I pull out my credit card. "He needs a weekend vacation wardrobe," I say. "Including a suit jacket."

The employee perks up. He sweeps his gaze over Jay, dollar signs lighting up his eyes. "Shoes too?"

"The works," I say.

The man walks in a circle around Jay. "Forty-two long jacket?"

"That's right," Jay says, sounding impressed.

When the man leaves, Jay pulls out his wallet. "You don't have to pay," he says. "I can expense it."

My brows furrow. "I can't believe the county is paying for this. I've seen the budget."

Jay starts to reply, but doesn't get a chance before the salesperson is back with an armful of clothes. He leads Jay to the corner of the store where they disappear into the men's changing area.

While Jay tries on the clothes, a linen shirt with a floral pattern catches my eye. Jay would look so cute in it, I can't resist.

I peek my head around the corner into the changing area. All the doors are open except the one in the back, and I can see Jay's bare feet and legs clad in gray slacks poking out from under the partition.

I knock lightly on the door. "How's it going in there?"

"This is the men's dressing room," Jay says.

I lower my voice. "No one else is in here."

Jay steps out wearing a pair of slim-cut gray slacks and a pale blue button-down shirt. I don't recognize the man in front of me. Dressed in something other than his typical tough-guy black wardrobe, he still looks every inch the bad boy.

Except somehow even hotter.

"What do you think?"

My tongue feels too thick for my mouth, and I shove the floral shirt at him. "Try this."

He pulls his hand away as if the shirt burned him. "No way."

"Just try it," I say.

He looks down his nose at me. "I don't think so."

I step closer, pressing the shirt against his chest. "Take the shirt, Jay. It's perfect."

"I draw the line at flowers." He unbuttons the shirt he's wearing and tosses it aside.

I can't tell if he's trying to distract me from the floral shirt by disrobing, or if he's just being efficient with time considering the mall closes soon. Either way, I can't think when faced with so much of his exposed flesh.

He turns around and grabs a dress shirt in his preferred color of black, giving me a view of his excellent ass in the fitted pants and the tattoo that completely covers his back.

My breath catches as my gaze travels over the angel, with its wings spread, standing over the form of a slain man. The intricate artwork reminds me of something I've seen at museums. My fingers itch to trace the detailed lines of the angel's wings inked across his broad back. I lift my gaze and find him watching me in the mirror, a sparkle of amusement in his eyes.

"See anything you like?" The arrogant tone in his voice is my breaking point.

I shove my way into the dressing room and pull the door closed behind me. "Stop being such an asshole. We have to spend the weekend together, remember?"

He scowls at me in the mirror, and *damn* if it isn't the sexiest thing I've ever seen. "I remember. I have to pretend to be your boyfriend while wearing these stupid, preppy clothes and keeping my hands to myself while you look at me like you want to devour me whole."

Shit. I guess he's caught me looking more than once. Do I want to devour him whole? Yes, yes, I do. "Maybe we stop pretending for the weekend. Have a little fun."

I stalk closer, watching his entire demeanor change in the mirror. His shoulders stiffen, his back straightens, and what just might be the beginning of a wicked smile, curves his mouth. He turns to face me, and I don't know where to look. His gorgeous face, that sexy smile, or the carved lines of his lean torso covered in ink.

Yanking on the black shirt, he turns to face me. "You should get out of here before we get in trouble."

A laugh tickles my throat. "Is bad boy Jay Sanchez afraid of mall security?"

He steps closer, reaches behind me, and opens the door. "No, but I am afraid of you, Mia. You look a little feral right now."

"Fuck you," I say.

"Yes." His laugh sounds as he ushers me out of the dressing room. "I believe that's what you're asking."

"Are you seriously turning me down?" I shove my arm into the open space of the door, prying it open. "You seemed pretty eager last time."

He looks me up and down, his gaze molten hot as he leans on the door between us. "I'll think about it."

The way he's looking at me makes me tingle in all the right places. I smile slowly, enjoying the sizzle of chemistry between us. "See that you do."

Jay gives me one more heated glance, then steps back. "Let me get dressed," he says. "I still have to pick out your outfit."

"Okay, but we are buying this." I hold up the floral shirt as he closes the door. "I can't wait to see you wearing it."

"Over my dead body," he says.

Under the partition, I see his pants drop to the floor. Heat scorches through me as I imagine him standing nearly naked on the other side of the door. For the first time since I got the invitation, I'm actually looking forward to my little brother's wedding weekend.

CHAPTER 23

Champagne Talking

"First Class Virgin?" Mia asks.

"I'm ruined for life." Stretching out my legs, I kick back in the seat and get comfortable. There's plenty of room for my legs, and with only two seats in the row, my shoulders aren't bumping anything but air.

Mia gives my outstretched legs a smile. "Pretty fucking sweet, isn't it?"

"Anyone ever tell you for such a pretty woman you have a very dirty mouth, Ms. James?"

She laughs, a low, naughty sound that makes my blood hum every time I hear it. Reaching up, she presses the call button for the flight attendant.

"I'm on my first vacation in years, and I am about to get tipsy on free Champagne." She points at her cherry red lips, slick with gloss. "The mouth is gonna get a lot dirtier."

I can't tear my gaze away from her mouth. Ever since she'd told me to think about having sex with her, I've done nothing but think about having sex with her. Starting with kissing her dirty mouth.

The flight attendant approaches, and Mia orders two glasses of Champagne, then looks at me. "Care to join me?"

"Isn't one of those glasses for me?"

"Nope." She wags a finger at me. "Get your own."

It's pretty early for me to start drinking, but I'm also on my first vacation in years. And it's all expenses paid. And it's with Mia. "I'll have tequila on ice."

Mia leans back and crosses one leg over the other, which hikes her short dress up her thighs and makes my blood pressure rise. I look away and shift in my seat, trying to ease the tightness of my jeans. This is going to be the longest two hour flight I've ever experienced.

I've never crossed the line with a client before. But technically, Mia isn't a client this weekend. Thanks to the mysterious celebrity, there is no danger on Serenity Island.

The flight attendant returns with our drinks and two bowls of premium nuts, one for each of us.

"To traveling in style," Mia says, lifting one of her Champagne flutes to me.

"I'll drink to that." I raise my glass, then take a sip of the tequila, savoring the burn as I swallow.

Mia downs her Champagne in one gulp, and I eye her skeptically. "You're not playing around."

She sets her empty glass down and raises a brow at me. "Don't tell me you're one of those boyfriends who counts his girlfriend's drinks, and gives her a hard time for having fun."

I scowl at the description. "No, definitely not."

She sips from the second glass, then reaches under the seat for her carry on. "Before you get too far into that tequila, you need to memorize this printout."

My brows raise as I take the folder and flip through the report. It's multiple pages long, listing all Mia's relatives in order of importance.

Her father, Owen, age sixty-five, a professor of economics who lives in Raleigh, is head of a philanthropic group that donates millions of dollars every year. Her mother, Janet, is a pre-school teacher, also sixty-five, and of Raleigh, North Carolina.

Her brother Malcom, known to the family as Max, is thirty-two, a sports agent, and lives in Atlanta, Georgia.

"Are you close with them?" I ask.

"I have thirty-eight cousins, and I'm close with around three of them."

"That's not a very high percentage."

"There are a lot of cousins." She selects a cashew and pops it in her mouth. "But don't worry, most of them aren't coming." She leans over to point out the names highlighted in yellow. "Those are the important ones."

"Thanks." I close the file and turn toward her. "Tell me about your brother."

"It's just the two of us, so we are super close," she says. "We grew up in a neighborhood where we were the only two people under the age of thirty, so we had no one to play with except each other. We sort of had to be close."

Considering most of the kids in the trailer park where I grew up went barefoot because their parents couldn't afford shoes, or chose to spend their paychecks at the local dive bar instead of Payless Shoes, a neighborhood devoid of playmates didn't seem that bad.

"Are you close now?"

"As close as we can be living four hours apart. Max is impossible not to like. It's actually very annoying. He's handsome, charming, and successful. He's also extremely humble for someone who is handsome, charming, and successful."

"Annoying," I agree.

She shrugs. "Every single person in my family is an over-achiever."

Between the cousin who's a professional soccer player, a former Miss America aunt, and the uncle who's head chef at a restaurant in New York that's so popular even I've heard of it, saying her family is full of over-achievers is definitely an under-statement.

Mia also has a cousin who is an Olympic gold medalist in

swimming, not to mention the mystery celebrity responsible for shutting down the island for the weekend.

"I'm kind of the loser of the lot of them." She sips her Champagne with a pensive expression, not meeting my gaze.

"You're joking, right?"

Picking through the nuts in her bowl, she finds a peanut and holds it up. "This is me," she says. "A lowly peanut. The rest of my family? They're macadamia nuts and cashews."

I pluck the peanut from her fingers and pop it into my mouth. "I prefer peanuts."

She laughs, and I feel that familiar pull in my belly every time I hear the sexy sound.

"My little brother is getting married before me, which makes me a loser."

Her frown deepens, and the feisty, quick-witted woman I've gotten to know has been replaced by someone I hardly recognize.

Someone who doesn't know her own worth.

I cover her hand with mine. "You know you're incredible."

She looks down at our hands. "You don't have to say that just because you're my pretend boyfriend."

"I mean it."

Her gaze finds mine again, and she smiles. "Thanks."

"Don't mention it."

"There's one more thing," she says. "I think we should have nicknames."

"I already have one."

"I don't think *The Savage* is going to go over well with my family."

"What did you have in mind?" I ask. "Darling? Honey?"

She scrunches her nose. "Too boring."

I'm warming up to the idea. "How about, Cupcake?" I lace our fingers together and squeeze. "No, I've got it. ShortCake."

She glares at me. "I don't know."

"It's perfect." I toss back a gulp of tequila. "What about mine?"

She taps her fingernail to her lower lip. "How about Lovebug?"

I narrow my eyes at her. "Lovebug?"

"It's perfect." Mia smiles wickedly.

"It's horrible."

"It suits you." She leans over the armrest, closing the distance between us.

I hold perfectly still as her lips brush the outer shell of my ear.

"Have you thought any more about this weekend?"

My heart jumps to my throat. It's all I've thought about. "Maybe."

"I don't know why you're resisting." Her hand drops to my thigh, fingers tracing a pattern on the dress pants she picked out for me. "You're the one who suggested I have some fun."

Now she's done it. My dick strains against my cotton dress pants, which are far more revealing than denim. "Technically, you're not my client while we're on the island."

"Technically, it would be a lot easier to fool my family if we weren't pretending." Her teasing fingers slide closer to my seat belt. "Everyone already thinks we're a couple," she says. "We might as well be one."

I drop my hand to hers, capturing her fingers before they can explore any closer to my eager dick. We are in public, but if I had her alone, she would be naked already. "Is that the Champagne talking?"

She shrugs. "Maybe."

"I like the way Champagne talks," I say.

Mia takes a sip of my drink and winks at me. "Wait until you hear what tequila has to say."

CHAPTER 24

Your Room Or Mine

It's still winter in Mossy Oak, but it's always summer in Miami.

The warm breeze caresses my bare skin, and the booze I consumed on the flight heats my blood. I feel free for the first time in months. No more looking over my shoulder, or being scared of my own shadow. No more jumping to do Jordan's bidding, or pretending with Jay.

For the next few days, its palm trees, sunny skies, and a broad-shouldered man who looks just as biker badass in cotton and linen as he does in denim and leather.

Aviator-style sunglasses cover his eyes, and his hair is loose, falling in thick, textured waves to his shoulders. His purposeful stride eats up the sidewalk, forcing me to double-time in order to keep up. He's dragging two suitcases—one black, one fuchsia—behind him, because he insisted on me not lifting a finger, but it doesn't slow him down.

"Stay close," he says, sweeping his gaze around the area.

My stomach flip-flops. He is still in bodyguard mode, and it is even hotter in Miami than it had been in Mossy Oak.

"If you would slow down a little, I could keep up." I point at my high-heeled sandals. "These shoes weren't made for running."

Jay slows down when we get to the ride share line. Glancing

over his shoulder at my shoes, his mouth tightens with disapproval. "You don't ever quit with the heels," he says.

"Nope." I raise a brow at his attire. "And you still managed to wear all black."

"This is gray," he says, nodding curtly at his shirt.

"Charcoal is basically black."

His gaze moves up my bare legs like a hot caress, lingering on my thighs. "Come here," he says.

My feet move automatically at the sound of his low command. A sizzle of awareness races down my spine in anticipation of his touch. He drops the handle of my suitcase and reaches for me, tugging me to his side.

"Stay close," he says. "It's crowded."

I'm not sure whether to be annoyed or turned on by his overprotectiveness. "We're not in Mossy Oak anymore. You can relax."

Jay lowers his sunglasses, pinning me with his dark, serious gaze. "I'll relax when we get to the island."

"I'm looking forward to seeing that."

The corner of his mouth lifts in a faint smile that's quickly replaced by his brooding scowl. "Let's just get there in one piece first," he says, ushering me toward our ride.

The driver hops out of the car, and Jay chats with him in Spanish as they load the bags into the trunk.

Jay opens the door for me, and I slide into the backseat. "I didn't know you spoke Spanish."

"There's a lot you don't know about me." Jay gets in beside me and says something else to the driver I can't understand.

"What did you say?" I ask, looking from Jay to the driver, who is grinning at us in the rearview mirror.

Jay takes off his sunglasses, pinning me with his big, dark eyes. "I told him I was about to kiss my girlfriend." His fingers skim over my collarbone, then curl around the back of my neck. "Is that okay with her?"

Despite all the liquid courage I consumed, I'm suddenly scared shitless.

This kiss is going to change everything.

It will mean no more pretending I don't want him and he doesn't want me. No more steeling myself to resist him.

What am I getting myself into?

Jay captures my chin between his thumb and index finger, lifting my face until our gazes collide. The gold streaks in his brown eyes shimmer in the bright sunlight. "I'll still keep you safe," he says. "Always."

My chest squeezes, and a slow hum throbs through my body. Jay can't keep me safe from my own heart. It was my idea to be a real couple this weekend, but now I'm seeing just how dangerous it's going to be.

The pad of his thumb traces my lower lip, causing a low thrum of pleasure to radiate through me. "Can I kiss you, Mia?"

I can't seem to find words, but my body knows how to answer. I lift my face and nod.

"I prefer words, but that's good for now." His thumb brushes once more across my lower lip, teasing it open before he replaces it with his mouth. He kisses me softly, the tickle of his close-cropped beard making me shiver with anticipation of it scraping softly over other parts of my body.

His kiss is slow and mesmerizing, heating me from the inside out until I feel smoke in my veins, a furnace building in my chest. His tongue stokes the fire inside me, each gentle glide making me yearn for more.

"Excuse me," the driver says, opening his door. "We're here."

Somehow Jay managed to make one long, languid kiss last the entire drive to the marina. He eases back and looks down at me, eyes dark with desire. "I can't wait to get you to that private island."

"Where I'm safe?"

He kisses me with surprising tenderness. "Where I can get you alone in a hotel room."

My heart launches into a sprint at the hunger in his gaze. "Technically, we have adjoining rooms."

"Whatever." He reaches for the door. "Your room, or mine, doesn't matter."

I take his hand and let him help me out of the car. "Too bad you have golf and I have a bridal luncheon."

"Tonight, then." His arm slides around my waist and he tucks me close to his chest. He dips his chin to whisper in my ear. "I can wait."

But I'm not sure I can.

As we walk down the dock and board the private boat waiting to take us to Serenade Island, my mind spins, trying to come up with a way for us both to get out of our commitments. Every part of me longs for more of Jay, more kisses, more touches, even more of his rough commands.

On board, we are greeted by a uniformed crew member letting us know we are the last to board and we will be setting sail in a few minutes. He leads us to a covered area where half a dozen passengers are mingling with drinks. I don't recognize any of them, so they must be Samantha's guests.

Out of nowhere, a man in a hoodie and sunglasses rushes up and grabs me, lifting me off my feet in a bone-crushing hug.

Jay is on him in an instant, yanking him back by the throat and pinning him to the railing, threatening to throw him overboard with a low growl.

"Wait." I grab Jay's arm and try to pull him back, but Jay is about as easy to move as a concrete slab. "This is my cousin. He's okay."

Jay shakes his head, slowly backing off and releasing Brad. "Sorry, man."

Brad yanks off his sunglasses and sizes Jay up. "*You're* Mia's boyfriend?"

"Brad," I say, stepping between the two men. I can only imagine what is going through my cousin's mind. Jay is big and intimidating, plus he just tried to toss Brad over the side of the boat. "This is..."

"Jay Sanchez," Brad finishes for me, reaching out to grasp Jay's hand. "I saw you fight in Vegas for the championship. It was legendary." He whips out his phone. "Can I get a selfie?"

Jay nods once, his sunglasses hiding his expression. I know him well enough after spending the last month with him to see the reluctance in his posture. He wants to take a selfie with Brad as much as he wants to go golfing with my family. But he'll do both, because underneath all the gruff, Jay is a big teddy bear.

Brad lowers his hoodie and poses for a selfie with Jay.

"Nice to meet you," Jay says. "My mom is a huge fan."

Brad laughs good-naturedly. "But I guess you're not, since you were about to toss my ass overboard."

I step up, taking Jay's hand. "He was just looking out for me," I say.

Brad raises his eyebrow at me. "Since when do you need anyone to look out for you?"

I've never been the type not to fight my own battles. I give Jay a look that tells him I told him so, and he laughs softly.

"She's pretty fierce," Jay says. "And I'm a bit overprotective."

Brad grins. "If I'm gonna get tossed from a boat, at least it's by *The Savage.*"

So much for Jay's nickname being too much for my family.

"Brad!" a woman's voice calls from the lounge. "Get in here before someone spots you."

Brad rolls his eyes. "It's Miami, Anna. No one cares about me."

"Just get in here," she says. "I'm not in the mood to hide from the paparazzi."

Brad heads toward his wife with a shrug. "No mystery who wears the pants in this family." He laughs at his own joke, showing a mouthful of perfect white teeth. "Get it?" he asks, glancing from me to Jay.

"We get it," I say. "His wife is an underwear model," I whisper to Jay.

Jay nods. "I don't live under a rock."

"Mia!" a voice calls from a few feet away.

I peer over Jay's broad shoulders to see a man I didn't expect to confront until much later. "Dad!"

"Your one and only," Dad says, striding forward to give me a hug. He stops short and glances at Jay. "You're not going to throw me over, are you?"

Jay's chin lifts. "No, sir."

Dad opens his arms, and I give him a hug. He smells exactly as I remember. Tobacco and mint. I'm pleased to note that he feels fit and strong. Dear old dad never lets anything get in the way of his golf game, and it keeps him in shape.

There are a few more lines on his face, but otherwise he looks tanned and healthy. "I thought you weren't coming until tonight."

"I was able to get an earlier flight." He glances between me and Jay, his gaze sharp. "You must be the boyfriend I've heard so little about."

Jay steps forward, extending his hand. "Jay Sanchez," he says. "Nice to meet you, Professor James."

I'm pleasantly surprised Jay remembers my dad's profession. Considering he only looked at my printout for a few minutes, I thought the chances of him retaining any of the information were slim.

"It's Owen," Dad says. "Let's leave Professor James back in North Carolina."

"Happy to leave our jobs back in Mossy Oak." Jay slips his arm around my waist and squeezes. "Right, ShortCake?"

At the sound of my nickname, I force a smile. Dad is never going to buy this. He knows how much I've always hated my height deficit.

To my surprise, Dad nods with approval, a grin on his face. "It's nice to see Mia so happy."

Jay's hand slides up my back to my shoulder. His gaze meets mine, the gold flecks in his brown eyes sparkling in the bright sunlight. "I agree."

It looks like Jay has passed the first test with flying colors.

But the real test is yet to come. He hasn't met my mom yet.

CHAPTER 25

Clock's Ticking

For the first time in a month, I don't have to worry about Mia. No one is going to hurt her here on the island.

More than likely, I'm the one in danger.

This woman is going to wreck me. Every moment with her makes her harder to resist. And for the next few days, she's mine. What that means for when we return home, I don't like to think about. I don't have to. Not yet.

Alone in my room adjoining with Mia's, I change into my golfing clothes and pull out my phone to send a quick text to my mom.

Jay: You're never gonna believe who I just shared a boat ride with.

Mom: Who is this?

Jay: Your son

Mom: Jay?

Jay: You only have one son, Ma

Mom: since you never call, I wasn't sure

Jay: I talked to you on Sunday

Mom: Who did u share a boat with????

Jay: Guess

Mom: Barack Obama

Jay: No

Mom: Brad Shelton

Only my mom would guess Brad Shelton right after a former President.

Jay: Yes. R u a witch?

Mom: Call me ASAP

Jay: I can't. I have to go play golf. With Brad.

I swipe my phone off with a grin, which quickly disappears as I catch a glimpse of myself in the mirror. I hardly recognize myself in slim-cut khaki pants and a lavender button-down shirt.

A knock on the divider door, distracts me from my reflection.

When I open the door, Mia is standing with her back to me, the creamy skin of her back exposed.

"Zip me up, will you?"

My heart knocks against my chest as I step forward and drag the zipper up, pulling the dress tightly to her slim waist and back.

She turns to face me, the ghost of a smile on her lips. "Thanks."

"Anytime." My voice sounds scratchy, and I clear my throat.

Her gaze drops over me, and a smile lifts her lips. "You look almost preppy."

I stalk back to my open suitcase and sort through the clothes. "I look like a dork."

Mia snorts. "You could never look like a dork," she says. "Not with those biceps."

I glance up to find her looking at me like she's starving and I'm the only thing on the menu. Teasing her, I flex my bicep, and watch her eyes go wide.

"You look..." her words trail off, and she presses her fist to her mouth. "You look like a hot banker."

I can't tell if she's laughing or salivating behind her hand. "Don't ever call me a banker again."

"Why?" she asks, definitely laughing. "What's wrong with bankers? I like bankers."

"No way I can wear this now." I sort through my clothes, looking for something less colorful.

Mia comes over and puts her hand on my arm. "Don't change," she says. "You look great."

I turn and look at her, giving her a thorough glance from head to toe. She's wearing a pale pink sundress with a halter top and a full skirt. High heeled sandals give her an extra few inches of height, and her hair and makeup are perfect. She looks like she is ready for a photo shoot, not as if she's been traveling all day, drinking more than her fair share of Champagne.

"Don't look at me like that, or I won't leave."

It's on the tip of my tongue to tell her not to leave. Instead, she should stay here and let me help her out of her dress. But, like any self-respecting not-pretend boyfriend, I put Mia first and walk her to the door.

Golf is more enjoyable than I'd thought. Max is exactly as Mia described, and Brad doesn't act anything like a celebrity. I'm paired with Mia's dad, and he keeps me entertained for hours with stories about Mia.

"She's always been unstoppable," Owen says, launching into a story about how Mia started volunteer clubs in middle school, was the president of her sorority in college, and was the first woman in their family to earn a law degree.

Max has stories to add about how he'd paid Mia to write his college essays, and Brad chimes in about the time she secured fake I.D.s for all of them before they were legal.

When we are finished with the game, Owen pulls me aside and tells me how happy he is Mia and I found each other.

"I have a good feeling about you two," he says, shaking my hand. "Don't screw it up."

"I won't, Mr. James."

"It's Owen," he says, striding off through the lobby.

When I get back to my room, Mia is standing on my balcony, looking out over the spectacular view of pristine white sand and turquoise ocean.

She's still wearing the dress she had on earlier with the tricky zipper, and I wonder if she can't get out of it.

I'm glad to volunteer my services.

"Why is your view better than mine?" she asks, turning around to look at me.

I step out on the patio and slip my arm around her waist. "I'm just lucky, I guess."

She turns and wraps her arms around my neck. "How was your day, dear?"

She's asked me the same question nearly every day for a month, but it feels different here on the island, where we are really a couple. "I spent the whole day hitting a tiny ball and listening to stories about you as a kid."

She rolls her eyes. "Sounds terrible."

"Max is exactly as great as you warned me he would be."

"He's happy."

"I hope so. He's getting married."

Mia narrows her eyes at me, her fingers combing through my hair. "How come you aren't married?"

I take a long time to answer. "I'm not the marrying kind."

She smiles sadly. "Neither am I. Marriage is overrated. The divorce rate is nearly fifty percent. Why bother?"

"I agree."

"I thought we were opposites when we met," she says. "But we actually have a lot in common."

I tighten my fingers at her waist. "Brad told me I helped him win a bet with his wife."

"How?"

"She bet I'd be an accountant, and he guessed I'd be a tech entrepreneur."

Mia's brow scrunches. "So neither one of them was right."

"Yeah, but she was so sure of herself she said if your boyfriend was anything other than an accountant or a real estate agent, he would win."

"I should have brought Harrison," she says. "I hate when Brad wins."

I lower my head and kiss her bare shoulder. "You don't mean that."

She runs her fingers through my hair, tugging my head back. "Don't start kissing me. It will lead to more than kissing, and we will never make it to the rehearsal on time."

I kiss a path up her shoulder to her neck. "It doesn't have to lead to more than kissing. I like kissing you."

She arches her back, giving me more access to her neck. "What if I want more than kissing? More than just your mouth."

I bite gently on her earlobe. "But my mouth is very talented."

She chuckles. "I don't think your mouth can give me every-thing I want."

My competitive nature kicks in. "I bet it can."

She clutches my shoulders. "I'm not that easy."

"I know how to kiss."

She leans back and looks at me, an amused glint in her eyes. "You've got ten minutes."

"I'll take that bet."

"And if you lose, you have to wear the flowered shirt tonight."

"It seems like a win-win situation for you."

She rises up on her toes to kiss me. "Seems that way, doesn't it? But if you're not up for the challenge, I understand."

"I'm up for the challenge." I'm not telling Mia, but there's no way I'm wearing that shirt tonight, because I didn't even pack it. "If I win, you have to wear the outfit I bought you."

She loops her hands around my neck, and I back her into my room. "I'll take that bet."

She shoves her fingers into my hair, loosening the tight tail as she drags my mouth back to hers. "Clock's ticking," she says. "I hope that shirt doesn't need ironing."

I nibble at her bottom lip and slide my tongue into her mouth as I push up her dress. My fingers skim softly over her smooth skin, drawing closer to the paradise between her legs.

"You don't know how much I've been dying to get my hands on you." I draw my fingers up, tracing a pattern over the top of her panties, then from one hip bone to the other. "There's something I've been dying to do for weeks," I say, slipping my fingers under the sides of her panties and easing them down her legs.

She moans, her back going flat against the door as I help her step out of her panties. "What?"

I drop to my knees. "Taste you."

I press my face between her thighs. The scent of her arousal makes me feel drunk. I breathe her in, savoring how delicious she smells as I rub my bearded cheek against her inner thigh. My tongue darts out, and I taste her, just a quick tease.

She moans and jerks her hips back, but there's nowhere to go. She's trapped between me and the wall, and it's all she can do to hold still as I blow softly on the swollen bud of her clit.

Her fingers find my hair again, and she guides my head exactly where she wants it.

Don't worry, ShortCake, it's exactly where I want to be too.

She's soaking wet, so slippery with desire I want to bury more than my tongue inside her. She tastes even better than I imagined. So ready for me, so responsive, so delicious. I lick her greedily, sucking and biting until I'm devouring her with no restraint.

She cries out, burying her fingers in my hair. "Holy shit," she pants. "You're so fucking good at this. It's not fair..."

Her voice trails off as I slide one finger inside her, stroking her hard and eating her until she's making incoherent sounds and shaking so hard I have to hook her leg over my shoulder for support.

Harder, faster, deeper, I stroke her and suck her, savoring every sound of pleasure tumbling from her lips. I'm so hard, I want to reach down and free my aching dick, but I hold myself back, doubling down on my efforts to make her come. Time is running out, and there's no way I'm losing this bet.

I drive her to the edge, and then push her right over. She bucks wildly against me, calling out my name as she comes on my tongue.

CHAPTER 26

The Man of the Hour

My mother looks Jay up and down with a critical gaze. "You must be the young man who's making Mia so happy lately," she says.

My cheeks burn as I remember just how happy he made me a few minutes ago, using nothing but his very talented mouth. I can't find my voice, but Jay steps in smoothly, reaching out to take my mom's hand.

"It's an honor to make Mia happy," he says, his voice full of smooth satisfaction. "She makes me happy, too."

"Mom, this is Jay."

"It's very nice to meet you, Jay." Her gaze lands on me. "You look lovely, Mia. I didn't think black was your color, but it suits you."

It's just like mom to give me a backhanded compliment. But I'll take what I can get from her. At least she hasn't started with how sorry she is for me that it's not my wedding.

After an awkward silence, Mom excuses herself to have a word with the wedding planner.

"You look gorgeous." Jay's hot gaze slides over me. "I knew that dress would be perfect."

The short, fitted dress hugs me in all the right places. It's classic with just a hint of sexy. The square neckline shows a glimpse of cleavage, and the capped sleeves add a touch of flair.

"You did an excellent job," I say.

His lips curve in a quick smile that is gone nearly before I catch sight of it. "Don't sound so surprised."

"I'm going to see you in that flowered shirt before the weekend is over."

He slips an arm around my waist. "You want to make another bet?" His palm spreads over the small of my back. "I'm game."

Serenade Island is one of the most romantic spots I've ever been in my life. The balmy heat, the scent of the ocean in the air, and the sound of waves crashing against the sand in the distance make this the perfect place to get married.

Or kiss your tatted-up, motorcycle-riding, bad-boy boyfriend.

I stretch up on my toes and wrap my arms around his neck, not caring who is watching or what they think. Our lips meet in a soft promise of more bets to come. Bets I wouldn't mind losing.

"Get a room!" Brad's voice booms from nearby.

Jay eases back. "I should have tossed him overboard," he says, loudly enough for Brad to hear.

"Calm down, Lovebug." I pat Jay's arm. "Brad isn't worth the trouble."

"Speaking of trouble," Brad says. "I have some weed gummies if you want one." He reaches into his jacket pocket. "Don't tell Anna."

"Don't tell Anna what?" Anna asks, coming up behind her husband.

"Nothing," Brad says, turning to greet Anna. "I'm just making sure Mia is signed up to sing at karaoke tonight."

"I don't sing," I say. "You know that."

"But this is family," Anna says. "No one is going to laugh at your horrible voice."

"Mia doesn't have a horrible voice," Jay says.

Brad bursts out laughing. "Tell me you haven't heard Mia sing without telling me you haven't heard Mia sing."

"Her shower voice is impressive," Jay says.

A blush rises on my cheeks. "You heard that?"

Jay nods. "Your Taylor Swift impression is spot on."

Brad thinks this is hilarious. "So I'll put you down for a Taylor Swift song?"

"Mia is singing?" Max asks, coming up behind me and linking his arm through mine. "Who are you, and what have you done with my sister?"

"I am not singing," I insist.

"Not even for me at my wedding?" Max asks.

"Not even for you at your wedding."

"Jay? Are you down?"

Jay shakes his head. "I don't sing."

"But, Lovebug, you're an amazing singer." I actually have no idea if Jay can sing or not, but teasing him is too much fun to resist.

"Not as good as you, ShortCake."

Brad laughs so hard he snorts. "ShortCake? You've got some balls calling Mia short."

"I like this guy," Max says, nodding at Jay.

Yeah, I know the feeling.

* * *

After the rehearsal, Mom ushers us to the family table where, to my annoyance, Chelsea Taylor and her date are already seated.

I'm still not used to the idea that the biggest gossip in town is going to be one of my relatives.

"Good to see you, Jay," Chelsea says. "I'm glad you could make it."

"Me too." Jay pulls out a chair for me.

"I hardly recognize you in all those clothes," she says, letting her gaze drop over him.

I nearly choke on my tongue, but Jay handles it with his usual stoic charm. "Mia was pretty specific about the attire." He takes the seat next to mine. "No gym clothes allowed."

"You know each other from the gym?" Chelsea's date asks.

"Jay is the owner," Chelsea says. "I told you that, Craig."

Craig lifts his shoulders in a shrug. "Yeah, probably."

"What kind of gym?" Dad asks.

"It's a boxing gym," I say. "And they have a kids' program called 'Champion's Corner' that benefits the local youth."

Dad hones in on Jay. "My dad used to box. It's a good sport for strategy and discipline."

Jay nods. "We teach the kids respect, integrity, balance. Some of these kids come from homes that don't even have running water. They are isolated in the mountains with no chance of a better life. Champion's Corner gives them a chance."

As Jay finishes, silence settles over the table. He's passionate about the kids' program, and it shows.

"How long have you two been dating?" Craig asks.

"A few months," I say.

"You never said how you met." This is from Mom, who is looking at us with undisguised curiosity.

"I'm sure I told you." I wave her off. "It really isn't very interesting."

A server approaches with our dinner plates, and while everyone is distracted, I scoot closer to Jay. "We never talked about how we met," I say in a hushed voice only he can hear.

"Let's just tell the truth," Jay suggests, lacing his fingers with mine under the table.

"But the truth is embarrassing," I say.

"Okay, so not the truth." Jay leans closer to me so our thighs brush under the table. "We could always tell them I'm your bodyguard."

I smack him on the shoulder. "Don't joke about that."

Mom's eyes are on us from across the table. "Are you going to keep us in suspense? Or tell us how you met?"

Jay and I look at each other. "Go ahead," I say. "You tell her."

Jay pauses and takes a sip of his drink. "I tricked Mia into dating me," he says.

My mouth drops open. "You did not."

"I'm sorry," he says. "But I did."

He meets my gaze, and *oh holy shit*, he's telling the truth.

Mom laughs. "I'm not surprised. Mia never knows what's good for her."

I ignore my mom's underhanded barb about my decision-making skills and squeeze Jay's hand under the table. "Tell the story."

Jay runs a hand through his hair, looking uncomfortable. "I got rid of her date so she would have dinner with me."

A laugh escapes my mouth. "You did that?"

Jay nods. "I knew as soon as I saw you I wanted to get to know you."

I shift closer to him, mesmerized by the golden flecks in his dark eyes. "I can't believe you did that."

He smiles. "I should say sorry, but I'm not."

I'm dying to know more about what happened, but it will have to wait.

Brad takes the stage to a round of applause, and it's impossible to continue the conversation.

"Thank you all for coming here tonight to celebrate Max and Samantha," Brad says. "I know most of you probably know who I am, but don't worry, there will be no interruptions from paparazzi this weekend. The island is secure."

The crowd laughs weakly at his lame attempt at a joke. As he strolls to the far right of the stage, the projector screen lights up with a life-size photograph of my brother and his future wife.

"This weekend is all about Max and Samantha," Brad says.

"Get off the stage, then," comes a good-natured catcall.

"Give me a minute," Brad says smiling. "First, I'd like to propose a toast."

Servers walk around with trays of the signature cocktail, something pink with an umbrella. Jay takes two and hands one to me.

We raise our glasses as Brad toasts the bride and groom, and everyone drinks.

"It wouldn't be a celebration without karaoke. We all know how much Max loves it. Our first brave soul to sing tonight is cousin Marty. Everyone give him a hand."

The crowd erupts in cheers as an older man comes on the stage. He selects a Celine Dion classic and sings with remarkably good pitch.

Next is a young cousin barely out of her teens who does an emotional Billie Eilish impression.

"Here's the man of the hour," Brad says as Max strolls onto the stage.

He's wearing a tropical print shirt, shorts and flip-flops, and he looks more relaxed than he should on the eve of his wedding. My brother has always been more comfortable in front of a crowd than he is one-on-one. He loves being the center of attention.

"This one's for you, baby," Max says as the first notes of John Legend's "All of Me" begins to play.

Max opens his mouth, and the crowd falls silent, listening to his amazing voice. Mom tears up as she watches her son pour his heart out on the stage.

Jay leans closer to me. "He's good."

"Yeah, I know." My darling brother is good at everything.

When Max finishes up to a loud round of applause, Brad announces the next singer.

"Mia, come on up!"

A lump forms in my throat, and my stomach clenches. I don't think I can move.

Jay squeezes my hand. "You don't have to do it."

But of course, I do.

If I don't, everyone will think I'm a loser.

I make my way up to the stage with shaky knees. While Brad launches into a quick story about the first time he met Samantha, I leaf through the book of songs. Nothing seems quite right, then I land on the Taylor Swift song I like to sing in the shower.

I make my selection and wait impatiently while Brad wraps up his monologue to another round of applause.

"Knock 'em dead," he says, winking as he passes me the microphone.

Growing up, Brad could never get enough of teasing me. My inability to carry a tune or play any sport involving a ball were sources of great amusement to everyone in my family.

The music starts, and a quick glance at the audience assures me all eyes are on me. My mom is leaning forward in her seat, a worried look on her face. My dad is smiling hopefully as if I magically learned how to harmonize since the last time he heard me sing.

I'm going to disappoint him and everyone else who thinks all members of the James family are like Brad and Max.

Nope, there's me. Smart and sassy, but hopelessly untalented.

Anxiety races through me, and I'm tempted to drop the mic and run off stage as fast as my high heels will allow.

The song is well into the first verse, and I have yet to open my mouth. I should be singing, but instead I'm frozen on the stage.

My gaze flickers over the audience and lands on Jay. His warm brown eyes are a balm to my frazzled nerves. I open my mouth, but no words come out, and before I know what's happening, Jay is striding onto the stage, taking the microphone from my hand and pointing at the stool for me to sit.

He sings the first line, and I'm blown away. I'm glad I'm sitting down, because Jay's rich, smooth baritone is enough to make me swoon for the first time in my life.

Maybe it's the liquor talking, but I might just be in love.

CHAPTER 27

Bedtime Routine

After karaoke, Mia leads me around the patio, introducing me to more cousins and friends. I play the role of attentive boyfriend with more dedication than Brad Shelton on the hunt for an Oscar.

We consume far too many signature wedding cocktails. I'm feeling more than a little drunk, and Mia wobbles on her feet. When she begins to slur her words and cling to my arm, I suggest we go to bed.

"Your room or mine?" she asks.

I'd be crazy to turn down a sure thing with Mia.

I guess I'm crazy.

"Let's get you into bed," I say, steering her around the pool to the hotel entrance.

"Wait, there's my cousin, Daniel." She points to a tall man with a head of curly hair and a thick beard. "You have to meet him."

"The Olympic swimmer?" I ask. "Two-hundred-meter butterfly gold medalist?"

Mia looks impressed but doubtful. "You remember?"

"I have a knack for remembering things I've read."

"Do you have a photographic memory?"

"No one has a photographic memory. That's a myth."

"Lots of people claim it."

"Lots of people are liars."

Mia widens her eyes at me, challenging. "What's his wife's name?"

I search my memory. "Amy."

Her mouth drops open. "Shit. You're for real, aren't you?"

"Nope. I'm a figment of your imagination."

She gives me a little shove. "I mean you're really smart." Her hands flatten out on my chest, unapologetically feeling me up. "You've got an incredible body. And you can sing." She squints up at me, no doubt seeing double. "You never said you could sing."

"You never asked."

Mia laughs and presses herself against my arm. I feel the soft swell of her breasts and think twice about taking her to bed.

"Daniel," she says when we approach the former Olympian. "This is Jay, my boyfriend."

Warmth spreads through my body at Mia's introduction. I could get used to the sound of being called her boyfriend.

"Great to meet you," I say, shaking hands with Daniel.

"You're Jay Sanchez, right?" he asks, narrowing his eyes at me. "*The Savage?*"

I haven't heard the nickname in years, and now I've heard it twice in one day. "Yeah. That's me."

Daniel pumps my hand, a huge smile on his face. "I'm a big fan."

"Likewise," I say. "It's not every day I shake hands with an Olympic athlete."

"Why did you retire?" Daniel asks.

Tension knots in my gut. "It was time for a change."

"You should have kept fighting," Daniel says. "A lot of fans were disappointed."

"Leave him alone, Danny," Amy says. "You should understand how much pressure it is to be an athlete."

Daniel looks chagrined. "Sorry, dude."

"No worries."

We say goodnight to Daniel and Amy, chat with a few more relatives, and then I finally get Mia in the hotel.

When we are alone in the elevator, Mia pokes me in the chest. "You're famous." She pokes me again. "Why didn't you tell me?"

I grab her finger before she bruises my chest. "I'm not famous."

"Everyone knows who you are," she says, plucking at the top button of my shirt.

"Not everyone." I slip my arm around her waist as she wobbles on her heels. "Only those who paid attention to boxing a decade ago. I'm old news, ShortCake."

Her lips twitch into a smile. "That nickname is growing on me."

"Maybe we can keep it when we get back home?" I want to keep the name and a lot more.

She slides her hands into my hair. "Okay."

I bend my head to kiss her, but the elevator stops before our lips can touch, and I come to my senses. It wouldn't be smart to kiss her now, it would lead to more, and she's tipsy.

Tightening my arm around her waist, I lead her out of the elevator and into the hall.

"Key?" I hold out my hand for her room key.

Mia leans against the wall for balance as she fumbles in her purse for the key. When she finds it, she tries to fit it in the slot, but her hand doesn't cooperate. I take the key from her and open the door.

Mia giggles and pulls me inside. Sober Mia would never giggle, but it's very cute.

"My room has a horrible view," she says, tugging me toward the balcony. "Want to see it?"

"Not particularly."

Whirling out of my arms, she nearly stumbles on her way to

the mini-bar. "I bet your room doesn't have one of these." She yanks open a cabinet revealing several rows of tiny bottles.

"All the rooms have mini-bars." I grab her hand before she can pluck one of the bottles off the shelf. "I think we've reached the limit on booze."

She licks her bottom lip, and I watch the tip of her tongue trace the fullness.

Damn, she's tempting.

She wiggles out of my grasp and grabs a bottle of tequila, brandishing it like a trophy.

"Don't open that." I reach for a bottle of water instead. "Have some of this. You'll thank me in the morning."

Mia sets the bottle of tequila down on the dresser with a thunk. "You're right." She taps her finger to her forehead. "So smart." She takes a step, and I grab her before she can trip. Another giggle bubbles up from her throat. "And strong." She squeezes my bicep in appreciation. "And talented."

"Thank you." I can't hold back a smile. She's such a cute drunk. "You're all those things, too."

Her face falls. "Not smart enough." She kicks off one shoe, then the other. "I can't get that fucker. He's too slippery."

I wrap my arm around her waist, catching her a moment before she falls. "You'll get him," I say, lifting her into my arms. "But, right now you need to get ready for bed."

She wraps her arms around my neck. "Now we're talking."

I set her down on the tile floor.

"Why are we in the bathroom?"

"Wash your face and all the other stuff you do."

"What?"

"You're gonna be pissed in the morning if you skip your bedtime routine."

She grins and plants a kiss on my cheek. "You're so sweet."

"I'm a fucking saint." I back out of the bathroom to the sound of her laughter.

When she emerges a few minutes later wearing the hotel

bathrobe and a pink fluffy headband, my heart skips a beat. She's so beautiful like this, without the perfect hair and makeup.

"I love this robe." She fluffs the collar around her neck. "You need one, too." She pushes me toward the door. "Get your robe on and meet back here for a movie. And tequila."

I swipe the bottle of tequila off the counter and hold it out her reach. "I don't think more tequila is a good idea."

"It's an excellent idea." She takes a step forward and flops onto the mattress with a groan. "The room is spinning."

"It's not the room, it's your head."

"I don't feel so good."

"Just lie still on the bed. You'll feel better in a few seconds."

She moans. "I'm drunk."

"Yes, but you're a nice drunk."

She smiles, then grimaces. "Ugh. My eyeballs hurt."

I brush her hair away from her face. She's so still she looks like an angel. "Get some rest."

She reaches up and takes my hand. "Stay."

When I try to pry my hand from hers, she tightens her grip and tugs me down on the bed.

"Stay." She wraps her arm around my waist and presses her face to my chest. "Please."

I settle my back against the headboard and pull her into my arms. "For a few minutes." I kiss the top of her head. "Because you said please."

"Please, Jay."

For fuck's sake, I want to hear her say please when I'm deep inside her. The thought makes every muscle in my body tense, but I manage to suppress my desire. A moment later, when I can move again, I reach over and turn off the light.

"Thanks." Mia sighs and scoots closer. "For everything."

"Of course." I plan to stay until she falls asleep and then leave quietly, but a long time passes and I'm still lying there, listening to the steady sound of her breathing.

Eventually, I kick off my shoes and pull a blanket over us.

Every passing moment with Mia brings me closer to losing my heart. I should go back to my room, leave her to sleep it off on her own, but instead I rub my hand down her back and fit her closer to my chest.

"Goodnight, ShortCake."

She's so still, I think she must be asleep, but then I hear her quiet response. "'Night, Lovebug."

CHAPTER 28

A Very Cute Drunk

A faint rumbling noise stirs me from sleep. It's a soothing sound, like the hum of the engine on an old beloved truck.

I open my eyes and discover the old beloved truck is Jay. He's snoring.

Growing up, we had a big, goofy golden retriever named Happy, and he had a soft, sweet snore just like the one vibrating from Jay's throat.

The sound and the soft cotton beneath my cheek are soothing, but Jay makes a better brick wall than a pillow, and his arm is a vice around my shoulders, holding me so close I can hardly move.

Not that I want to.

It's pitch dark, the middle of the night, and there's no place I'd rather be than tucked in tightly against Jay "The Savage" Sanchez's hard, male chest. My leg is hooked over his hip, and my entire body is pressed against his side.

I'm wearing nothing but a high-quality fluffy robe, and my naked leg pins Jay's hips to the mattress.

My cheeks heat. Was I humping him?

A bottle of tequila on the nightstand catches my eye, and the memories of the night before come crashing down on me.

Failing at karaoke in front of my entire family.
Hundreds of eyes on me.
Drinking way too many cocktails.

Then I remember Jay's song. Smooth and rich, his baritone mesmerizing everyone in the crowd, especially me.

When we'd left the stage to a thunder of applause, there had been shots of tequila, many more signature cocktails, and a flurry of family and friends I hadn't seen in years.

I remember Jay carrying me, my face pressed to his chest as my head attempted to whirl off in a dangerous spin.

"'Night, ShortCake."

He'd stayed with me when I'd begged.

How fucking embarrassing. I'm never going to live this down. He'd seen me at my weakest. There was a giant chink in my facade.

Fucking tequila. I'm never listening to it again.

I try to extricate myself from Jay's embrace, but it's not easy. I don't want to wake him. I'm not ready to own up to my horrible behavior. And I also kind of like being so up close and personal with Jay.

I lift my head and feel the brush of his beard against my forehead. He's so different when relaxed in sleep. His normally fierce expression is gone, the lines on his face softened. When I shift, his arm tightens around me, securing me against his side.

I don't know how old Jay is, but he looks much younger in his sleep, like he doesn't carry the weight of the world on his broad shoulders.

Skimming my fingers over his face, I delight in the hard edge of his jaw, the softness of his beard, the carved lines of his mouth. I kiss him softly, barely brushing my lips over his beard.

Emotion catches in my throat, and the truth claps me over the head. I'm kissing this man in his sleep. I'm falling for him. It's not just his body that I want. Although it being a work of art doesn't hurt. I want his solid presence, his quick wit, his easy silence.

What the hell have I gotten myself into?

I pull back, shivering as a breeze drifts in through the open door to the balcony.

Jay stirs in his sleep, his hand stroking down my arm. "You cold?"

I stiffen and jerk away. "How could I be next to you? You're like an electric blanket."

Jay shifts on the mattress. Turning to face me, he finds my gaze in the darkness. "What's wrong?"

"N-Nothing." I choke on the word, clear my throat and try again. "I'm fine."

His bearded chin rubs my cheek in a soft caress. "You're crying."

"No, I'm not. I'm fine." My voice wavers, and I'm mortified by the sound. I push against the wall of his chest. "I need some space."

As soon as the words leave my mouth, the mattress dips, and Jay's warmth disappears. Through my blurred vision, I see him move through the darkened room and out of sight. I hear the creak of the door open and the soft click of it shut a moment later.

Wow. I know I told him to go, but I didn't expect him to light out of here like the room was on fire.

Then again, I did ask for space.

Be careful what you wish for.

I let go of a sob, and tears flow down my cheeks. Curling into a ball, I hug my knees to my chest.

I never cry. The physical pain of it surprises me. *It actually hurts.* And I don't even know why I'm crying.

Maybe it's the pressure of convicting Mattson. Or the realization that I'm a complete failure next to Max.

Maybe it's Jay, and the feelings I have for him. I've been denying them for a month, but I can't anymore.

Something blessedly cool and wet bathes the heated skin of my forehead. I open my eyes and see Jay's silhouette in the darkened room standing over me.

Once again, I hadn't heard his movements. Jay moves like a panther, with grace, elegance, and hardly any sound at all.

He helps me sit and presses a plastic bottle into my hand. "Have some water."

I sip obediently, letting the cold trickle of water soothe my parched throat. It tastes so good. I gulp nearly half the bottle before Jay eases it away.

He presses a couple of tablets into my palm. "Aspirin will help too."

Swallowing the aspirin, I mumble a thanks and close my eyes in mortification.

The mattress dips as Jay sits beside me. "It's still early. Try to go back to sleep for a bit."

A sob sneaks up on me out of nowhere. "I don't know why I'm crying."

"It's okay," he says. "You're drunk. You don't know what you're doing."

My chest pinches. "I'm not drunk. Not anymore. And I'm sorry about that too. I'm sure I said something stupid."

He brushes away the hair stuck to my cheek. "It's okay, Mia." His voice is a soothing balm, the deep baritone resonating low in my belly. "You didn't say anything stupid. And you're a very cute drunk."

"I shouldn't have kissed you while you were asleep." I pull in a breath before another sob can escape. "I'm sorry."

Jay scoots me over and stretches out beside me on the bed. "It's okay, I didn't mind." He puts his arm around my shoulders and pulls me onto his chest. "And I wasn't asleep."

"You were snoring."

His fingers link with mine, settling over his belly. "I don't snore."

I laugh so hard it comes out as a snort. "You definitely do."

Jay pulls me closer. "This is dangerous territory," he says.

I sift my fingers through his hair. "Worried you're gonna fall in love with me?"

His dark eyes gleam. "I don't worry about something that's already happened."

All the breath leaves my lungs. My heartbeat roars between my ears. My belly flutters, and I feel like I'm floating on air. A thrill races through me, followed quickly by the sting of wariness. I'm not a naïve young girl anymore. I know how men operate.

"You don't have to say you love me to get me to have sex with you."

His brow creases. "Who said anything about sex? We are just lying in bed together."

"Which leads to kissing. Kissing leads to sex. Sex leads to us being happy for a short time until we both realize we aren't right for each other and somebody gets hurt." *Probably me.* I push against his immovable form. "You know what? Never mind. I'm tired."

"I bet you're exhausted. We just went from kissing to sex to breaking up, all in the span of ten seconds." He rubs the back of his neck. "I think I have whiplash."

I give him a little push that does nothing to budge him. "I'm going back to sleep."

"And for the record, I didn't say I loved you." His hand rubs up and down my back in a soothing gesture. "When I tell you I love you, it's gonna be special. Not because we're in bed together."

When I tell you I love you.

Not "if," but "when." As if it's already been ruled on.

His lips brush my temple, warm against my cooled skin, and my laugh dies away. Other ideas bloom to life as his hand trails up and down my arm. Heat sparks in my chest, and I lift my face, eager for the softness of his mouth against my skin. His lips skim down my cheek, then finally, finally find mine.

CHAPTER 29

Old Habits

Mia is laid out on the mattress, her blonde hair spread on the white sheets, her skin kissed by the early morning light.

Mine.

I've pictured this moment so many times, it's hard to believe it's real.

Except for the fluffy robe. I never pictured that.

"Take this off." I slide my fingers down the middle of the robe, parting it.

She sits up and lets it fall off one shoulder. Her eyes sparkle like ice on a clear mountain lake, so bright blue they're almost silver. Running her fingers down the middle of the robe, she parts it just enough to give me a glimpse of her soft, full curves.

"You said I could call the shots," she says.

The look in her eyes makes my heart stutter, then slam in my chest. Anticipation spikes along every nerve in my body. Need saturates my blood. I force in a calming breath and meet her hungry gaze.

"What do you want?"

She cocks her head to the side, looking at me as if she wants to devour every inch of me. Her gaze scorches a path over my face, then down the length of my body. "You," she says, pointing to the mattress. "Lie back."

Goddamn.

Heat thickens the air. Tension sizzles between us. And my heart just might explode before she even touches me.

She climbs onto my lap, and the robe parts around her thighs. I reach out to touch her, but she grabs my hand, pinning it to the mattress by my side with a shake of her head.

"No. Don't move yet."

Since I outweigh her by about a hundred pounds, I could easily break free of her grasp, but I made a promise. She's in charge. I relax my hands and let her unbutton my shirt, one slow glide of her fingers after another, until the fabric gapes at my sides.

She traces a path across the tattoo that spans my upper chest from collar bone to collar bone.

"So much ink," she says, trailing her fingers from the scripted letters to the proud eagle etched across my chest. "I want to lick every inch of it."

My pulse races, sending all my blood south, straight to my dick.

She feels me stiffen, and the corner of her lips curl up in a wicked smile. "I've never licked a tattoo before."

The innocence in her voice makes me itch to touch her, but the warning gleam in her eyes is enough to make me hold still as she drags her fingernails lightly down the center of my chest.

My breath comes quicker as she bends over me, tracing the path of her fingernails with her tongue. She licks down my chest, flicking and swirling her tongue over every feather of the eagle's wings, then the center of its body, down to the talons inked above my navel.

The hot glide of her tongue strokes across the tops of the letters visible above my waistband, then pauses while she unfastens my pants and pushes down my briefs.

My dick rises eagerly between us, moisture already beading at the tip. She gazes up at me, locking her eyes on mine as her tongue darts out to lick me clean.

I suck in a sharp breath as she wraps her hand around the base and squeezes.

"Not tattooed everywhere," she says, almost to herself. "But still delicious."

"Fuck." I grit the word between clenched teeth as she shoves my pants down and climbs on top of me.

The early morning light is a halo behind her. No makeup, hair a little wild, eyes hooded with desire—she's the sexiest woman I've ever seen.

Except for the goddamn robe. She's purposefully taunting me by keeping it on, but I let her have her way.

Next time it will be my turn.

She leans down to kiss my mouth, her tongue pushing between my lips. Her hot hand fists my straining dick, pumping it with a slow rhythm that makes my hips jerk off the mattress for more. Faster, then slower, she works me with her hand until the ache of pleasure is almost too much to bear.

She slides forward, teasing the tip of my dick through her wet folds. She's so slick, I easily slip inside.

I gasp as she slides down one inch, then two, then eases out again.

"Condoms," I groan as she teases me mercilessly.

"No need," she says, kissing a path across my jaw, down my neck.

Her words send a shiver of lust down my spine. I'd like nothing more than to bury myself inside her without a barrier, but...

"I always use condoms."

"I know." She leans back, a glint of anger flashing in her eyes. "But you don't need one." She lifts a brow at me. "Trust me?"

I swallow thickly. I know better than to leave anything up to chance. But this is Mia. I've never known her to lie.

"I trust you."

"Good." A siren's smile curves her lips. "I want your cock inside me."

"Yes." The word becomes a hiss of released breath as she slides down on me in one swift move. "Jesus. Mia. You feel so fucking good."

She groans, bracing her hands on my chest as she rolls her hips forward to take me deeper. Her tight, wet heat surrounds me, turning the edges of my vision hazy.

Sweat beads on my brow as she begins to move, rocking slowly. That determined expression I love so much steals over her features. Her gaze fixes on mine, and her lips part. The tip of her tongue peaks out to touch her top lip, and it's all I can do not to reach up and drag her down for a kiss.

But this is about Mia being in charge. So, I let her take control. I let her ride me, use me to forget everything.

"Touch me." She grabs my hand and brings it between us. Her robe parts, giving me a visual of her full breasts and peaked nipples that will last me a lifetime. "Here."

But my fingers don't need directions, I find the swollen bud of her clit and press.

She trembles, and a quake of pleasure vibrates through us both. Shifting forward, she grinds against me, finding just the pressure she needs.

"Holy fu—"

Her dirty words die off in a groan as I shove her robe aside and close my mouth over her nipple. I suck her hard flesh into my mouth and flick my thumb over her clit.

It's exactly what she needs. The tight sheath of her pussy flutters, clenching around my throbbing dick. A tidal wave of ecstasy threatens to consume me as she comes with a loud cry.

I don't wait until she's done. Grabbing her hips, I flip her onto her back and drive into her, coaxing another orgasm from her just as the first one subsides.

With slow, deep thrusts, I fuck her until she writhes beneath me, begging me with nearly incoherent moans.

More. Faster. Harder.

She asks for what she wants, and I give it to her, making her come over and over. I would give it to her like this every day if I could. Keep her coming back for more.

Her moans dies away, and she collapses back against the mattress, letting her arms fall limply at her sides.

The sight of her sweat-slicked body laid out on the mattress is a fantasy come true. It's too much. I can't hold back anymore.

Desire rips through me, tightening every muscle in my body. I drive deep inside her, careful not to lose control. Prolonging the pleasure, I drive again, then pull out at the last second. One pump of my fist. Two. Then, everything clenches, and I spill in a hot arc across the curve of her belly.

My heartbeat thunders in my ears and my vision clouds, then sharpens on Mia lying there. She's glistening with my cum, goose-bumps rippling across her skin.

My dick stiffens in my fist.

I swear, this woman is gonna kill me.

CHAPTER 30

Not In This Lifetime

It's bright the next time I wake up. The sun is shining into the room. Jay is already awake beside me. Although he is hardly moving, this time I know he's awake. There's something in the air. A charged energy that is purely Jay. You just can't miss him when he's in the same room.

A glance at the clock assures me I haven't overslept, but I need to get moving in order to make my eleven o'clock appointment at the spa.

"Don't get up." I press a hand to Jay's chest as he shifts to sit up. "You don't have to be anywhere until twelve."

A smile lifts the corner of his lips, and he stretches his arms over his head. He looks good enough to eat with the sheet draped over his hips. "I could get used to this."

I grab my robe from the floor and pull it on. "Don't get too used to it. In two days we'll be back home in Mossy Oak, and you will be back to guarding my body twenty-four seven again."

He grabs the sash of the robe and tugs me towards him. "I like guarding your body."

His strong arms close around me, and before I can protest, I'm tumbling onto the mattress. Jay leans over me, pinning me on my back. The sheets tangle around us as he parts my robe and kisses a path down the center of my chest.

He already knows how to play my body perfectly. His kisses are warm and soft, his beard rough against my skin. I tangle my fingers in his thick hair as he places little love bites on my belly.

I would stay in bed with him all day if I could, but I can't today. With a sigh of frustration, I tug his hair until he lifts his face. "I have to go get beautified for the ceremony."

He pushes open my robe and cups my breast, lazily stroking my hard nipple with his rough thumb. "Ten more minutes won't hurt."

There's no way ten minutes with Jay would ever be enough time, but I can't deny how much I want him. He brushes a light caress from my breast to my belly and lower.

I gasp as he dips one long finger inside me. I'm already slick with wanting him. "Okay," I say. "Ten minutes."

* * *

Ten minutes turns into twenty, and I am nearly late when I rush out the door.

"The zip lining adventure starts at noon."

Jay is sitting up in bed, reading the book I left on the nightstand. He drags his gaze up from the book, his brows drawing together. "The fuck it does."

"You said you didn't care what I picked for your activity," I say, grabbing my bag and checking to make sure I have everything. "So, I picked zip lining across the island."

Jay barks out a laugh. "You won't catch me dangling from a rope over a mountain range. Not in this lifetime."

A teasing smile curves my lips. "You're not afraid, are you?"

"Hell yeah, I'm afraid." His shiver of displeasure is definitely not fake. "I can't stand heights."

"*The Savage* is scared of heights?"

"How about working on my tan at the beach?" He flips a page in my book, a historical romance set on the high seas. "I might take this book with me. It's not half bad. For porn."

I check my lipstick in the mirror. "It's not porn. It's a historical romance."

"Hmm." He flips back a few pages and reads out loud, "'Julian got on his knees and pressed his tongue to Liza's most treasured pearl of passion—'" He lifts his gaze to mine. "What do you think a treasured pearl of passion is?"

My stomach clenches at the thought of Jay on the beach, in all his tattooed glory. What if my mom sees his prison tattoo? I'll never hear the end of it.

"If you go to the beach, make sure you keep your shirt on," I say. "Like we emailed about."

He puts the book down on the nightstand. "I thought you were kidding."

An awkward silence fills the room. We stare at each other through the thickening tension. "I wasn't kidding."

"It might be hard to get a tan with a shirt on."

"There's always zip lining."

With narrowed eyes, Jay gets up from the bed and walks toward me. He's wearing briefs and nothing else. The long muscles in his thighs ripple and flex as he strides across the room with effortless grace. His hair is loose around his shoulders, slightly disheveled from my fingers, and his eyes are darker than melted chocolate.

"What are you afraid of?" he asks, stopping inches from me. "Your family seeing my tattoos?"

A flush spreads up my chest. I know I look like a real bitch, but I can't lie. "Yes."

He looks down at his delectable chest, covered in designs. "They've probably seen tattoos before."

"Probably, but not on one of my boyfriends."

"Accountants and bankers have tattoos," he says.

I glance down midway on his right arm, and he stiffens.

"You don't want your family to know you're dating an ex-con?"

Jay knows the answer, but still he waits with infinite patience for my response.

"It's Max and Samantha's day," I say, changing the subject.

Jay's dark eyes narrow on me. "You're ashamed of me."

My jaw clenches, and I grind my teeth. "It's not that."

Jay shoves a lock of hair behind his ear. "Good thing I'm not your real boyfriend."

A chill runs through me as I feel him pull away, throwing up walls between us where none had been before. I reach up to touch him, but he flinches.

My heart squeezes. "We'll talk about it later."

Jay shrugs. "Whatever you say, Boss."

I frown. "Don't call me that. I'm not your boss."

"You're paying me," he says, walking back to the bed. He stretches out, picks up the book, and resumes reading. "Is it okay if I order room service?"

"Jay, don't be like that." I put my bag on my shoulder. "I have to go. Just be careful today."

He flips a page. "I'll wear plenty of sunscreen."

"You know what I mean."

"Don't worry. I'll be the perfect upstanding boyfriend worthy of Mia James." He puts the book down and glances up at me, his gaze guarded. "You better go. Don't want to be late."

My stomach knots. I don't have time for this conversation, but I can't leave Jay like this. I walk over to the bed and sit next to him. My feelings for him are hopelessly tangled.

Part of me wants to shove his past aside and accept him, but there's a big part of me that can't forget he's a criminal. And there's a bigger part that tells me it doesn't matter. Our relationship is temporary, at best.

I drop my gaze to the letters tattooed across his upper chest. RESPECT. The inked lines stand out against his tawny skin. "We're too different."

He closes the book and sets it aside, giving me his full attention. "If you're trying to apologize, you're doing a shitty job."

Frustration mounts in my chest and I grit my teeth. "I'm not trying to apologize."

His brow lifts. "Okay then, what are you trying to do?"

"I'm trying to..." My words die away, and I drop my gaze to his chest. So much ink. So much hard, lean muscle. He doesn't even look real.

"You want to go another round?" he asks, his voice a cold, hard edge. His eyes are even colder.

Anger churns inside me. "Dammit! I'm not trying to have sex with you, either."

He folds his hands across his belly, completely unaffected by my emotional outburst. "It's okay that you're ashamed of me," he says in a perfectly neutral voice. "It doesn't matter."

And then he says the words I've been thinking. The ones I've been dreading.

"None of this is real."

I rise from the bed and walk out of the room, holding my head high as I slam the door behind me.

CHAPTER 31

Just Being Nosy

Relaxing is impossible. All I can think about is the look on Mia's face before she walked away.

Disgust. Anger. Regret.

It was so easy to see everything Mia was thinking. Unlike me, she hasn't mastered control of her features.

I pretend to be absorbed in the book I'm reading as Craig walks by on the beach, holding two cups in his hands.

"Hey." He stops in front of my lounge chair. "They gave me two drinks instead of one," he says. "Want it?"

I turn back to my book. "Not really."

"I hear you! A little too many signature cocktails last night?"

Without asking, he settles himself in the lounger beside me. "You doing any of the activities today?" he asks.

I flip the page even though I haven't read a single word. "Nope."

"I just got done with horseback riding. I've got ten minutes to suck these drinks down before I have to be at the cooking class."

"Good luck with that."

He sucks noisily on his straw. "Aren't you hot in that shirt?"

"I'm good." I reach down and grab my phone and my room key. "I'll catch you later."

"Holy crap," he says. "Now there's a sight for sore eyes. Too many good-looking women to decide where to look."

I glance down the beach to where Craig is pointing with his cup. The bride and her attendants are standing ankle deep in the turquoise surf, posing for a photographer.

There are five gorgeous women, but Mia is the only one I see.

She is a head shorter than everyone else, but what she lacks in height she makes up for in curves.

"Chelsea's boobs are worth every cent she paid for them, but that Mia is a hot little piece of...."

Craig doesn't finish his sentence because I'm standing over him, my bulk blocking his view of the women.

"Don't even think about looking in Mia's direction again, or you're gonna be eating your fucking teeth." I loom over him, barely restraining myself from following through with my threat.

"She's in a swimsuit," Craig says, shading his eyes with his hand as he looks up at me. "This is a beach. You better get used to people looking at your woman. She's asking for it with a body like that."

My fist clenches, and I force myself to breathe deeply. "You better go, or you're gonna miss that cooking class."

Craig scrambles up, and hurries off in the direction of the hotel without a glance back at me or the beach. When he's a safe distance away, I turn my attention back to the photo shoot.

Mia is nearly naked in that tiny swimsuit. Memories of last night cloud my mind. Everything had been so good between us. Then this morning, she'd treated me like shit.

My pride still stings from her rejection, but it doesn't stop me from wanting her. Wishing there was a way to make it work between us, against all the odds keeping us apart.

Mia tosses her hair off her face and catches me staring. She freezes, and I swear I can feel the emotion in her gaze from across the beach before she turns away and smiles for the camera.

When the photoshoot is over, she says something to the

others, then heads my way. She sits on the chair Craig just vacated and laces her fingers together. "We should talk."

My heart leaps into my throat. This sounds suspiciously like a break up preamble. But we aren't really together, so there's no breaking up to do.

"Why?" I adjust my sunglasses and lean back in my chair. "I think you made everything crystal clear."

"As did you." She clears her throat, lowering her voice. "The thing is, we only have one more night. Maybe we should try to make the most of it. Remember the swings on the playground? This is supposed to be fun."

The swings had been my brilliant idea. But instead of keeping things light and fun, I'd gone and fallen for Mia.

That wasn't her fault.

"Last night was fun," I say.

To my surprise, Mia laughs. The sound sneaks up on me and wraps a fist around my heart. Squeezes.

"Well, I liked that thing you did with your tongue," she says. "That was definitely fun."

Desire flares, heating my blood. Mia in that tiny bikini talking about what we did in bed last night makes me *almost* forget the things she said this morning. Almost.

I nod at the bridal group gathered on the beach a few feet away, staring at us. "Are they waiting on you for more pictures?"

"No," she says. "They're just being nosy."

"Maybe we should give them something to talk about."

Before she can react, I lean forward and close my lips over hers. It was meant to be a quick, punishing kiss because I'm still more than a little angry. But the second our lips touch, my body gets better ideas. I coax her mouth open and slide my tongue between her lips.

The little sound of pleasure she makes has me spinning. I want everything this woman has to give, even if it will never be enough.

Wrapping my hand around the back of her neck, I deepen the

kiss. She responds with another soft moan, fisting her hand in my shirt.

"This is better than swinging," she says, her breath a soft puff on my lips.

"Hey, Mia!" a woman's voice calls across the beach. "You're messing up your lipstick."

Mia smiles up at me. "Should I tell her to fuck off?"

"Yes."

I kiss her again, and the bridal party catcalls and whistles.

We are attracting so much attention; I release her.

"I'd kill for an espresso right now," Mia says. "Someone kept me up half the night."

"Someone kept me up, too."

"Chelsea already bitched me out over the bags under my eyes. She said I'll ruin the pictures."

"There's no way you could ever ruin a picture."

She shakes her head. "You lie."

Frustration pinches my chest. "You know better than to believe that."

A frown creases her forehead. "This whole weekend is a lie."

The sadness in her voice sends a shiver down my spine.

"I should go," Mia says, rising to her feet. "I have to have my hair done and get dressed with the others before Chelsea loses her shit."

I stand and pull her close to my chest, kissing her one last time. There are so many unspoken words between us, the air practically vibrates with them.

Maybe it's better that way.

CHAPTER 32

I Won't Fall

Brad folds me into a hug as soon as I walk up to him in the lobby. "You look amazing," he says. "But don't take me down in those shoes."

I squeeze his shoulders and release him. Sweeping my gaze over his wedding ensemble, it's hard not to be affected by his star quality. Brad's long, lean physique is accentuated by the slim-fitting suit. The dark blue color brings out the cobalt in his eyes, and the open neck of his crisp white shirt shows off his deep tan. His hair is expertly styled into tousled dark waves. It's easy to see why he's been a heartthrob for years, but it's hard to forget he's also my annoying cousin who doesn't miss a chance to pick on me.

"I won't fall," I say, swatting him on the shoulder. "I've learned how to walk in heels over the years. Plenty of practice."

He holds me by the shoulders and smiles down at me. "You ready?"

I nod. "I think so." I can't believe my little brother is actually getting married. It's hard not to think of him as the kid who rode his bike with me to the neighborhood pool in the summer, or the shy ninth-grader who had a hard time making friends.

Max is all grown up now, and he's about to become a husband.

Maybe some elder sisters would be envious that their little brother was getting married before them.

Not me.

I'm happy for Max and Samantha. She's the woman I'd always hoped would fall in love with my brother.

Memories of me and Max as kids flash before my eyes. Max at Christmas, unwrapping a toy guitar. Max getting his permit and learning how to drive while I cling to the passenger seat door for dear life. Max breaking down in tears at our grandmother's funeral. The look of pure murder on Max's face when I told him what happened to me Freshman year.

Max and all the trouble we got into as kids, all the experiences we shared, the love we gave, the bond that could never be broken.

He's so much more than a brother to me. Max has always been there for me. He's one of the best friends I've ever had. My hopes and dreams for him and a happy future are even more than what I have for myself.

I feel the threat of tears and I haven't even seen my brother yet.

Brad and I line up with the other attendants and get ready for the big moment. Chelsea and one of Samantha's male cousins step up behind us, and behind them is Samantha. She looks stunning in her gossamer white gown.

At the cue from the wedding director, Brad and I step out of the lobby and cross the courtyard to the beach. We turn the corner and walk along the white carpet laid over the sand, dividing two sections of white chairs in rows.

Lights strung from the palm trees twinkle against the pastel-colored sky, and white tiki torches glow along the path.

Max stands under an archway decorated with tropical flowers, his blond hair stirring in the ocean breeze. He looks so handsome and hopeful in his white suit. He takes my breath away.

As we step onto the white carpet, the wedding guests turn and look at us. I scan the familiar faces, spotting my mom and dad in the front row. Directly behind them is Jay.

Our eyes meet, and I feel him looking all the way through me down to my soul. He sees past all the barriers I erect, all the bullshit I pile up so nobody gets to know the real me. No man has ever looked at me the way Jay looks at me, as if I'm the most important person in the world.

I stumble a little as Jay's mouth shifts into the tiniest of smiles. I didn't think he ever smiled, but now I realize I've been wrong. I just had to get to know him better to catch his subtle gestures. His face barely changes, but I can see the faint crinkling of his eyes, and the twitch of his lips. His joy is all the more special because of how stingy he is with expressing it.

Emotions pinch my chest, and I feel the rise of tears clouding my vision.

"Don't cry, ShortCake," Brad says in a low voice.

I suck back my tears and jab my cousin in the ribs. "Don't call me that."

Brad elbows me back. "Only Sanchez can call you that, huh?"

"That's right."

"You two gonna be the next wedding?" Brad asks.

I purse my lips to keep from saying something I might regret. "Shut up, Brad."

"Can I be in the wedding?"

Frustration mounts inside me. I have no intention of marrying Jay or anyone, and right now, all I want is for Brad to mind his own business.

"It's not serious between us." *It's not even real.*

Brad's eyes twinkle with a knowing gleam. "You brought him to a wedding, but it's not serious?"

I can't admit to Brad that Jay and I are fake, but how else can I convince him to leave me alone? "It's not what you think."

My mom is giving us the death glare, and I can only imagine what Chelsea is going to have to say about Brad and me chatting it up the entire walk down the aisle.

"I think he's the exact opposite of everything you say you want in a man," Brad continues, oblivious to the laser beams of disapproval shooting from my mother's blue eyes. "So, he's basically perfect for you."

My toe hits an uneven lump in the carpet they've laid over the sand, and I nearly stumble.

Brad squeezes my elbow, supporting me as he walks me to my place. "You're the most stubborn woman I've ever known," he whispers. "Just admit you're in love with him."

"I'm not..."

"Shh!" Chelsea hushes me before I can finish denying my love for Jay.

Brad winks at me and saunters over to his place on Max's side.

I'm not in love with Jay.

I don't do love.

As my previous boyfriends would attest to, I'm incapable of love.

But there's something about Jay that makes me feel fizzy. I'd break every rule I've ever made for myself for Jay.

My mouth goes dry, and my heart is a dull thud between my ears.

Jay is everything I ever wanted in a man. He's sweet, and funny, and he's the kind of solid that rivals the Blue Ridge Mountains.

Jay isn't just a rock of strength. He's an entire mountain.

My mountain.

The wedding march starts up, and all heads swivel in Samantha's direction. All eyes are on her, but Jay is looking at me, and I'm looking at him.

Something bright and beautiful passes between us. Something very real.

CHAPTER 33

What Are You Thinking, ShortCake?

After spending so much time with Mia, I can usually read her expressions like a book. I know whether she's had a good day or a bad day without her having to speak a word. Her big, expressive eyes give her away, even if she doesn't realize it.

But, for the first time, I have no idea what Mia is thinking.

Whatever it is has a hard grasp on her. She's thinking so hard, she doesn't hear the officiant's cue. The rest of the bridal party turns and faces the couple, but Mia's gaze is locked on me.

I raise a brow, concerned that something's wrong. Did she eat some bad fish for lunch? Is she still hung over?

She has the funniest look I've ever seen on her face. Her eyes are wide, and her cheeks are pink. She looks like she's seen a ghost.

What are you thinking, ShortCake?

Chelsea bumps her from behind, and Mia turns with a start to face the couple.

I hardly listen as Max and Samantha exchange their vows, promising to love each other forever. I'm thinking hard now, too, wondering what it would be like to have someone in your life worthy of forever. Someone who felt the same way about me as I felt about her. Someone who wasn't ashamed of me.

The newlyweds kiss to an enthusiastic round of applause, and the ceremony is over. While Mia and the rest of the bridal party leave to take photos, I'm left on my own. It's the longest half hour of my life.

I'm trapped in conversations about the weather, Ivy League colleges, and the cost of Samantha's dress. It's the worst kind of hell. When I finally make my way to the bar, Anna corners me.

"How long do you give it?" she asks.

I count the heads in front of us and then assess the bartenders, who are moving with lightning speed. "Five minutes at the most."

She laughs. "Wow. You're even more of a cynic than me. I was gonna say six months at least."

It takes me a moment to realize she's talking about the length of the marriage, not the wait time for a drink.

"Everybody thought Brad and I wouldn't make it longer than five minutes, too." She inches forward, invading my personal space again. "But look at us, now. Five years later and still just as strong as ever."

I shuffle up in line, pretending to study the drink selections. "Congratulations."

She presses close enough to brush the back of my arm. "Do you want to know the secret to our marital success?"

She's too close, and there isn't anywhere for me to go. She doesn't wait for my answer.

"We don't limit ourselves," she says.

A cold trickle of sweat runs down the back of my neck as I get her meaning. This woman is unbelievable. Even though it's almost my turn to order a drink, I abandon the line, not wanting to stand next to Anna any longer than necessary.

"Hey!" she calls after me. "Where are you going?"

I don't answer, walking along the stone path away from the celebration as fast as possible. Snippets of conversations reach my ears as I make my way to a dark corner where no one will see me.

"I heard her dress cost twenty K."

"My little Tommy is heading to Harvard in the fall, can you believe it?"

"I feel so sorry for the older sister. Seeing her little brother get married first must be humiliating."

Fucking assholes. I'd love to say something to shut them up. But it isn't my place. And Mia doesn't need me to defend her. She's fully capable of taking care of herself.

I spot Mia before she sees me. There's never been a moment when she's entered a room and I haven't been instantly aware of her.

As if she senses my stare, she lifts her head and our gazes collide. She gives me a look I recognize immediately. Anticipation, excitement, relief. It's the same look I've seen on her face nearly every day when I greet her after work.

"Let's get out of here," she says as I approach.

"Are you sure?"

"Positive."

That's all I need to hear. I take her hand and lead her from the party, taking the quickest route possible to the hotel.

"Everything okay?"

A humorless laugh escapes her mouth. "I'm not sure."

A stone settles in my gut, as I can only imagine she heard some of the mean-spirited gossip of the guests. "What happened?"

We step into the elevator, and Mia presses the button for our floor. "I've been thinking."

I wait until the doors close, making sure we are alone before asking, "What about?"

She lifts her head, pinning me with her intense blue gaze. Energy crackles between us.

"I think I might be falling for you," she says.

My heart takes off at a gallop. "That's what you were thinking about during the ceremony?"

She nods. "I don't know what to do about it."

I hold back a laugh and match her serious tone. "Maybe I can help you figure it out."

Her gaze drops over my face, lingering on my mouth. "I'd like that."

Excitement races down my spine. "First, why don't you list all the things you like about me?"

She shoves me in the chest, and I allow her to back me up against the wall. "You're funny," she says.

"That's not one I hear a lot."

Winding her arms around my neck, she presses against me. "And kind."

My hands find her waist, spread up her back. "Most people think I'm too harsh."

She rubs against me. "Not me."

I dip my chin, stopping just before our lips meet. "Anything else?"

"You have a very nice..."

The door opens, cutting Mia off before she can finish. From the naughty gleam in her eyes, I have a good feeling what part of me she was going to pay a compliment.

I tug her out of the elevator, down the hall to her room, walking so fast she has to jog to keep up with me.

CHAPTER 34

I Wasn't Done Yet

Jay's lips are on mine as soon as we close the door to my room. He reaches around and unzips my dress, unhooks my strapless bra and peels off my panties.

"Not fair," I say, shoving his jacket off his shoulders. "You're wearing way too many clothes."

He unbuttons his shirt and tosses it to the ground, then pauses as he reaches for his belt buckle, his eyes devouring me from head to toe.

I'm suddenly shy, not only because of my state of undress, but because of my confession. Jay knows how I feel about him now. There's no taking it back.

"Jay?" A shiver runs through me as I second guess telling him how I feel. He hasn't said a word about how he feels about me. I can only hope I haven't scared him off. "Is everything okay?"

He nods, his gaze dark and dangerous. "You're so fucking beautiful."

Heat spreads up my body. He's not so bad himself. Standing there, shirtless, with his hand resting on his belt buckle, he looks like a sex god.

"Turn around," he says.

186

My muscles turn to water, but somehow I manage to make my feet move. I turn around, giving him a view of my backside.

"Gorgeous." His voice is husky with desire. "You're my girl," he says. "All mine."

He reaches for my waist and pulls me against him. His front is pressed to my back, and I can feel the hard length of his cock through his pants. "Feel what you do to me?"

I reach back to touch him, but he spins me around and walks me backward until I'm on the bed. He unbuckles his belt and unzips his pants. I reach for him and push his briefs down. My fist closes around his hard flesh, and he lets out a long moan.

His eyes drift shut, and he says my name with a guttural groan. "Fuck, Mia. Your hands feel so good."

Power surges through me, making me slick with desire.

"Your mouth," he says, sucking in a harsh breath. "Take me in your mouth."

There is no time to think, no time to do anything other than obey his command. I pull him forward so that his magnificent erection is right in front of my face and lick my lips.

I've wanted his cock in my mouth since the first time I saw him. Now's my chance to take it.

I lick the tip, tasting salt, then run my tongue around the fat crown. He hisses out a long breath, fisting my hair in his hand. Urging me back with a tug, his dark gaze meets mine.

"Suck me."

Fire races through me at his deep growl. Normally I hate being told what to do. But it's so hot coming from Jay, hot juices drip down my thigh.

With him, none of the rules apply.

Wrapping my lips around him, I hollow out my cheeks and pull him deep. I take as much of him as I can, but his impressive size makes it challenging.

His hand spreads over the back of my head, urging me to take as much as I can. I suck harder, drawing a moan of pleasure from him.

He rocks against me, and I feel the vibrations of his restraint. He's giving the orders, but it's me in charge, setting the pace. I pull back, sliding my mouth over his rock hard flesh.

Needs builds inside me. My pussy gets wetter each time he moans, and trembles spread up my spine with each gasp of pleasure I draw from his lips.

His hands slide from my hair to under my arms, and he urges me off him, sliding me back so that I'm lying on the mattress.

"I wasn't done yet," I say, sounding like a child who's toy has been taken away.

"You can have it again very soon," he says. "But now it's my turn to taste."

His mouth closes around my nipple, and his hand covers my mound. He pushes a finger deep inside me, and I buck my hips off the bed, needing so much more.

He strokes me as he tongues one nipple, then the other, working me into a state of desire that borders on desperation.

I'm slick with wanting as he slides in and out, his thumb brushing my clit with every stroke.

Then, in a sudden move, he takes his hand away and replaces it with his hard cock.

He fills me with one long stroke, and we groan in unison at the pleasure it brings. I can't seem to make up my mind if I want to move, or lay perfectly still so I can freeze this moment forever in my mind.

Then, desire takes over, and I move. My hands find his perfect ass, and I urge him deeper. He thrusts into me.

"You feel so good." His voice sends a thrill down my spine. He sounds so hungry for me. It's the sexiest thing I've ever heard.

I rock against him, feeling the coarse hairs on his chest rub against my peaked nipples. I'm kindling, eager to burn if it means he's burning with me.

He's in control now, and I let go, allowing him to press my knee up to my chest and take me deeper with every thrust. He fucks me hard, a growl building in his throat as he plunges into me.

My head bangs against the headboard, but I hardly notice the discomfort as pleasure unfurls deep inside me. He sets an unrelenting pace, drawing me closer to release with each thrust. I brace my hands against the headboard, lifting my hips to meet him stroke for stroke.

He knows exactly what I need. Speeding up, then slowing down to drive deep, each drag of his heavy cock inside me makes me tighten and arch my back.

His name falls from my lips in a chant as he prolongs the throes of ecstasy. The headboard bangs against the wall with every slam of his flesh against mine. I'm close, so close, then he pulls out and leaves me bereft and begging.

He grips my hips and slides me down away from the headboard, then flips me over so I'm on my belly. His fingers dig into my flesh as he yanks my hips up in the air.

"Such a sweet ass," he says, running his hand over one cheek before giving it a light slap.

I quiver with need, crying out his name.

"This is what you need?" he asks, giving me another swat that makes my entire body throb.

"Yes."

He slaps me again, a sharp clap ringing in the air. And then he plunges so hard and deep inside me, I shatter with release at his first thrust.

Jay picks up his pace, grabbing my hips to drive himself home. I know he's close. "Come inside me."

He grunts. "You sure?"

"Yes. I want to feel it."

I can feel his hesitation, but then pleasure overtakes him, and this time he trusts me. His hot seed fills me as he pumps harder and faster, coming with a muffled roar.

He eases out and leaves the room, coming back a moment later with a wet cloth.

"Mia?" he whispers against my heated skin after we've cleaned up.

"Yes?"

He tucks me against his chest, rolling so my back is nestled to his chest. His arms wrap around me, and he holds me with a reverence I'm sure I don't deserve.

"You have my heart," he says.

CHAPTER 35

A Story I Don't Tell

Her fingers trail over my chest, chasing the swirling lines. "Which one was your first?"

I take her hand and guide it to the letters inked below my navel that spell out the word LOYALTY. "This one."

She strokes the letters. Her manicured nails tracing the top of the capital L, then traveling down the bold, gothic font to my lower abs.

I lace our fingers together, stilling her exploration.

"I didn't even want a tattoo. It was my sister's idea." Her mouth is close enough to kiss, and I indulge myself before continuing. "She convinced me to use our fake I.D.s to get tattoos, and then she went with two tiny butterflies on her ankle. I wanted something bolder."

She pulls her hand free to trace the wings of the eagle covering my pecs. "Which one hurt the most?"

I sigh and lift my arm, showing her the large spider web that spirals out from the center of my elbow.

The tattoo prisoners get to signify their time waiting to get out of jail.

I shift onto my back to put some much-needed distance between us. Touching Mia makes me lose my train of thought, and I need to be clear-headed to answer her questions. Because Mia won't stop with one question. She won't stop until she gets the full story. That's just her. My magnificent Mia always gets to the bottom.

An unbearable heat builds in my chest, a knot of anger burning inside me until it threatens to consume me.

I roll over onto my side then sit up, my entire body aching with frustration and regret.

Then I feel Mia's hand on my arm. Her touch is a soothing balm, a cool breeze on a hot day, a drop of water to my parched soul.

Her fingers trace the lines of the tattoo that made her ashamed of me. The pain from each of my tattoos is a distant memory, but this one still makes me wince sometimes. That's the whole point of it. To make me remember.

"Tell me what happened."

Her voice is soft in my ear, and it makes every wall I've built come down.

"It's a long story."

"I'm not going anywhere," she says.

A shudder runs through me at the thought of laying myself bare. This is a story I don't tell. No one knows everything. Not even my lawyer. "I don't know where to start."

Mia's voice is calm and steady, the voice of reason. "Start at the beginning."

A harsh laugh slips from my throat. She doesn't need to know how our dad abandoned us and we ended up living in a trailer park. A single-wide at first with only one bedroom the three of us shared. We had one bed, but it was enough.

"My mom raised me and my sister on her own," I say. "We didn't have much."

That was the understatement of the year. We didn't have a pot to piss in. We didn't have Christmas. We didn't have back-to-school shopping or regular haircuts. But we had each other.

"I already told you fighting became my way out." I take a deep breath, pushing through the painful memories of hunger and cold. "Once I started training with a coach and winning tournaments, I started to make some real money."

In my mind, I'm back in the ring, taking out my fury on my opponents, smelling the blood, sweat, and fear in the air.

"It landed me in jail."

The air vibrates with tension. "What do you mean?"

"I almost killed a man with my bare hands." I've never said the words aloud before. Never told anyone what happened.

"Why?" Mia's voice is full of confusion.

"My sister's boyfriend beat her so badly she ended up in the hospital."

The memories crash over me like cold, hard fists. I nearly lost my mind when I found out what my sister's boyfriend had done. I hadn't thought about myself, I'd only seen blood- red rage. I'd gotten in my car, driven straight to his house, and nearly killed him.

"I broke his nose, his jaw, several ribs, and was choking him when they pulled me off. A few more minutes and I would have killed him."

"Jay," she says. "You didn't mean to do it. You were blind with rage."

A rough laugh escapes my mouth. "I wasn't sorry. I wished I would have killed him. He deserved it."

A dozen years later, and I'm still angry. I would beat him again if given the chance, even knowing it would land me in jail.

The mattress shifts as Mia moves closer. Her hand trails up my arm to my shoulder, and then I feel the press of her soft breasts against my back, the brush of her hair against my neck. Her arms slide around me, holding me, but she's the one who's crying.

I turn and pull Mia into my arms, settling her on my lap. Stroking her hair away from her face, I kiss away her tears.

"I'm such a bitch," she says, framing my face within her hands. "I judged you, Jay."

"It's okay."

Her fingers run through my hair, tugging. "I had it all wrong," she says. "You're a hero."

Her words shake me to the core. "No. I'm not."

"I could have used someone like you when I got assaulted in college. But no one stood up for me. No one even believed me."

"I'm sorry."

She shakes her head, her gaze trapping mine. "I didn't think I could forgive your crime, much less understand it. But I do."

Tears flow down her cheeks, smearing her makeup. Her hair is messy from my hands, and she's a far cry from her usually perfect appearance. "Can you forgive me?" Her voice is so soft I can barely hear her.

"There's nothing to forgive."

She kisses me, claiming my mouth with a fierce passion that I'm all too ready to return. We roll back onto the bed. Tears and apologies are forgotten when we start touching each other.

CHAPTER 36
The Elephant on the Plane

The next morning, we have a goodbye brunch with the other guests.

After we finish eating, we wait in the lobby for our courtesy shuttle to take us to the airport.

My mother squeezes me tightly as we say goodbye.

"Try not to be too upset, sweetheart," she says.

I'm not upset, but her comment grates on my nerves, and now I *am* a little upset, although I would never give her the satisfaction of seeing it.

I'm trying to come up with a response when Jay appears at my shoulder, his hand a reassuring presence at my lower back.

"You ready, ShortCake?" he asks. "Our car is here."

We say one last goodbye, and when we leave the lobby and settle into the back seats of a Ford Explorer, I let out a long sigh of relief. "Thank God that's over."

Jay runs a hand through his hair. It's long and loose, the thick strands still damp from his shower. "I think I might take up golf," he says. "You think I should get a membership at Emerald Hills?"

I smile and pull out my phone, checking my messages. I can't imagine Jay swinging a golf club at the country club, but now that my brain goes there, it is an enticing image. Those tight- fitting golf pants would look excellent on him.

Jay leans over and cups my cheek, pulling me close. "You have the sexiest grin on your face right now," he says, kissing me.

I lower my phone and kiss him back before realizing, we don't have to do this anymore. We are officially done with our act for the weekend. We can go back to being client and bodyguard or whatever it is we were before Serenade Island.

I'm not sure what we will be when we get home. Not sure what I want. But at least I won't have to make a decision right away. When we get back home, Jay will come to my house. We will have an early dinner, and if he insists on staying the night to protect me, I will talk him into doing it from my bed instead of the couch.

We are almost to the airport when I remember to check my messages. There are two from Jordan, both of them from early this morning while Jay and I were languishing in bed on our last few hours of vacation.

There's urgent news on the Mattson case, and he wants me to call as soon as possible. Elena isn't due to confront Mattson until I get back, so nothing could have gone wrong there.

When I try to call him, it goes straight to voicemail. I frown and hang up. Jordan's usually more straightforward. He's not one to leave me guessing, but his texts are cryptic and send a shiver of anxiety down my spine.

"Everything okay?" Jay asks, reaching for my hand.

"I'm not sure," I say. "I can't reach my boss and he said he had some news."

"Hope it's good news," Jay says, giving my hand a squeeze.

Me too. I smile absently, my mind already focused on home and what I will need to do to put Mattson away. Now that Max's wedding is over—he and Samantha are already on a plane to Paris —I can concentrate all my energy on my job again.

Jay squeezes my thigh. "Winston Churchill said, 'If you're going through hell, keep going'."

His words fill me with confidence. Jay is so sure of me, so convinced that I'm smart and capable, that it's easy to believe it's true. Of course, I *know* it's true, I'm excellent at my job, but having someone believe in me makes a difference.

After spending the entire weekend fending off passive-aggressive comments of disapproval dished out by my mother, it's nice not to have to hold up a shield.

A glimmer of happiness shines in my heart, spreading out through my chest. Jay is my shield, my protection.

When we get to the airport, I try Jordan again while we wait to board. I leave another voicemail, but by the time we have to turn our phones on to Airplane mode, I haven't heard back from him.

There's nothing I can do until we land, so I try to forget about it for the next few hours. Jay makes it easy. He asks me questions and listens to the answers as if I'm the most interesting person he's ever known.

He asks me if I remember my first kiss and doesn't judge when I admit it was my third cousin once-removed who did the honors. If only I hadn't judged him that first night we met, things would have been different from the start.

We could have skipped over pretend and gone straight to couple. But I wouldn't have been ready to be a couple with Jay then. I don't know that I'm ready now.

"Favorite flavor of ice cream?" he asks, lacing our fingers together.

"Pistachio."

He wrinkles his nose. "That's not a flavor," he says.

The memory of cold creamy sweetness floods my mind. In the summer of my sophomore year in college abroad in Italy, where pistachio was the most popular gelato.

"Have you been to Italy?" I ask.

"I haven't been anywhere in Europe."

The fantasy of traveling with Jay plays in my head like a romantic reel. Strolling along the stone streets in the floating city of Venice, sharing a bottle of Chianti in Tuscany, watching the sun set on the Amalfi Coast over a candlelit dinner. Jay and I would visit everywhere I'd been when I was nineteen.

Only this time, I would be in love.

"We should go," he says, watching me intently. "My passport is current."

My mind spins with the possibilities. "We would both have to get time off work," I say, my heart skipping happily.

"That's one of the perks of owning the place. I can take time whenever I want." He leans close, brushing my cheek with a kiss. "I want to take time with you."

My pulse jumps, and my imagination runs wild. "It will have to wait until after Mattson is put away," I say, really thinking about it. I can almost taste the rich espresso and smell the salty air.

"Okay," he says softly, kissing a path to my ear.

My pulse kicks up a notch as his lips brush the sensitive spot below my ear.

"Lunch is served," says the flight attendant, a smiling young woman who can't take her eyes off Jay.

We pull down our trays, even though I wouldn't mind skipping lunch for a little more of what Jay is serving. As I pick at my salad, because I'm still full from pancakes at brunch, the reasons we can't go to Italy start adding up in my mind.

There's not only time off from work, there's the money. Who's paying? I have plenty of money in savings, but what about Jay? We've never discussed finances. It could lead to an awkward conversation. What if he's one of those men who's threatened by a woman who makes more than him?

But, no, Jay isn't like that. He wouldn't care if I made more, and come to think of it, maybe I don't. He might be killing it at the gym, and private security is a very lucrative profession from what I've seen.

And then there is the elephant on the plane. If we go to Italy together, what does that make us? Officially a couple?

And then what? Get married? Have a family?

My blood runs cold. At least half of that is off the table.

Besides, I'm not ready to be a girlfriend. The last thing I want is someone prying into my life, telling me what I can and can't do, sharing my private space.

But, Jay has been sharing my private space for weeks, and I've never minded. And he isn't the kind of man who'd try to control me. He might pry into my life, but only because he wants to keep me safe, and he loves me.

My heart slams to a stop before starting up again, as if the plane is crashing.

He loves me. And apparently, I feel exactly the same way about him.

I'm not ready for this. Any of it.

I glance at Jay, who seems as lost in thought as I am. He eats neatly, cutting his chicken and taking pristine bites off his fork, but his mind is elsewhere.

He catches my eye and puts his fork down on the plate. "I know," he says.

And it's enough. He does know. This is just another example of how I thought we were complete opposites, but we are really so much alike.

The flight attendant gathers our half-eaten plates of food, and Jay takes my hand again as soon as the tray tables are put away.

"We'll figure it out," he says. "Together."

Suddenly, all my fears bloom at once. Jay is thirty-six years old. He can't afford to be wasting time with me if he wants a family. Our relationship will be doomed from the start.

Still, I want to try.

"I can't have kids," I say, my voice quiet, barely audible over the faint rumbles and creaks of the plane.

His fingers tighten on mine. He doesn't judge, doesn't even react with anything but a quiet question. "Do you want to talk about it?"

Surprisingly, I do. I keep my voice neutral as I tell Jay how I put off getting married and having kids while I got my career started. "Then it was too late," I say.

"What do you mean?" He joins our hands, squeezing mine gently.

"I'd been getting these severe pains for a while, but I just ignored them. Then one day while I was at work, I couldn't ignore them anymore." I take a deep breath, reliving that horrible day at the hospital. "I had an ovarian cyst rupture, and I had to have a procedure."

"I'm so sorry."

I try to shake off the traumatic memories of the operation, the recovery, the shame, but they will always be with me.

"What if I told you I don't want my own kids?" Jay asks. "I have plenty with Champion's Corner."

I close my eyes, fending off the wave of regret that washes over me. "You might be fine now, but what about a year from now? Five years?" The fear grows, spreading through my chest and clogging my throat so that I can hardly speak. "What if you change your mind?"

Jay's hands cup my cheeks. "Stay with me in the present, Mia. It's pretty good right here."

He kisses me with sweet, tender passion, holding my face as his talented mouth coaxes a reaction from me. His tongue seduces mine in a dance that instantly sparks my desire. The future might be uncertain, but he's right about one thing—the present is pretty awesome.

"I don't know where we are headed in five years," he says. "But tonight I'll be back on guard duty, and I'm looking forward to guarding your body all night long."

He kisses me again, angling his head to claim more of my mouth, and hint at what the rest of the night will bring.

CHAPTER 37

The Threat is Over

As soon as we get off the plane, Mia's phone rings.

"It's Jordan," she says.

The hair on the back of my neck stands up at the mention of her boss's name. There's something about the guy I don't like.

"I need to take this," she says.

"Of course." I know she's hinting for some privacy, but she's not gonna get it. We're back in Mossy Oak now. There could be danger lurking. "Answer the phone, Mia." I glance at the phone in her hand with Jordan's name scrolling across the screen.

That stubborn look I love so much crosses her face, but it's fleeting. She knows I'm right. I'm not going anywhere as long as Mattson is roaming free.

She swipes the screen and holds the phone to her ear. "Jordan, I've been trying to reach you. We just landed."

She falls silent, listening while Jordan talks. Her eyes widen and her steps falter. "When?"

I stop next to her, my gaze scanning the airport around us. I'm not expecting anything to go down in the six-gate airport. There are some people waiting to board at a few of the gates and some customers browse in the gift shop, but other than that, it's quiet.

"Is she in custody?" Mia's voice is sharp. The color has

drained from her face, and her shoulders are tense. When her eyes collide with mine, they are cold and calculating. Fiercely determined.

I cock my head at her and raise a brow. She raises both brows in answer, then hangs up with Jordan. She drops her phone in her purse, then strides with purpose toward the luggage pickup, leaving me to follow in her wake.

I catch her in two long strides. "What happened?"

She glances over her shoulder at me. "I'll tell you in the car."

I'm instantly on high alert. Jordan should have called me immediately about a threat. I step closer to Mia, shielding her with my body. "Are you in danger?"

She checks the time. "How long do you think our luggage will take?"

I sweep my gaze over the other travelers, nearly ready to pluck Mia off her feet and carry her to the car if something looks out of place. The older man with the cane looked innocent enough a few minutes ago, but now I see he's only pretending to look at the postcards in the gift shop. What's he really up to?

"Forget the luggage," I say, grabbing Mia's hand and tugging her toward the exit. Whatever was in those suitcases isn't worth risking Mia's life.

Mia pulls her hand from mine and strides toward the luggage pickup. "You don't have to protect me anymore," she says. "Mattson is dead."

"What?"

Mia sighs. "I'll tell you everything in the car on the way to your place."

"My place?" There go our plans for a quiet evening of lounging in her bed, planning trips to Italy and ordering in.

"I have to go into the office," she says. "It's a mess, and Jordan needs me."

"Yeah, I'm sure he does."

Mia misses my sarcasm as she studies the luggage carousel. Her mind is focused on work, and I doubt she would notice if a fire broke out in the airport, much less my disappointment that our plans are ruined.

In her car, Mia explains that the young woman who accused Mattson of rape, the one who was deemed an unreliable witness, stabbed and killed Warner Mattson and is now being held in Azalea County jail without bail.

She delivers this all with no expression or emotion, driving as if she's on autopilot.

I realize that she's already thrown up her walls. It's obvious to me she cares about this woman, but she's all business now, the cold, calculating attorney.

We are quiet on the drive back to town, the interior of the car humming with unspoken words.

"Don't worry about dropping me off," I say as we pull into town. "I can walk from your office."

Mia stops at a traffic light, but doesn't turn to look at me. "What about your luggage?"

"I'll get it later."

Mia finally looks at me. Her face is a mask, every emotion hidden away. When we arrive at the courthouse, I make Mia wait in the car while I check out the parking lot. There are less than half a dozen cars in the lot. I see Jordan's BMW is one of them, and my nerves fray.

"I'll walk you in," I tell Mia, opening her door.

"No need." Weariness creeps into her voice as she stands. "The threat is over."

"Let me finish the job." I step aside so she can get out of the car.

"There's no need." Her voice is hopeless.

I place an arm on the car behind her, boxing her in. "What if I have a need? I want to see you tonight."

Mia's breath hitches. She leans into me, and I can feel her softening, her body melting into mine. "I'm not sure what time I'll be done."

"That's okay."

"It might be late."

I won't sleep until I see her again, until we talk a few things over. "Just text me."

We stand there staring at each other, trapped in an awkward moment with the security guard as our interested audience.

I wait for her to make a move. To kiss me, or hug me, or even a wink to let me know we are still the same people who discussed taking a trip to Europe together earlier today.

She extends her hand. A polite smile is on her lips, and her eyes are twin pools of glacial blue. "It was nice working with you."

I take her hand in mine, my palm engulfing hers. I feel that jolt, same as always, when we touch, and I can't help wondering if she feels it too. She pulls her hand free without another word, and a moment later, disappears into the building.

CHAPTER 38

My Ass on the Line

I march straight to Jordan's office, where I find him talking on his office phone. He acknowledges me and points at the chair opposite his desk. I take a seat and cross one leg over the other, feeling out of place wearing jeans and a sweater in the office. I might as well be naked without my power suit and heels, but Jordan's appearance is even more revealing. I've never seen him with as much as a strand of hair out of place, but his hair looks like he's been running his hands through it half the night. It stands up in wavy tufts that are usually gelled back to within an inch of their life. He's wearing a wrinkled button-down shirt with the sleeves rolled up. He has bags under his eyes and a five o'clock shadow, even though it's only a few hours past lunch.

I'd come in here ready to cuss Jordan for letting this happen, but as soon as I see him, I know he's already told himself everything I'm about to say and worse.

He ends the call and shakes his head at me, looking forlorn. Reaching into the top drawer of his desk, he pulls out a pack of cigarettes and a lighter.

"Join me for a smoke?" he asks.

"I thought you quit."

Jordan stands up and runs his hand through his hair, mussing it even more. "Come on. Let's go up on the roof."

I never knew there was roof access from the top floor of the building, but I follow Jordan through the escape door and onto the tar roof where we stand at the edge looking out over the charming downtown of Mossy Oak. It's a gorgeous early spring day, with a slight chill that won't last another week. Snow is behind us, and spring is in the air. The dogwoods are blooming and cherry trees spread pink-blossomed branches over Main Street. In the distance, puffy clouds hang over the slabs of gray mountains cutting into the blue sky.

Jordan lights a cigarette and hands it to me, then lights another for himself.

"This is all my fault," he says, exhaling a long stream of smoke into the air.

I take a drag off the cigarette, holding the smoke in my lungs as I consider my answer. Jordan's my boss. He runs this office with an iron fist. I don't want to get on his bad side. But he made a bad call, and we both know it. "How do you plan to fix it?"

He jabs a hand through his dark hair. "I can't believe this happened."

I resist the urge to say I told you so. "How is Elena?" I ask.

"Lawyered up." He takes a drag off his cigarette and flicks ashes over the roof. "She got Morris Birchland."

"Morris Birchland?" He takes advantage of his clients, barely winning a case unless someone screws up on the other side of the aisle. "Fuck that. She needs someone better."

"The cops had her this close to confession." He holds his thumb and finger an inch apart, his cigarette dangling from his lips. "Then Morris Birchland shows up out of nowhere."

My shoulders inch up to my ears. None of this should be happening. She wasn't supposed to talk to Mattson until this week. I can't help feeling it's all my fault. "I need to see her."

Jordan squints at me over the cloud of smoke. "What good would it do? She won't say anything to you."

I scowl, turning all my inner anger on him. "Maybe I want to say something to her."

"Don't look at me like that. It makes me feel like I'm less than human."

I sigh and put out my cigarette. After an entire weekend of not smoking, it isn't as great as I remembered. And, hearing how hopeless Elena's situation is makes me wish I had any other job in the world.

"What happened?"

"I don't know all the details yet."

"This is all my fault. I asked her to talk to Mattson."

Jordan's eyes narrow. "What?"

My chest pinches, and I can barely force out the words. "I thought if she confronted him and got it on tape, we would have a case."

Jordan drops his cigarette and stamps it out under his shoe. "You didn't tell her to gut him with a knife."

"What if she didn't do it? What if something else happened? Or it was self defense?"

"It was premeditated. Cold-blooded murder."

Despite the chill in the air, I'm burning up with emotion. "Which could have been prevented if we would have done our jobs. If Mattson was behind bars, he wouldn't be dead, and Elena wouldn't be left without a future."

"She killed him," Jordan says, his eyes glassy as he stares off into the sky.

Below us, the townspeople of Mossy Oak enjoy a bright spring day. The cobblestone sidewalks are filled with window shoppers, and people wander into popular restaurants for a late lunch. I feel a million miles away from it all, observing through a cold, hard lens. The fact that some people are enjoying a late lunch at a sidewalk cafe while young girls like Elena are forced to take justice into their own hands because they were too unreliable to have a voice makes me want to scream.

"She never had a chance in life," I say, shifting my gaze back to Jordan. "Did she?"

He bends down to pick up his cigarette butt and stuffs it in the pocket of his jeans. "She never did. And even if we would have sent Warner Mattson to prison, don't think she would have been free. Warner's father would have made her life a living hell, in one way or another. The Mattsons are untouchable in this town."

I lift a brow. "Unless they're dead."

Elena did the world a favor by offing Warner Mattson, and the thanks she gets is a jail cell.

"You didn't have to come straight from the airport," Jordan says. "It could have waited until tomorrow."

"No way I was going home without finding out more." I turn on my heel and start back towards the stairwell. "I want to see all the evidence."

"Why?" Jordan takes my elbow, stopping me. "What good will that do? Elena is going to jail, and you are going to help put her there. It's your job."

I shake him off. "No."

"Mia." Jordan's voice is pitched low.

Then he does something unexpected. He takes me in his arms.

I'm so stunned by his sudden embrace, I freeze. My heart beats frantically in my chest, and I feel like ants are crawling all over my skin.

His arms tighten around me, and he lowers his lips to my ear. "I'm so relieved I don't have to worry about you anymore."

I had no idea Jordan had spent a spare ounce of energy thinking about me. Although he'd been the one to insist on Jay, I'd thought he was just doing his job. "You were worried about me?"

"Of course." Jordan leans back enough to look at me. "I'm glad you're back in one piece and the threat is gone. You don't have to hang out with Sanchez anymore. You don't have to pretend he's your boyfriend."

I take a step back and lift my chin. "What are you talking about?"

"I know you were pretending he was your boyfriend, so you didn't look weak."

"That's none of your business."

He cocks his head at me. "It is when I'm the one signing his paychecks."

My jaw falls open. "What?"

"I hired Jay to protect you," he says. "You don't think the county would foot that kind of bill?"

I *had* thought it was odd that our usually frugal budget allowed for personal security, but I'd believed Jordan. "Why did you lie?"

Taking a step closer, he closes the distance between us and places his hands on my shoulders. "I care about you, Mia."

My breath freezes in my lungs. "You're my boss."

He shakes his head, smiling slightly. "I try to look out for you."

I ease back from him, putting a few feet of space between us. My head is spinning from his admission. "You don't look out for me, Jordan. You try to make me look bad every chance you get. You give me the shit jobs and take credit when they go well. If they don't, it's my ass on the line."

A muscle in his jaw tenses. "I do that for your own good. I'm trying to make you stronger, so you'll be ready when it's time for you to shine."

When he reaches for me, I jerk away from his touch. "I'm as strong as I need to be. I don't need your favors."

"Mia, don't be like that. You have so much potential, but you aren't there yet."

"Oh?" I glare up at him, squinting against the bright sun. "I just need a few more years under your thumb?"

He smiles, completely missing the sarcasm laid over my words. "I wouldn't put it like that, but you do need more time. To develop."

"I should go," I say.

"Where are you going?"

I push past him and wrench open the door to the stairwell. "Home," I say.

But as I open the door, I realize it's not where I'm going, but to whom. There's only one person I want to see right now. Only one person who can make this nightmare fade away. I drive straight to Out of the Box, just in time to see Laura closing up the gym. Jay isn't there. He's gone on a ride and she doesn't know when he'll be back.

CHAPTER 39

Trying To Get Lucky

The wind on my face, the sun on my back, the smell of blooming flowers in the air. This ride through the mountains is exactly what I need to clear my head.

When I get home, it's nearly dark, and the gym is closing for the night. I thank Laura for keeping everything smooth in my absence.

"That's what you pay me for, Boss," she says in her usual cheerful manner. Her optimism used to annoy me, but I've gotten used to it and I don't know what I'd do without her.

After she's gone and the gym is locked up for the night, I head upstairs for a shower. I check my phone while I unlock the door, but Mia hasn't called or texted. She's probably still at work, grinding out a strategy to deal with a case that might break her. With Jordan.

I don't trust that man, and neither should Mia. But if I try to warn her, I will look like a jealous boyfriend.

Maybe that's what I am.

Inside my apartment, I shed my jacket and throw my keys on the counter. The air is stale and all the lights are off. I open a window and check out the meager contents of my fridge.

I'm supposed to be sharing takeout with Mia, but instead, I'm alone and missing her like crazy. It's odd to be away from her. I've gotten so used to shadowing her, I don't know what to do with myself.

The buzzer sounds from the back entrance, and I instantly perk up.

It must be Mia, coming over to see me. I press the intercom. "Hello?"

"Hey, Coach," says a young male voice I don't recognize.

My heart sinks. "Who's this?"

"It's George," he says. "Can I talk to you?"

I sigh and buzz open the door. A moment later, I open the apartment door and find not only George standing there, but another kid standing slightly behind him. They look enough alike to be family, and I assume it's his brother.

"Thanks, Coach," George says, coming in when I open the door wide. "This is Tyler. My little brother."

"Hi," the kid says.

"What can I do for you?"

The kids look at each other, and then George finally speaks up. "We were hoping we could crash here tonight."

I don't know what I expected, but it definitely wasn't that. "What?"

"Our dad kicked us out for the night. He's got a date and she'll probably stay over, so he told us to get out."

I think of a few lessons I'd like to teach George and Tyler's deadbeat dad. "Where does he think you are?"

George shrugs. "He doesn't care. He just told us to scram."

"He's trying to get lucky," Tyler says.

"He sounds like a great guy," I say.

"We just need a place to crash. We won't bother you."

"I was just going out," I say. It's not entirely true. Mia still hasn't texted. I check the time and realize she should have by now. Why hasn't she called?

"Perfect," George says. "You won't even know we're here. We can sleep on the floor."

I roll my eyes. No way am I gonna have a teenager and a kid sleep on the floor. "The couch pulls out into a bed," I say. "And there are some sheets in the closet."

George brightens. "You mean we can stay?"

"Yeah, you can stay."

George swallows roughly. "Thanks. You won't even know we're here."

George reminds me of myself when I was that age. A kid in a man's body, he's bigger than the other teens in the program. He's a good fighter and can make something of himself if he stays focused. But staying focused isn't easy when you have a parent who tosses you out on the street every time he has a date.

You and your little brother.

"Did you eat?" I ask, going to the pantry again. Maybe there are some chips or a loaf of bread, but it doesn't look any more promising than it did ten minutes ago.

"We could eat," Tyler says, following me into the kitchen.

"Shut up, Tyler."

"I was just about to order take out." I grab my phone. "Pizza or Chinese?"

"I thought you were going out," George says.

"In a little while."

But Mia is still silent. I try not to get annoyed, but it's hard to imagine her and Jordan huddled over a desk together. The man wants her. There's no ifs about it. And Mia would be a lot smarter to date a guy like Jordan than me. So what if he's her boss? They are perfect for each other.

"You okay, Coach?" George asks.

"Yeah." I clear my throat. "Pizza or Chinese?"

I eat dinner with the boys while we watch an NBA game.

Tyler wants to join Champion's Corner when they get enough money for a membership, and I tell him he can fill out the scholarship form.

"But he's only nine," George says. "He's not old enough until next year."

"I'll make an exception." I made an exception for Summer Carleton, and she is also nine. But she's a paying member, so honestly, I would have taken her at eight. Paying members make it possible for kids like Tyler and George to be part of Champion's Corner. "You're big for your age," I say.

Some kids grow up with advantages, while others grow up in trailer parks or with parents who would rather get laid than take care of them. Kids like George and Tyler, who've had to scratch their way up in the world, have a natural chip on their shoulder which makes them better prepared to dig deep in the ring.

"Don't you have to be somewhere?" George asks, reaching for the last egg roll.

I check my phone and see Mia still hasn't reached out. "Not yet," I say.

George eyes me critically. "You're not wearing that, are you?"

"What's wrong with it?" I'm in jeans and a T-shirt. Both black.

George scoffs. "Nothing if you're going to a funeral."

I gather the food containers and toss them in the trash.

"He's going on a date," Tyler says from the living room.

"Why do you think that?" I ask.

"Because that's what grown- ups do," he says. "That's what Dad does."

Something twists in my gut.

"Do you want us to get out?" George asks, his voice cracking.

"But he said we could stay," Tyler protests.

I come back into the living room, a stern expression on my face. "I don't go back on my word,"

Tyler punches his brother in the arm. "See?"

George schools his features into a mask. "Thanks again."

"No problem."

"We can clean the rest of this up," Tyler says, grabbing shoes and jackets in his arms.

"And I'll make up the bed," George offers.

Mia still hasn't called by the time the boys are settled in for the night, with a movie on the big screen television. I give in and type out a text, but hit delete before I press send. Maybe it's best to show up at her place. If she isn't home, I'll just wait. I'd been planning on staying the night, but I don't want to leave George and Tyler alone.

"I'll be back in a few hours," I say.

"Do you want some help picking out your clothes?" George asks.

I tug at the hem of my T-shirt. It's so worn it's faded into a dark gray. And suddenly, I know exactly what I'm going to wear to impress Mia.

CHAPTER 40

Get Rid of Him

Once back at home, I check my messages again before getting in the shower. I need to talk to Jay, but I also need to find out what's going on with Elena.

Jordan is mistaken if he thinks I'll have anything to do with prosecuting her. He will have to do it himself.

I take a long time under the hot spray of the shower, trying to rid myself of the dirty feeling deep inside. It's my fault Elena is in jail. She might not see her kids again for years, and it's because of me.

Wrapping myself in my robe, I grab my phone and call a number I never thought I would dial willingly. When Morris Birchland answers the phone, he is just as wary to talk to me as I am to talk to him.

"I want to meet with you as soon as possible," I say.

"Concerning what?"

"I want to talk about your client, Elena..."

He cuts me off. "I have nothing to say."

"You don't understand." I pace across my bedroom, finally giving in and going outside on the balcony. I find that the urge to smoke a cigarette is gone, but I still want to be outside under the

216

cloak of night. Looking at the mountains in the distance brings me a sense of peace. "I want to help her."

After a few more protests, Birchland agrees to meet me for coffee and discuss Elena's case. I hang up feeling better than I have in hours, but still there are no messages from Jay.

If he doesn't text soon, I'll have to take matters into my own hands and show up on his doorstep again. It might come off as a bit desperate, but I need to see him. Scrolling back to the text I sent him over an hour ago, I realize it is still unread.

Is he ignoring me?

I head downstairs and grab my laptop. Until Jay arrives, I can busy myself starting a new spreadsheet. A new database is exactly what I need to calm my mind, but when I go to start a new project, the page won't load. A message comes up telling me I'm not connected to the wifi. I go through the steps of reconnecting, but I get the same results. The server can not be reached.

I grab my phone and check the connection. Sure enough, no wifi.

Hope soars in my chest. No wifi means my text to Jay didn't go through. He isn't responding for a reason.

My fingers fly over the screen, scrolling to settings to turn on my data plan. I'm about to click the button to turn on my data plan when my doorbell rings.

My heart races and I jump up from my chair. Jay is here.

As I reach for the door, I peek through the peephole, but it's too dark to see more than a large male shape. I think to check the camera feed on my security system, but the wifi is down.

I pull open the door, ready to launch myself at Jay, and tell him my plan for a new start when I see it isn't Jay.

It's a tall man with graying hair and broad shoulders. His handsome features look familiar, and then I recognize him.

Eric Mattson. Warner Mattson's dad.

I narrow the gap in the door and take a step back. "What can I do for you, Mr. Mattson?"

He's aged since the last time I'd seen him sitting next to his son in the courtroom. His hair has gone gray overnight, and his cheeks are sunken, but he musters up a snake oil salesman smile and steps closer to the gap in the door. "Why don't you let me in? We can have a nice long chat."

Fear tremors through me like an earthquake, but I hold my ground. "I don't think so. I have company."

His smile turns into a snarl. "That's a lie, counselor. Like all the other ones you told." The silver barrel of a handgun flashes in the darkness as he pushes it into the crack of the door. "Let me in."

My stomach clenches, and I try to remember everything I'm supposed to do in a fight, but my brain freezes. Eric Mattson slams his hand against the door, and I have no choice but to stumble backward and allow him in. I feel like I'm back in college again, helpless and confused. But then I remember I'm an adult, and I have a lot more experience dealing with assholes of the world like Eric Mattson.

He might think he has the upper hand, but I'm not helpless. I'm not terrified like I was when the boys from the lacrosse team threatened to hold me down until they were done with me. I've been dealing with criminal minds for years.

"Can I offer you something to drink?" I ask, moving toward the kitchen and my phone.

Eric Mattson takes a look around my apartment, holding his gun in front of him and gesturing with it. "This place is a dump," he says.

"You think so?" I survey my boring apartment with a nonchalant glance. "I think it's nice."

He points to a stool by the kitchen counter. "Sit down."

My heart is pounding out of my chest, but I take a deep breath and slowly make my way to the stool. My phone is on the desk next to my laptop, only a few feet away. If I could manage to grab it...

"Don't even think about it," he says, giving me that fake smile again. He points to the stool and drags a backpack off his shoulder.

When I see the backpack, my blood runs cold. I can only imagine what he has planned for me. Nothing good, I know that much. I start talking. Anything I can think of to get him distracted. He seems eager to spill his story and starts blabbing about what a good kid Warner was. How he was just like his grandad. Good at baseball, the women loved him, he could talk anyone into anything. Blah, blah, blah. As he waxes on about how amazing his son was, my mind whizzes into action. He has a gun, but I'm younger and smarter.

When he pauses to remember the details of Warner's home-coming football game, I slide off the stool and saunter into the kitchen. "I have a good chianti waiting to be opened," I say. "Maybe you'd like a glass?"

He hesitates, his eyes glassy with far- off memories. There's a fine sheen of sweat on his forehead and his skin is so pale it has a greenish tint. He nods, wiping the back of his hand over his brow. "Wine would be okay," he says.

I open several drawers, pretending to look for the opener as I palm a vegetable peeler and push it under the sleeve of my sweater. The peeler isn't much use against a gun, but maybe if I get him relaxed and drinking wine, I can take it from there.

"Warner could have been somebody," he says. "He wanted to run for president. Did you know that?"

I struggle to keep my eyebrows in place. Just what our country needs, an attempted rapist in the most powerful position of government. "Wow," I say, schooling my features to seem impressed. "That's ambitious."

I grab the bottle of wine and consider chucking it at his head, but he's too far away, and my aim is terrible.

The doorbell rings and both of us freeze. Hope bursts in my chest, because this time it has to be Jay. But did I send that message before Mattson rang the bell? I can't remember. It doesn't matter. It's the opportunity I need.

Eric storms across the room and grabs me by the shoulder. It's the first time he's touched me since he came into the house, and it makes my skin crawl. "Answer the door," he says, dragging me through the living room. "But don't try anything funny, or I'll shoot you."

He positions himself behind the door and waits while I look through the peephole. My chest fills with hope as I see Jay standing on my doorstep. The darkness cloaks him, but I recognize the set of his broad shoulders, the way he holds his head. Everything about him is familiar in the most reassuring way.

"Whoever it is, get rid of them," Mattson says.

I glance at the gun, and sweat beads on my brow. I have to get rid of Jay, or he could get hurt. Eric Mattson is unstable.

I pull open the door a few inches and my heart melts. He's wearing the flowered shirt I bought him. Tiny wings of longing flutter in my chest. Even in the darkness, I can see his hopeful expression. Him wearing that shirt is better than all the bouquets of flowers in the world.

"Hey," he says. "You never texted."

I must not have hit send, which works out perfectly. If I'm going to get Jay to leave, it's better I never sent the text telling him to come over.

He glances up at the spotlight over my door. "What happened to your lights?" he asks.

I shake my head, trying to come up with a way to get him out of here so he's safe. "I don't know."

His brows draw together and his chest puffs up like he's ready to go Mr. Fix-it on me.

"I'm tired," I say, feigning a yawn.

He stands straighter, transferring his helmet from one hand to the other in a betrayal of his nerves.

"We should probably talk," he says. "We left things unfinished."

Matsson pokes me with the gun, and mouths for me to hurry up. I tear my gaze away from him and look back at Jay.

"Call me later," I say. Mattson jabs my ribs with the gun, shaking his head. I take a deep breath and smile at Jay. "Maybe tomorrow?"

The hopeful expression on his face turns to frustration. His jaw clenches and he puts a hand on the door to stop me from closing it in his face. "Tomorrow?" he asks. "What's wrong?"

I sigh heavily. I've got to get rid of him so he won't be in danger. If anything happens to Jay because of me, I'll never forgive myself. I already have Elena rotting in a jail cell because of me. I can't take another tragedy on my soul.

"Nothing I can't handle," I say.

Jay squints at me, his eyes gleaming with suspicion. He tries to look past my shoulder into the apartment, but I block his view.

"Is someone else there with you?" he asks.

I shake my head quickly, lowering my gaze so he won't see my lie.

"Mia." His voice is a low grumble. "Don't lie to me."

I give him my brightest smile, pleading with him. "Just go, Jay. We'll talk tomorrow."

He steps forward, then shakes his head and retreats. "If that's what you want."

"That's for the best." Part of me is disappointed at how quickly Jay gives up, but the other part is relieved. At least he is out of harm's way.

As Jay takes another step back into the darkness of the parking lot, Mattson slams the door shut. Grabbing my shoulder, he shoves me toward the kitchen. I stumble over my feet and fall on the hardwood floor of the entryway. A muffled cry escapes my mouth as I land painfully on my side.

Mattson stands over me, pointing the gun straight at my face. "Get up," he says. "You owe me a glass of wine." He laughs bitterly. "And my son's life."

I get to my feet and make my way into the kitchen, trying to look as demure as possible. If he thinks I'm helpless, he will underestimate me. And that will be his downfall. At least Jay is safe. As I open the wine and get ready to negotiate my way out of this mess, that's all that matters.

CHAPTER 41

Instincts Never Steer Me Wrong

What the fuck just happened? I stalk back to my bike, feeling like someone has just knocked me out with a surprise punch. Anger and confusion make my head spin as I approach my bike. Then something prickles on the back of my neck. Something's not right.

All the lights are on over the doorways of the condos. All except Mia's. It was working last week, so it's strange that it's out.

I don't like strange.

I backtrack to the door and peek up at the light. The bulb is shattered, and that's when I hear it. A thump and a muffled cry.

My jaw clenches, and I glare at the door. Pulling out my phone, I'm about to dial Mia when I think better of it. If she would have wanted me to come in, she would have asked. I pace back and forth a few steps, glancing around the parking lot. There are the neighbors' usual cars that I've gotten to know over the last few months. But at the curb is that dark Lexus I noticed around Mia's office. Not Jordan's BMW, as I'd first assumed when I thought Mia had company.

A prickle of fear runs down my spine. Mia is in danger. I need to get inside her place. Instead of knocking on her door again, I think of another way. Walking next door, I stand at the window of the condo for sale and dial the number for the real estate agent.

After a few rings, Chelsea answers in a bright, professional tone.

"Hello? You've reached Chelsea Taylor."

I grit my teeth. The woman's cheerful voice sets me on edge. "Chelsea. It's Jay Sanchez."

"Oh. Hello, Jay." Her voice is full of false cheer. "What can I do for you?"

"I was wondering if you could let me in the condo you're selling in Frog Level?"

She's quick to agree. "I could show you the place this week," she says. "What day is good for you?"

"I was thinking right now."

"Right now?" Her voice is disbelieving. "I'm in the middle of dinner."

"Maybe you could just give me the code and meet me over here after dinner?" I ask, trying to use my most persuasive voice.

"That's not the way it works," Chelsea says, laughing.

"Well, I'm standing outside the condo right now, and I really want to get in. But there's another place I'm interested in across town. In fact," I pause dramatically, my heart racing as I wonder what's going on behind Mia's closed door. "I think I'll just head there now."

"That won't be necessary." Chelsea practically chokes, trying to get the words out. She rattles off the code, then tells me she would never do this for anyone else.

I punch in the numbers, and the door unlocks. "Don't worry, I won't touch anything."

The only room I'm interested in is the main bedroom with the second floor balcony that neighbors Mia's. I race up the stairs, kicking myself for not insisting I stick by Mia even after the threat was over. My instincts tell me she's in trouble, and my instincts never steer me wrong.

In the main bedroom, I fly through the room to the French

doors that lead to the balcony. Just as I remember, it's an easy climb for a man of my height from one balcony to the next. I jump onto the landing of Mia's balcony and hope her bad habit of smoking hasn't ended, and she's been out here since she got home. My racing heart calms as I see a fresh pack of smokes and the French doors slightly ajar. I ease them open and sneak into her bedroom.

Best-case scenario is I'm a paranoid motherfucker, and Mia is curled up on the sofa watching television. Worst-case scenario, my gut is correct, and she's in trouble.

I creep down the hall, listening keenly as I near the stairs. Voices drift up from the lower level, and my stomach clenches. Mia's voice is too bright, and the following deep male answer is gruff and angry.

I prepare for the worst and inch down the stairs. The closer I get, the worse I feel. I knew something wasn't right in the parking lot, but now that feeling has multiplied a thousand times. I press my back to the wall and creep closer, my skin crawling with the idea that Mia is in danger.

I should have insisted on staying with her instead of dropping her off. I should have seen this coming. I should have known.

"You should have wised up and dropped the case," the man's voice says. "But no, you had to keep pushing."

Mia's soft chuckle sounds. "Just doing my job, Mr. Mattson. You shouldn't take it personally."

"Bitch," he responds.

Anger explodes inside me, and I see red. Motherfucker. I'm going to make him regret talking to Mia like that.

There's a loud pop, and my stomach turns. I would know a gunshot anywhere. My heart thunders so loud in my ears that all other sounds are drowned out. I storm into the kitchen, no longer thinking clearly as I fly around the corner. My mind is filled with horrific scenes of Mia lying in a pool of blood, her pale face terrified.

But what I see is far different. Mia stands over a man with a gun pointed at his head. Her face is a mask of calm, her feet are spread apart in a secure stance, and both of her hands are firm on the gun.

He tries to get to his feet, and she steps closer, pointing the gun at his forehead. "Make one move, and it's your last."

"You wouldn't kill me."

Mia tosses her hair off her face and glares at him. "You raised a rapist," she says, her eyes gleaming. "Maybe I *should* kill you."

I've never seen Mia look so fierce. I realize she means it. She's really thinking about killing him. I don't blame her, but I also don't want to see her do something she'll regret for the rest of her life.

"Mia," I say softly from the hallway.

She turns her head toward me. The mask of indifference fades, and emotions flicker across her face. "I told you to go away."

I stride into the room. "I didn't listen."

"I have this under control," she says, swiveling her gaze back to the man in the kitchen.

"I can see that."

Her hand shakes. "I really want to kill this bastard right now."

I stride across the room and place my hand over hers. "No, you don't. Trust me."

The gleam in her eyes dies out, and she shifts her gaze from the man to me. "You shouldn't have come."

The need to pull her into my arms is strong, but first I want to deal with the intruder. "Got anything I can tie him up with?"

"Masking tape. Top drawer."

I pull open the drawer and grab the roll of tape, ripping off a long piece as I cross the kitchen. "Turn around and put your hands behind your back."

"My leg," he says. "She stabbed me."

"I don't give a fuck about your leg." I step closer, wrenching one of his hands behind his back.

He cries out as I bind his hands with no mercy. "I just wanted to talk to her," he says.

"That's why you cut her wifi, and held her at gunpoint? Sounds like you had more in mind than a chat."

"You don't know what you're doing," he says. "You should just let me go and we will forget all about this."

"That's not gonna happen," Mia says.

"You have no idea who you are messing with." He groans with pain as I shove him into a chair. "I know people."

"It doesn't matter who you know," she says. "You broke the law. You're gonna end up where you belong. I'll see to that."

His bitter laugh sounds despite his compromised position. "You don't have a great track record when it comes to prosecuting my family, counselor."

"Call the cops, Jay," Mia says, holding the gun steady on the man's face.

I pull out my phone and dial nine-one-one. "You're a badass," I say, waiting while the phone rings.

A small smile lifts her lips, but it doesn't reach her ice-blue eyes. "I know."

CHAPTER 42

Damn Good To Be Alive

The police show up in less than thirty minutes and take Eric Mattson away.

As soon as I close the door and lock it, I feel like I'm going to pass out. My knees wobble, and Jay grabs me around the waist.

"I've got you," he says.

He guides me into the living room, where I sit down on the stiff couch and stare at the bullet hole in my wall. I might have killed him if Jay hadn't been here. The thought makes me doubt everything about myself.

"Tea or tequila?" Jay asks, pulling one of my throw blankets around my shoulders.

"Tea." My stomach is too unstable for liquor. But as he walks away, I have a flash of standing over Eric Mattson, struggling with the temptation to take justice into my own hands. "Tequila," I call out.

Jay opens cupboards in the kitchen with the ease of someone who knows his way around and comes back a moment later with a bottle of Jose Cuervo and two glasses. He pours us both a healthy shot, and we lift our glasses.

We knock back our shots, never taking our eyes off each other. A shudder passes through me as I swallow.

"I wanted to kill him."

"Yeah. I don't blame you."

I feel a surge of energy, a hyper-awareness about everything in the room. For the first time, I see my home with fresh eyes. It's completely devoid of personality, and now it has a bullet lodged in the drywall.

"Hell of a night," Jay says, following my gaze to the scarred wall.

I study his profile. The dark line of his brow, the slope of his nose, and full lips framed by a neat black beard. He's so gorgeous it's a shock to look at him. "Why did you come back?"

He shakes his head, and a stray lock of hair falls from the knot at the back of his head. He pushes it away in the slow, patient way of his before meeting my eyes with his intense stare. Our gazes collide, and I feel a jolt to my system, a deep knowing that pulls low in my belly.

"I felt something was off. But then there were too many things that were out of the ordinary. Your light was busted. The wifi was down. You were off."

"I was trying to protect you."

"That's my job." His voice is a sharp bark, full of guilt. "You didn't let me do it."

He sounds angry, but I know it's just the adrenaline charging through him. I feel it too, and it makes me feel a little wild with excess energy.

All my senses are heightened. I can smell Jay's scent, like winter wood, and feel the surge of energy that vibrates from his body and cocoons us both. I lean closer, desperate for the heat of his fingers on my chilled skin.

Jay meets me halfway, closing the distance between us with an arm around my shoulders. He pulls me close and I press my face against his chest.

My mind spins as I try to put the pieces together. Everything is a blur. After I sent Jay away and Eric shoved me to the ground, everything happened so fast. I remember stabbing him in the leg with the wine opener, then grappling with him for the gun. I hardly remember punching him, or taking possession of the gun, but I know that's what must have happened because my right hand hurts like hell.

I turn my face up to Jay's. "How did you get in here?"

He smooths my hair from my face, a tiny smile curving his lips. "Chelsea."

"What?"

"She gave me the code to the condo next door. I climbed onto your balcony. You left your door unlocked."

A laugh vibrates through my chest, and I feel all the emotions I've suppressed come spiraling through me.

"What's so funny?"

"Smoking saved my life," I say.

"I wouldn't go that far."

"If I hadn't left the door open when I went out for a cigarette, you wouldn't have gotten in."

"I would have found another way." His body tenses, and I feel the shiver run through him. He drags in a deep breath. "I didn't save you. You had everything under control by the time I got here. All I did was tie him up." He kisses the corner of my mouth, then trails a path along my jaw. "I'm so proud of you." His soft chuckle vibrates against my throat. "But I have to admit, I've never been so turned on in my life. You were like a superhero."

My heart slams in my chest as he kisses the sensitive spot he's found just under my jaw. I savor the feel of my pulse quickening, and the desire pooling in my belly. It feels damn good to be alive.

In Jay's arms.

My phone rings, but I am happy to ignore it. I sift my fingers through Jay's hair as he kisses a path to my shoulder. There is blessed silence as the call goes to voicemail. Then it immediately starts ringing again.

"Do you need to get that?" Jay asks.

I glance at my phone and see my boss's name tick across the screen. "It's Jordan."

Jay eases back. "Go ahead and deal with him. I need to call Chelsea."

"You're going to ruin her night."

"I'll let her down gently." Jay rises and leaves the room, giving me privacy to deal with Jordan.

"Hello?"

"Mia!" Jordan's voice sounds high-pitched with panic. "Thank God."

Oh, God. He knows. I'm not surprised, because Jordan knows everything that happens in this town. Reaching for the tequila, I take a long swig before answering. The liquor burns a path down my throat.

"What the hell happened?"

"What do you know?"

"Only that police were dispatched to your place, and Eric Mattson is in custody."

"That's pretty much the bullet points."

"You shouldn't be alone right now. I'll come over."

"I'm not alone," I say. "Jay is here."

"I thought you were done with him? What's he doing there?"

My spine stiffens. "That's none of your business."

"Mia." He sighs in frustration. "I care about you. I don't want you to get hurt."

I glance into the kitchen where Jay is leaning against the counter, talking on his phone. The shirt I bought him looks good on him, even if it doesn't exactly go with the black jeans and motorcycle boots he's wearing. "Jay wouldn't hurt me."

Jordan scoffs. "He isn't right for you."

My fingers tighten on my phone as anger surges inside me. "You don't know anything about him. Or me."

"You don't know what you're saying right now," he says. "You'll be better tomorrow."

I clear my throat. "I'm not coming in tomorrow. I need a personal day."

There's a heavy silence before Jordan responds. "I understand," he says. "Take as much time as you need."

I end the call before he can say anything else and lie back on the sofa.

Jay comes out of the kitchen, and all I want to do is feel alive.

Suddenly, I know exactly what I want to do.

CHAPTER 43

Just Like This View

Mia jumps up and hurries to the window. Flicking the blinds open, she squints into the dark parking lot. "Did you ride your motorcycle?"

I rise from the sofa. "Yeah. Why?"

Her expression is excitement and terror rolled into one. "I want to go for a ride."

I hold back a laugh, but I know better than to question Mia. She knows her mind like no one I've ever met. After months of lecturing me on the safety of motorcycles, she's suddenly had a change of heart.

"You want to feel alive." It's not a question. I've known that feeling before. I've played with death and come out the winner.

Mia nods. Relief shines in her eyes.

Outside, the parking lot is lit by a full moon, and there is still a bit of winter in the air, even though it smells like spring.

"Where's your jacket?" I ask as we approach my bike.

"I don't need one," Mia says. "I like the cold. I need it."

I drape my jacket over her shoulders. "You'll want this. Trust me."

She looks like she's going to argue. A crease forms between her straight brows, but she nods quickly. "Okay. I do."

She threads her arms through the sleeves of my jacket and allows me to cover her head with my helmet.

"What about you?" she asks as I fasten the buckle under her chin.

I kiss her upturned lips. "Don't worry about me."

We climb on, and I show her where to put her feet, how to lean into the curves, and a signal if she wants to stop.

"Tap my thigh if you're scared and I will find a place to stop."

"I'm not scared." She hugs my hips with her thighs.

I wrap her arms securely around my waist. "You ready?"

"Ready. Where are we going? Your place?"

I shake my head. "I've got guests."

Her brow creases. "Who?"

"A couple of kids who needed a place to crash."

Her heart shines in her expression. "Jay."

"I know. I'm a softie. Don't tell anyone, okay?"

She leans forward and kisses my shoulder, the helmet cumbersome between us. I smile and start the bike. "Hold on."

She wants the wind on her face, the taste of freedom, the unknown curves ahead, and I know exactly where to take her.

It's a short drive out of town into the mountains. Night has settled, and there's no traffic climbing along the curving roads. It's too dark to see the majestic mountain view, but it doesn't matter. It's the thrill Mia seeks, not the scenery.

We climb high into the mountains where we are surrounded by pine trees, and the starry sky seems close enough to touch. I push the speed, taking the curves with skill and expertise. I don't want to scare her, but I do want her to feel the exhilaration.

She doesn't tap my thigh once.

She whoops with joy as we shoot up a hill, then zoom down the other side. She laughs and squeezes my waist, her hands sliding up my chest to embrace me from behind. I feel the thunder of her heart against my back and the quickening of her breath.

I envy her riding a motorcycle for the first time. There's nothing quite like the first thrill of speed and power.

I turn off the main highway onto a one-lane road that cuts a path between the giant trees. It smells like Christmas, and the damp air feels like rain. Mia's front is pressed tightly to my back, her arms circle my waist, and her thighs wrap around me.

We are headed to my favorite place in Mossy Oak, a lookout that spans Sapphire Lake. The first time I saw the view of the crystal lake tucked into the valley between the mountains, I knew I wanted to live in Mossy Oak. It's a view I can never get tired of, and tonight I'm sharing it with Mia. I stop the bike at the lookout and cut the engine. The lake sparkles in the moonlight, the still water reflecting the dark sky.

"It's gorgeous," Mia says, climbing off.

"Have you been here?"

She shakes her head. "It's a night of firsts."

I get off the bike and help her with the helmet. Tucking her hair behind her ear, I dip my head and kiss her cheek. I'm glad to be the one giving her these firsts. I want to see her face light up and hear her joy.

We walk closer to the edge of the lookout. Holding hands, we are quiet for some time, taking in the stunning view nature provides. The cool breeze stirs Mia's hair, and I wrap my arm around her shoulders.

She smiles up at me, but there's a tinge of sadness in her expression. "I wanted to kill him," she says.

I squeeze her tightly, remembering the look on Mia's face when she held him at gunpoint. "I know."

She shivers, and I pull her closer, tucking her head beneath my chin. "How can I uphold the law when people like Mattson walk free, and people like Elena are forced to take justice into their own hands? I failed her."

I ease back and look her in the eyes. "Don't blame yourself."

Her mouth pinches in a line, and she closes her eyes. "I don't think I can go back."

I grip her shoulders and force her to look at me. "What do you mean?"

"I can't do my job anymore."

I rub a soothing hand down her arms. "Take a few days to think it over."

"No. My mind is made up."

"But you love your job." Her job is everything to her.

"I used to love my job. But I can't prosecute people like Elena. I won't."

"You can't give up your life's work so easily."

"Don't you understand? It's not black and white to me anymore. Not since I met you."

"What do you mean?"

"Look at you, Jay. You're smart, honest, and the best guy I know. How did a guy like you end up in jail? For protecting his sister?"

I shake my head. I don't want to talk about me. "What do I have to do with you changing careers?"

"Everything was clear before I met you. I wanted to put away the bad guys at all costs." She pulls in a deep breath and turns to face the view. "But it's not so easy. Just like this view. The sky is reflected in the surface of the lake, but which one is real? It's not always easy to tell the difference." She sighs heavily, crossing her arms over her chest. "I'm not making any sense."

I pull her close to my side. "You're making perfect sense. You can do whatever you want with your life. But don't make any decisions after such a trauma. Let Jordan take over for a while."

"Jordan!" She spits out his name. "He thinks he knows what's best for me." She gives me a little shove on the chest that does nothing to budge me. "Why didn't you tell me he was paying your bill?"

"He asked me not to."

"Didn't you think it was strange that he told me the county was paying?"

"It's not my place to judge. He wanted to protect you. I can respect that."

"He hit on me," she says.

My spine stiffens. "He what?"

"He kissed me tonight."

Rage builds up inside me, but I've had years of practice. I keep my anger under control. There's no reason to be jealous of a kiss. Unless...

I peer down at her, watching the play of moonlight over her features. "What did you do?"

She fists my shirt and pulls my face down. Her lips smash against mine, and she kisses the breath from me. Her teeth graze against my lower lip, biting softly. She comes up on her toes and curls her hands around my neck.

"I only want to kiss one man," she says, tangling her fingers in my hair. "You."

My chest swells, my heart soars, my blood stirs to life.

The words mean so much. Yet, they aren't enough. I need more. I need to know this isn't a game or a bet. This is real.

Jay and Mia.

I dig deep, past my fear. "I love you, Mia."

She stares up at me, then a smile breaks out on her face and she begins to laugh. "God help me, I love you too."

I kiss her deeply, knowing for the first time, she's really mine.

CHAPTER 44

Emails from Mia to Jordan

Email message from James.mia@azaleacounty.gov
To Adler.Jordan@azaleacounty.gov

Dear Jordan,

Please accept the attached notarized document as my formal resignation. I will be working out my two weeks notice, and I would appreciate your support. Thank you for everything you've done for me. I hope there are no hard feelings between us going forward and that we can maintain a professional relationship.

I will be pursuing the opportunity to assist Morris Birchland in Elena's defense, so we may see each other on opposite sides of the aisle. It is my wish that we do this without animosity.

Regards, Mia

Email message from Adler.Jordan@azaleacounty.gov

To James.mia@azaleacounty.gov

Dear Mia,

239

As you are aware, resignations are not accepted over email in this county. Please make an appointment with my assistant to arrange for an in-person meeting.

Respectfully,
Jordan Adler

CHAPTER 45

Justice Served

Morris Birchland is late.

I'm friendly enough with the cops at the precinct to convince them to let me talk to Elena without his presence. Even though I'm not her lawyer, and she hasn't spoken to me at all, I cash in a few favors and within minutes, Elena and I are in a room together.

She glares at me from bloodshot eyes. "Where's my lawyer?"

"He's late."

"I'm not saying anything until he gets here."

I fold my hands on the table between us. "I'm not the prosecution. I'm on your side."

Leaning back in her chair, she crosses her arms over her chest. "You're the one who got me into this mess in the first place."

I want to point out that she wasn't supposed to go to Mattson's house until next week, but there was nothing to gain from beating her down. "Tell me what happened."

Elena looks over my shoulder. "I'll wait until my lawyer gets here. I'm not stupid, you know?" She laughs bitterly. "Or maybe I am. I trusted you. I thought you knew what you were doing."

The accusations sting. Probably because they are true. But Elena hasn't heard my story yet. "His dad came to my house," I say, feeling the anger and fear bubble to the surface. I've pressed everything down, but now I let it rise. "He wanted to kill me."

"What?" Elena's face pales. "Did he hurt you?"

I shake my head. "I got away." I lean forward, pressing my palms against the scarred wooden table. "But I know what it feels like to feel trapped. Helpless." I'm filled with the familiar anger that goes all the way back to college. "I'm here for you. I will make this right."

Her eyes are flat and cold. "You said that before, and look at me."

I press so hard into the table, I can feel the splinters in the wood. "Tell me what happened. I know you didn't do this on purpose, and I am going to find a way to get you out of here." My voice rises with conviction. "Justice needs to be served."

She covers her eyes with her hands. "What if I don't want to get out of here? What if this is the best place for me?"

Frustration makes me see red. "And your children? Where are they?"

A sob escapes her mouth. "They're with my mom. Better off. Or so she says."

Anger slices through my frustration. "Your mom doesn't know what she's talking about. They are your kids and they need you."

"Not according to her. She never fails to remind me of what a disappointment I am." She glances around the interrogation room with a sad smile. "And now this."

We aren't supposed to touch, but I reach out and take her hand. "Let me help you. Tell me what happened."

Tears leak out from the corners of her eyes, and she lets them fall without wiping them away. "I don't even know what happened. We were struggling for the gun."

Morris Birchland bursts into the room. "Don't say another word." He glares at me. "How dare you try to steal my client?"

"I'm not stealing her. You were late."

He runs a hand over his sparse hair. "I'm here now."

Elena locks eyes with me, and we exchange unspoken words. The tension in the room is so thick, it leaves a bitter taste in my mouth. I clasp my hands on the table, my gaze pleading with her to give me a chance to make everything right.

Finally, Elena gives me a small curt nod, then directs her gaze at Morris Birchland. "You can go," she says. "I choose Ms. James."

My chest swells with hope, and I nod back at Elena. Morris Birchland mutters something about crazy women and picks up his briefcase.

"I'm keeping your retainer," he says.

Elena's eyes widen and her face pales. "You can't do that."

"He can," I tell Elena, glaring at Birchland. "It's an asshole move, but he's an asshole." I stand up and show Morris Birchland the door. "Get out."

Birchland looks at Elena one last time. She nods at the door, and he scowls. "Your loss," he says.

When he leaves, Elena rests her head in her hands. "There goes my savings."

My chest tightens at the rough deal Elena has been handed. But I know she didn't kill Warner Mattson in cold blood.

I take the seat across from her and pull out my notebook. "Don't worry about the money," I say. "I'm doing this for justice."

Elena drops her hands and shoots me a look full of skepticism. "I thought you were on the other side. You're the one who puts people in jail."

If only it was that simple. "Innocent people don't deserve to go to jail."

"I'm not innocent." A sob catches in her throat. "I stabbed him."

"You've got to stay strong," I say. "Do it for your kids."

She blinks back her tears, and when she looks up at me with a determined glare, I know she's ready to start.

"Start at the beginning. Why did he come to your house?"

Elena runs a hand through her hair. It's thick and a little wild from not seeing a comb for more than a day. "He texted me. Said he wanted to talk." She picks one of her fingernails. "At first I didn't answer, but then I thought it might get you what you wanted. I thought I could trick him into a confession."

"Elena." Frustration brews inside me, and I tamp it down, force myself to remain calm. "That wasn't the plan. You were supposed to wait until I had more evidence."

Her jaw flexes. "I had an opportunity, I took it."

I grimace, but I'm not cruel enough to point out where her impulsiveness landed her. "What did you say when you answered?"

"I told him I'd meet him. My neighbor took the kids—" She holds back another wave of tears. "And I went to meet him at the park." Her shoulders tremble. "I was so stupid. I never should have gotten in his truck."

I bite my tongue. It's too late to lecture her now. "So, you got in his truck at the park?" *Bad move.* "Then what?"

"He started telling me how the office was falling apart without me. He begged me to come back." She swipes at her tears with the back of her hand. "So stupid. I fell for it. I thought, maybe it had been all in my head the way he treated me. The harassment, the sexual jokes, the way he pawed at me." She shakes her head. "It seemed like maybe I made it all up. I just wanted everything to go back to normal. It was a good job. The pay was great, and I could get time off whenever I needed to. If I would just let him touch my ass every once in a while, maybe cop a feel in the break room, I could be making eighty grand a year again. It wasn't so bad." Her lip curls. "Then he pounced on me."

My pen stills. "He did what?"

"He grabbed me and pinned me down. Forced my seat back and started groping me." The tears pick up their pace, sliding down her cheeks to splash on the table. "I grabbed around in the back of his truck. He had a bunch of hunting gear. Binoculars and gloves, a bunch of crap. I managed to get the knife unsheathed, and I—" She shakes her head, folding her lips together.

"Take your time." My pen races across the page as I try to keep up with taking notes. The bastard got what he deserved if you ask me, but I'm not the one Elena has to convince.

"There was so much blood. So much..." She presses the heels of her hands into her eyes as if trying to block out the image. "I don't even remember stabbing him."

My heart aches for the young woman sitting across from me. If I would have had my way, Warner Mattson would be sitting in a jail cell right now. Instead, he's in a casket.

The door opens, and District Attorney Jordan Adler strides in. He's wearing his navy suit and a pale blue shirt, his hair is perfectly combed, and he's carrying a tray with three coffees.

"Mia." A smile stretches across his mouth. "I brought you coffee."

I glare at him. How did he know I would be here? "I'm fully caffeinated, thanks anyway." I gesture at my to go cup I brought from home. "What are you doing here?"

He sets the tray down on the table and offers Elena one of the cups. I shake my head, indicating she should decline.

Jordan catches the exchange. "It's just coffee, Ms. Rogers." He takes a sip from his own cup. "You should take advantage seeing as you might not get anything of this quality for quite some time."

"What are you doing here?" I repeat the question with an edge in my voice.

"Ms. Rogers was getting ready to give her confession. It was all arranged with Birchland."

I rise from my chair. "Birchland is out, and she's not confessing. I'm requesting a bail hearing immediately. My client is innocent on grounds of self defense." I call for the guard to take Elena back to her holding cell. "I'll see you tomorrow," I tell her. "And try not to worry."

She gives me a resigned look, then walks off with the guard.

When she's gone, I open my laptop bag and take out the notarized resignation letter. "You saved me the trouble of coming to your office."

Jordan refuses to take the letter. "We're a team," he says. "We can make a difference together."

My heart pinches as I think about how that dream is dead. "I used to think so." I press the letter into his hand. "But now I'm just going to make a difference on my own."

His spine straightens, and he looks down at me. "You're making a big mistake. You'll be nothing without the district behind you."

Ice washes over me, filling my veins until my emotions are frigid. I shoulder my bag and reach for the door, tossing Jordan a look on my way out. "I'll see you in court."

CHAPTER 46

Welcome To Book Club

In a few months, Mia has gone from hating motorcycles to fully embracing the lifestyle. I take her on long drives through the mountains where we can lean into the curvy roads, exploring together.

When I pull up on my bike to get her, she's waiting outside, dressed in a leather jacket and boots. I cut the engine and get off the bike, striding forward to catch her in my arms and kiss her. That mouth on mine feels like home, and when she winds her arms around my neck and clings to me, there's no place I'd rather be.

"Hey, ShortCake."

"Hi, Lovebug."

"How was your day?" I ask.

"It wasn't bad."

Something in her tone gives her away. I cup her chin, tilting her face up to mine. "What happened?"

"You're looking at Elena Rogers' new representation."

My fingers tighten at her waist, and I set her back enough to look into her eyes. "This is what you want?"

She swallows hard, looking down quickly before meeting my eyes with a quick nod. "Jordan had some words."

I cup her cheek. "Fuck Jordan Adler."

She sighs. "I can do this."

"You can." There's no hesitation in my voice. I know Mia can do anything she puts her mind to.

"In other news, I heard from Max. They are back in the States and want to meet up for dinner in Asheville next month. If you're willing."

I cinch my arm around her waist. "Anything for you."

She presses tightly to me and buries her nose against my neck. "Maybe we should skip book club and just stay here."

I'm tempted, but I ease back, looking down at her. "No. We are going to your book club. I know it's important to you."

"In that case, I have a request." She glances at my motorcycle. "I want to drive."

"No way." I hand her the extra helmet and climb onto the bike.

"Maybe next time?" She shoves the helmet on her head and gets on behind me, scooting forward so that she's tight against my back.

I take her arm and cinch it tighter around my middle, then start the bike, heading for Thatcher's bookstore.

It isn't a long trip to Main Street, and soon we are pulling into a spot in front of the store. As we climb off the bike, a tall woman with pink and purple hair stops walking on the sidewalk to stare at us.

"I must be dreaming," she says.

"Kennedy!" Mia calls, taking off her helmet and shaking out her hair.

Kennedy eyes me, then returns her gaze to Mia. "Are you okay?" she asks.

"Never better."

"But you just got off the back of a motorcycle." Her gaze lights on me with suspicion.

"Kennedy, this is Jay. He's the newest member of our book club."

Kennedy lifts a pierced eyebrow. "I thought no men were allowed. Besides Thatcher, of course."

"It was Thatcher's idea," Mia says.

I hold up my hands, backing off. "I don't have to stay if you are uncomfortable with it."

Kennedy grins. "The more the merrier. As long as you like to read?"

"I mostly read non-fiction. Biographies and memoirs are my favorite, but I also love True Crime."

Kennedy nods. "You can crash our book club any day." She opens the door to the bookstore and slips inside. "Did you hear why Sloane isn't coming tonight?"

"Sloane never goes anywhere," Mia says. "She's always working."

"She's taking time off to get married," Kennedy says.

"Married?" Mia halts mid-stride, nearly tripping over my foot. "I didn't even know she was dating anyone."

"Me either! I thought maybe I missed the whirlwind romance because I'd been in Puerto Rico for six weeks." She looks at me, raising both eyebrows. "I missed a whole lot."

"I can't believe Sloane is getting married," Mia says.

Kennedy looks at me apologetically. "I hope you weren't here to discuss books, because all we're gonna talk about is Sloane and her weekend wedding."

"Maybe I should go," I say, hesitating at the door. "I don't want to ruin your party."

Kennedy links her arm through mine. "A few months ago, Mia would have run kicking and screaming from a man being introduced to our club. Now she brings you." She tugs me inside. "You're not going anywhere."

I glance down and see Mia grinning up at me, and I know it's true. I'm here to stay.

Epilogue

Max and Samantha's house is exactly what I'd thought it would be. Small and cozy, it's hidden from the street by flowering trees. It's the perfect place to raise a family. I can already imagine a couple of kids riding bikes down the long, winding driveway, and scaling the trees for hide and seek. Max and Samantha wasted no time getting their family started. It's only been six months since their wedding, and they are already expecting their first.

Mia stops her car in front of the house and turns to face me. Her mouth turns down in a frown. "Thanks for being here," she says.

"Of course." I curl my hand around the nape of her neck and pull her close, kissing her frown away. "There's no place I'd rather be."

"Really?" She wrinkles her nose. "I can think of at least a dozen. And I have a pile of work to do."

I squint down at her. "No work today. Don't even mention it."

She jabs a finger at my chest. "That goes for you, too. I don't want to hear a single word about boxing."

"Ouch." I grab her hand and drag it up to my lips. "That hurts."

She laughs and rubs her knuckles over my beard. "You're such a baby." Her hand slides into my hair. "You smell so good." She leans close, running her nose up my jaw. "How do you always smell so fucking good?"

My dick responds to the sexy tone in her voice. "You have the dirtiest mouth."

"You love it." Her tongue darts out, licking into my mouth.

"Mia." My hands slide down her bare shoulders. "Don't start."

She angles her head to kiss me deeper, sliding her hot tongue into my mouth and slipping her fingers through my hair. "Don't start what?" she asks, practically climbing into my lap. "It's not my fault you smell like that."

"Like what?" I'm not wearing cologne, so I have no idea what she's talking about.

She disengages her seatbelt and leans over the console, her hand sliding up my leg. "You smell like a man who is going to let me drive his motorcycle."

I reach down and stop her hand, circling her wrist with my fingers. "I don't let anyone drive my motorcycle."

"Except me." She wriggles her hand out of my grasp and lightly trails her fingers over the growing bulge in my pants. "You will let me drive it, right?"

There's not a chance in hell Mia is driving my bike, but I'm enjoying her trying to persuade me too much to argue.

A knock on the driver's window makes us jerk apart. "Fucking hell," Mia says. "It's Brad."

Brad Shelton pulls Mia's door open and pokes his perfectly styled blond head into the car. "Get a room," he says, cracking up at his own joke.

Mia scowls. "Do you remember my annoying cousin?" she asks.

It's hard to forget one of the most famous men in Hollywood. "What's he doing here?"

"I'm filming in Savannah," he says. "A quirky romantic comedy about a time-traveling werewolf and his sidekick witch."

"Which one are you?" Mia asks, letting Brad help her out of the car.

He folds her in a hug. "Shut up, cuz."

"Do you think it's a boy or a girl?" she asks.

"Definitely a boy," he says. "How about you, Sanchez? Got a guess?"

"I'm just here for the cake," I say, shaking his hand. "Anna with you?"

"She's at a runway show in Paris."

My shoulders relax. Anna makes me nervous. She got a little too close into my personal space at the wedding, and I'm pretty sure she was hitting on me in the drink line.

Brad leads the way into the house, and we are greeted by a dozen family members as soon as we cross the threshold. It's just as hectic and wonderful as I remember.

Mia is passed around for hugs, and everyone seems pleased to see me.

Owen wants to know if I've got time for a game of golf tomorrow, Brad wants another selfie, and Mia's mom corners me in the kitchen to ask me when Mia and I are going to tie the knot.

Mia and I never talk about marriage. The subject makes her prickly, so I tend to avoid any references.

"Come outside!" Mia bursts into the kitchen, grabbing my arm. "We're doing the gender reveal."

Everyone makes their way outside, where Samantha is lined up on the opposite side of the yard with a baseball in her hand. Mia leads me over to stand near her brother, who is holding a bat.

"There's powder in the baseball," Mia explains. "When Max hits it with the bat, it will explode in either pink or blue."

I nod, trying to wrap my mind around the huge production. We drove four hours for this party, so I won't speak a negative word about it, but in my mind, it's a tad excessive. Why not just wait until the baby comes and be surprised?

Mia grabs my hand, pulling me close to her side as Samantha winds up her pitching arm. I transfer my gaze from the mom-to-be to Mia. She's looking at me, and something passes between us. I know that no matter what happens in our lives, I want us to be together. Kids and marriage might not be in the cards for us, but that doesn't mean shit.

We are not bound by the rules of society. We make our own rules.

She smiles at me, and I smile back. Just then, something hard hits me in the chest, and I look down to see I'm covered in sparkling pink goo.

"It's a girl!"

It takes me a moment to realize Max has failed to swing at the ball, and it has hit me in the chest, exploding the contents all over my shirt.

"Are you okay?" Mia asks, brushing at my shirt.

It's no use, the pink goo isn't going anywhere. "I'm fine." I peel my shirt off my chest and smile down at her. "Looks like it's a girl."

Mia turns to glare at her brother. "You didn't even take a swing," she yells over the mayhem of everyone shouting congratulations.

"So, sue me," Max says, laughing.

Mia wrinkles her nose at me. "Come on, let's get something else for you to wear."

She takes my hand and leads me through the house to the owner's suite, where she marches into the bathroom and grabs a towel.

"Take that off," she says, pointing to my button-down shirt.

"If you wanted to get me naked and have your way with me, you didn't have to go to so much trouble." I strip out of my shirt.

"Max is a moron," she says. "How could he miss that slow pitch?" She dabs the towel over my chest, carefully wiping off all the sticky slop. "You're a little sparkly, but it only adds to your rugged good looks."

"You think I have rugged good looks?" I can't hide my grin.

She strokes my bicep, trailing her fingernail through the pink glitter stuck to my skin. "I think you're fucking sex on a stick." She lets her gaze drop over me. "Can I take a rain check on getting you naked and having my way with you?"

I bend down and kiss her. "Only if I can have my way with you first."

"Don't start kissing me," she warns. "We won't stop there, and my mom is going to walk through that door any minute."

I ease back, frustration mounting as I glance at the door. "Better find something fast," I say. She wouldn't want her mom to see me shirtless. We can't chance her seeing my tattoos, one in particular.

Mia strides over to the dresser and rummages through the drawers as I try to wipe off the glitter. When she comes back into the bathroom, she's holding a black T-shirt.

"I thought this would be great on you," she says.

I take the shirt from her, my brow rising as I inspect it. "This is short-sleeved." I try to give it back to her.

She pushes it into my hands, her eyes shining with emotion. "Hopefully it's not too tight."

I take the shirt and pull it over my head. It's a little snug, but that doesn't matter. "It's a perfect fit."

Acknowledgments

Thank you for reading this far! If you are still reading, thank you again. You deserve a cookie.

Only the true fans (and relatives) of an author read to the dedication. So, you all get cookies. Chocolate chip is my favorite.

Extra cookies go to:

Grace and Michael—you are always #1 to me.

Tara, Carrie, Angel, Vicki—thank you for all the late nights and encouragement.

Mickey and Tarzan—the long walks helped me more than you'll ever know.

Erin Spencer—huge cookie to you for finding my dream narrators every single time.

Jay Lam—for being a total sweetheart. Your kindness is a rare thing in this world. I hope to meet you in person one day and give you a dozen cookies.

To all my readers and listeners—I love hearing from you and chatting about books. I wish I could meet every one of you.

About the Author

Jill Brashear is a hopeless romantic and author of swoon-worthy contemporary romances that will leave you breathless. With a pen in her hand and a heart full of love, Jill weaves tales of passion, longing, and happily-ever-afters that will make your heart skip a beat.

From a young age, Jill has been fascinated by love stories, and she's never lost her passion for exploring the intricacies of the heart. Whether she's crafting steamy scenes that will leave you blushing or laugh-out loud moments that will tickle your funny bone, Jill's stories are always full of emotion, depth, and soul.

Also by Jill Brashear

ALOHA SERIES

Try Easy

Try Me

Try Right

Try Over

BLUE RIDGE BOOK CLUB

Love, Lacey Donovan

XOXO, Valentina

Blue Collar Crush

Sincerely, Thatcher Hayes

STANDALONES

Win, Lose, or Love

Jock Seeks Geek

Mr. Mistletoe

Small Town Spark

www.ingramcontent.com/pod-product-compliance
Lightning Source LLC
Chambersburg PA
CBHW071433200726
48294CB00002B/616